Praise for Heidi Cullinan

"Where other gay romances might be headlong dives into sex and love, Cullinan's are subtle and sneaky journeys that promise the real thing, not just a mirage."
—All About Romance

"It's not very often that I am charmed by a book almost from the first page—but this book blew a fresh wind into the rather overworked 19th century area of the m/m historical romance genre and I found myself won over and wooed."
—Speak Its Name on *A Private Gentleman*

"This is a fabulous little story. I pretty much can't recommend it highly enough."
—Dear Author on *Special Delivery* (A)

"A love letter to librarians as she shares small-town library life, with its ups and downs."
—Library Journal on *Sleigh Ride*

"This is a great book for any season, but for Christmas it's truly special. Highly recommended with extra heart."
—*USA TODAY* on *Sleigh Ride*

Clockwork Heart

Heidi Cullinan

SAMHAIN
PUBLISHING

Samhain Publishing, Ltd.
11821 Mason Montgomery Road, 4B
Cincinnati, OH 45249
www.samhainpublishing.com

Clockwork Heart
Copyright © 2016 by Heidi Cullinan
Print ISBN: 978-1-61923-395-9
Digital ISBN: 978-1-61922-723-1

Editing by Sasha Knight
Cover by Kanaxa

First Samhain Publishing, Ltd. electronic publication: February 2016
First Samhain Publishing, Ltd. print publication: February 2016

Dedication

For John, because it's all your fault.

Acknowledgments

To Nathalie Grey, Vanessa North, Juliane Taubner, Holli Klein and Martina Nealli for French, German and Italian translation help: *merci, danke, grazie*. I couldn't have done this without you.

Author's Note

This is a tale of alternate history.

Imagine Napoleon hadn't invaded Russia, that France hadn't lost Waterloo. That without this victory, the sun always set on the British Empire, and the United States developed without connection to most countries in Eurasia due to constant war. In this story's version of Europe, the French Empire stretches from half of Spain all the way to the far side of Poland, as far south as the Alps. Its only true challengers are Britain and the Austrian Empire, the former who essentially can at best keep France at bay, and the latter, which is in constant war with France.

Austria and its holdings contain the largest deposits of a newly discovered element called aether, which briefly allowed Vienna hope they might one day beat back France, but without the French Empire's advanced clockwork technology, they develop almost no technology, only maintain their army by selling aether as dirigible fuel. France dreams of a Europe united beneath its flag and ruled by Paris, to make a world power greater than the Roman Empire and forever unbeatable. It sees conquering Austria as step one of that quest.

In this version of European history, the war between France and Austria has gone on for almost one hundred years. Our story starts in the spring of 1910, still powering through the end of an industrial revolution where petroleum is ignored in the presence of noble aether, where intricate, aether-powered clockwork mechanisms are ubiquitous tools of everyday life, and where everyone, absolutely everyone, travels by balloon-powered airship.

I also invented a continent-wide habit of lacing absinthe with cocaine.

While this may have possibly occurred, it absolutely didn't to the degree it does in *Clockwork Heart*. Alas, in real life neither is absinthe as hallucinogenic as its reputation—but I'm confident lacing it with cocaine would close that gap.

Chapter One

March, 1910
Calais, France

Though Cornelius Stevens had thumbed his nose at his father's international conflicts since he was old enough to understand what the word *war* meant, the night he rescued the Austrian soldier from a pile of dead bodies was the first time his disobedience had gone as far as treason.

He'd gone out, as it happened, to spite his father, who had ordered Conny to attend the local magistrate's dinner party. "A good friend of mine will be there and is looking forward to meeting you," his letter had said, and then it had gone on to promise Cornelius a hefty raise of his allowance and the set of Italian tools he'd been coveting in exchange for his presence at the event. Normally that would have been enough to lure Conny into even the most dull official gathering, but the letter had arrived with the evening paper, whose headline celebrated the archduke's victorious conquest of Switzerland in the name of France. Cornelius had been put off his breakfast at the thought of how many innocent people had died so his father could supply the worthless, lazy emperor in Paris with cheap aether, and he'd burned the letter from his father in his brazier, vowing he'd join the Austrian Army himself before he'd attend a dinner party where he'd hear nothing but the glories of the French forces.

Cornelius was not his father. He saved lives instead of taking them. He was a tinker-surgeon, apprenticed to the best tinker in France. He was a master of clockwork. He saw at least three veterans of his father's horrible war each week, and he gave them surgeries for free and clockwork for cost, or for whatever the soldiers could afford. He was his father's son, but he was a bastard son, in blood and in spirit. He would never celebrate the Empire's appetite for war. He donned his white armband for peace with pride. He wouldn't attend a dinner party where he knew they'd be celebrating more death.

So that evening Conny dined with friends and drank wine, enough to make him glib about the sirens' warning of an invasion on his walk home, chalking it up to more hokum from his father. Until half a kilometer from his flat he heard the shelling.

Calais, the city that never saw much more than a dust-up between sailors on leave, was being invaded. Uncertain how to respond, Cornelius moved into alleys and side streets to complete his journey. He climbed barrels and stumbled over cats, sobering with every step as he made his way home through fog tinged with the tang of gunpowder. He wove his way into an industrial area, following the path of a service canal—and that was where he found the raft of dead Austrian soldiers.

At first he thought he was hallucinating. It happened more often than he cared to admit, if he worked too long without stopping to eat. But he'd eaten both lunch *and* dinner, and it had only been one bottle of wine, no absinthe. Also, he'd never hallucinated *smells* before. Gunpowder. Sea muck. Sweat. Blood.

Death.

As a tinker-surgeon, Cornelius knew the scent of life recently ended all too well. The small barge heaved with a stack of dead soldiers, almost six feet high. Each wore the same green-gray uniform with the Austrian insignia, now caked with blood and mud. Some stared sightlessly at the sky, some twisted to their side, gazing at a distant eternity. No one living rode along to shepherd the dead. They simply drifted along with the rest of the night garbage waiting to be disposed of downstream at the city incinerator. No need to guard dead enemies. No need to afford them courtesy.

It was the most horrific, *inhuman* spectacle Cornelius had ever seen.

This is the work of my father. This is the fruit of Archduke Francis Cornielle Guillory's terrible, endless war.

Cornelius swallowed the lump in his throat. He'd spent the day erasing the poor Swiss invasion victims from his imagination only to stumble upon barges full of fuel enough for a lifetime of nightmares. Hundreds of men, dead at his father's hand. It didn't matter how many lives Cornelius saved in surgery, how many wounded soldiers he gave new life to with surgical clockwork. He realized, standing on the bank of the canal, his entire life was but a pebble in his father's ocean of blood.

Shutting his eyes, Cornelius put a hand to his mouth and fought the urge to retch. A watery cough made him open his eyes again, and he saw a hand raise and lower feebly on the top of one of the piles of corpses.

One of the soldiers was still alive.

With a cry, Cornelius sprinted across the street, hopped over the rail and vaulted onto the barge.

He climbed the dead men, the soft squish of their faces and necks and creak-cracks of their bones making him shiver as he scaled the heap. Another cough from above spurred him on, and then, at last, when he grasped an arm for purchase, it tensed and flinched under his grip.

Life. I have found you.

"It's all right. I'm here." *So much blood.* The soldier's legs were broken at odd angles, and the right one had a seeping stain that told Conny it was bleeding out. Shrapnel protruded from the man's belly and chest, and one great piece of metal appeared to have gone through his left arm entirely. His left eye was a scarred, mangled mess—it wasn't missing, but it had been highly damaged. If he could see at all out of that side, it wasn't much. Though that wound wasn't fresh. However he'd partially lost his sight, it wasn't from this battle.

The soldier murmured something in slurred German and tried, weakly, to push Cornelius away.

Cornelius stilled him with one hand as the other continued his examination. "You're badly injured. But everything here is treatable, I think. Certainly I could give you a new eye without any trouble. Your left arm must go, and I can't promise good things for your right leg, but…well, you floated by the right one for the job."

The man gasped in pain and tried again to shove Conny. This effort was even weaker, though, and when Cornelius's hand brushed his, the soldier's fingers tightened around his own.

Cornelius threaded their fingers together. "I'm so sorry this has happened to you. This is wrong. This war is wrong, this *barge* is wrong—you shouldn't be here if you're alive. You should be at a prisoner-of-war camp, and you should be accorded respect." He swallowed a bubble of bitterness. "You should be *at home*. If you came to Calais, it should be for a holiday."

The man opened his good eye and gazed at Cornelius through a haze of pain. Though he spoke in German, no translation was necessary for the look on the soldier's face.

I'm going to die, and I'm afraid.

Cornelius drew the man's hand to his mouth and kissed the bloody, dirty knuckles. "You aren't going to die. I'm going to save your life."

Letting go of the soldier, Conny hurried down the corpses and up the bank with his blood pumping as his mind raced through potential plans. When he spotted a small surgery on the corner down the way, he dashed to it, picked the lock and burst inside. Needles, medicine, antibiotic went into his bag, as well as three rolls of bandages. The surgeons had a gurney as well, bless them. Leaving a hefty pile of bank notes on the counter by way of apology, he dragged the gurney outside and toward the barge, which had by now drifted almost out of sight.

His lungs burned as he climbed up a second time, and he feared he would find the man dead after all—but no, the soldier babbled slurred, panicked German as Cornelius arrived.

"*Calmez-vous.*" Cornelius wished he could offer reassurances the man would understand. He gave him an injection of painkiller, another of antibiotic, and then, to make things easier, he dosed the man with just the faintest bit of aether.

He was glad for it, because even with the gas, the soldier cried out as Cornelius tried to set his limbs. Unfortunately, Conny quickly realized all the soldier's extremities were crushed except for his right hand. Cornelius bound the wounds as best he could, devised splints out of bits of the ferry rail, and then, with great effort, rolled the man onto the gurney pallet and strapped him in, hoping against hope the shifting didn't incur too much additional damage.

Getting the pallet off the heap nearly sent them both into the canal. The soldier was broad and tall, and Cornelius was not. Essentially the only way to transport him was to slide the poor man on the pallet as if it were a sled. Clamoring after, Cornelius hoisted the pallet back onto the gurney, unlocked the wheels and rattled into the alley toward his apartments above Master Félix's shop.

Only God knew what Cornelius would have said if he'd run into anyone on the streets—but he didn't. Everyone hunkered in cellars, praying they weren't set upon by soldiers. There were no soldiers on the streets, however, save the one Conny wheeled into the night. Once back at the shop, he found Master Félix wasn't at home, and the maid was long gone for the night, so Cornelius simply rolled the gurney into the elevator in the back, primed the crank and rode with his patient past the first-floor general tinker shop into the second-floor surgery.

As an apprentice to the most celebrated tinker-surgeon in all of France, Cornelius had seen his share of dire patients, but he'd never faced anything as intense and critical as this soldier, and he'd never done such an intensive treatment alone. He did his best to push his nerves aside as he washed his hands, donned his surgical apron and dosed the soldier with so much aether he wouldn't feel any pain well into the next week. Once that was done, he stripped the patient down and cleaned him head to toe.

So many wounds. Shrapnel in his belly and chest—some had gone into a lung, Conny was certain of it. The legs did have to go. Both of them, sadly, though the left leg only to mid-calf. The left arm too. For a moment, Cornelius wondered if he shouldn't help the man cross over, instead of yanking him back to life. Then he remembered the look of naked terror on the man's face, and resolve gripped him like a vise.

No. I am a healer, a fixer. I hate war and weep for all humans in pain. I will save this soldier. Whatever it takes. And I will give him clockwork so grand he won't miss the flesh he's lost.

Amputating and cauterizing the man's mangled legs stopped the worst of the bleeding, though Cornelius did transfuse some blood into his patient to be certain he hadn't lost too much. Perhaps it had been a bit of fancy to use his *own* blood from the stored pints, but he *was* a universal donor, was he not? Cornelius got rid of the soldier's burned, crushed arm and sealed up that stump too. He wrapped the belly, then shifted his focus to the collapsed lung.

That was when he saw the bit of metal sticking out of the soldier's chest, right above his heart. It was so low he'd missed it the first time, tangled in the man's thick pelt of chest hair. But there was no missing it now.

It was the mortal wound. Conny skimmed his hand over the man's thigh, scanning his patient's body with new eyes, taking in the wounds old and new. It was the metal in the man's heart killing him. Cornelius had healed everything else. If he healed that too, and fixed the lung, the man wouldn't die.

Cornelius drew his bottom lip into his mouth as he stared at the stub of iron.

Seeing to *that* wasn't simply cleaning him up. It was surgery. Clockwork surgery. And to finish the job, Conny would need to give the man a clockwork heart assist. That would be *improving*. Organ upgrades barely allowed to the gentry, given to an enemy soldier.

That would be treason.

Cornelius sucked his lip deeper into his mouth, biting nervously on the soft flesh.

Going any further than what he'd done was too much. He should give the man an overdose of aether and send him sweetly into death. He should do his duty, then find a pretty thing in a dockside bar or a stalwart sailor willing to let him cry on his shoulder before making him forget the shadows of war.

Cornelius let his gaze rest on the soldier's big, battered body, his surprisingly pretty countenance beneath the scars, so innocent in sleep. Conny remembered the look of terror on his face and those whispered pleas. The weariness only war could bring. He thought of the dead Swiss men and women and children, who had done nothing but live in a country rich with aether the archduke needed to fuel his war.

He couldn't save those victims. But he knew, if he let himself cross the line, he could save this one.

Probably he'll die in surgery, Cornelius told himself as he washed his hands and sterilized his kit. *He'll die, and I can say I tried. Treason with no witness or lasting effect.*

Except Cornelius did more than simply *try.*

Putting the Austrian on the Lazarus machine when the surgery went south was wrong. Siphoning off another pint of his own blood was *foolish,* because it made him woozy. Setting a tiny assistant pumping mechanism into a dying man's chest was pointless—careless, even, since he'd end up burying thousands of dollars' worth of intricate machinery if the man died, which he was highly likely to do.

But breaking into Master Félix's vault to steal the clockwork heart once the pumping gear wouldn't turn—that was certainly the most terrible thing Cornelius had ever done.

The clockwork heart was Félix's masterpiece. He'd only shown it to Cornelius a month ago, after an evening of too much wine. "This is my masterwork, Conny, not that anyone can ever know about it. A clockwork heart. Not an assisting device but a fully clockwork organ, the first and only of its kind. Completely replaces an organ made of flesh, and very possibly functions better than the pump God gave us. It would run forever, until the body gave out. It might well make a body perform *better* than a flesh heart could. It could change the world."

"But that's wonderful!" Conny had touched the clockwork heart reverently, imagining all the good it could do. "It could save so many lives. You should make more of them."

"I will never make another one as long as I live, and no one will ever use this infernal machine. I only have it here because it was no longer safe where it had been hiding. Soon I must move it again. Unless I can work up the courage to destroy it." Félix turned to Conny, sodden with wine but burning with intensity. "You must never tell anyone about this. Not a single soul. Not ever."

Cornelius hadn't told anyone. Not even Valentin, his longest, dearest friend. But he knew the heart hadn't yet moved on to wherever Félix intended to hide it next, and he hadn't destroyed it. As the Austrian soldier lay dying, his heart of flesh too damaged to beat on its own, all Conny could think of was the perfect substitute locked away downstairs, lying useless with its owner vowing never to let it see the light of day.

Surely the safest place to hide the heart was inside of someone. A man who would not live without it.

Cornelius set the clockwork heart next to the mechanical pump, coaxed it into working independently before sewing it up inside the thin gold cavity he made in the man's chest. He made a flesh-seal and tucked the access port under the man's right arm, sealing it up with a cap that could pass for a mole to anyone who didn't get close enough to see this mole had a tiny hinge. He stood over his patient, his own still-human heart thumping madly as he realized what he'd done.

Then it occurred to Conny, since he'd crossed one line, there was nothing stopping him from breaking as many rules as he needed to not only save his soldier but give him every advantage in whatever the next chapter of life brought him.

And that is precisely what Conny did.

* * * * *

Johann Berger was fairly certain he should have been dead.

He couldn't yet be sure he *wasn't* dead, though that he had a headache and ached all over seemed a good indication he was probably still alive. Death seemed like it would either not hurt at all or hurt a hell of a lot more, to pardon the pun. But Johann's aches felt muted. Annoying, but tolerable. His left arm and his legs felt very odd. His mouth tasted like ash, and his chest felt…strange. He was warm, however. He lay in something soft and fragrant. Inhaling, he caught hints of lavender, sage and the lemon tang of a cleanser. He could not, for the life of him, imagine where he was or how he got there. Hoping for visual cues, he opened his eyes.

After drawing in a sharp breath, he closed them again. Tight.

When he opened them once more, his pulse beat hard against the back of his throat. He could see. Out of both eyes. Not a blurry haze out of his left which his right eye had to ignore. He *saw*, with crystal clarity, though his left eye saw everything with a sharp-edged tinge of yellow-brown.

He raised his hands to his face. Through the amber edging, he could see his right hand looking normal, his arm bare and scarred and marked with service tattoos. He also saw his left hand, which did not look like a hand at all. In any kind of light.

Oh, there were five fingers, true enough. But they were made of copper casings, not flesh. Tiny wheels held every joint in place and larger gears made up what he could only call a wrist. More wire and more clockwork comprised a forearm he could, technically, see through. What should have been his left arm was now a delicate machine. But even stranger than his new appendage was the discovery that when his brain told his left arm to move, his left wrist to turn, the fingers of his left hand to curl—*they responded in kind.* He let out a shaking breath and touched his left hand with his right. The clockwork arm didn't register sensation in the way his right hand did. It felt like a slight fuzzing on his brain, an odd tickle that resonated more in his elbow than in his substitute fingers. He noticed, too, that his movements weren't as smooth or dexterous with the mechanical arm as with his real one.

This was clockwork. *Incredible* clockwork. He'd seen some clumsy versions on a few officers who'd lost limbs, and once his unit had been stationed near Italy, where Johann saw a nobleman wearing gears on his flesh arm, but the kind of clockwork fused to Johann was like nothing he had known could possibly exist.

How had this happened? He tried to recall his last memory, but everything felt blurred and confused in his head. Had he ended up back with Crawley? He couldn't see how. The pirates had left him, the commander had found him, and they'd put him straight onto the front lines. Onto a special assignment, the regiment sent to storm Calais.

A suicide mission. He remembered now. A distraction so the English airships full of Austrian troops could land on the eastern shores. Something about destroying a weapon. Or finding it. Or something. Nothing to do with him—*his* job was to be cannon fodder for the French.

So how had he ended up in a nice-smelling, soft bed with a yellow eyeball and a clockwork arm?

His belly curdled as he remembered the rumors, the warnings the sergeants had taunted them with at camp. *The French are turning their war prisoners into automatons. Don't let them catch you alive, or they'll make it so you can never die and can't do anything but fight for Archduke Guillory.*

Terror brought back missing pieces of Johann's memory. It had been fear of that story that had made him fake death and swallow his cry of pain as the French soldiers had tossed him onto the corpse barge. He remembered lying cold and trembling in the foggy night, waiting for death, knowing being burned alive would be better than the future they had in store for him as a prisoner of war.

And then a pretty young man had climbed the corpse heap, touched his face and whispered in French.

The curtains around Johann's bed parted, and the pretty Frenchman from his recollection smiled down at him, head backlit by gaslight, his features outlined in a strange amber hue in Johann's left eye.

"*Voilà, vous êtes réveillé enfin.*"

The Frenchman sat on the edge of the bed and smiled kindly down at Johann. As he spoke more lyrical words Johann had no hope of comprehending, he touched Johann everywhere. His face. His neck. He laid a hand over Johann's chest, pressing gently—it was then Johann realized that flesh was slightly numb.

They have captured me and turned me into their slave. That is why I have the clockwork arm and God knows what else. I am an automaton. He began to panic.

The pretty man shushed him, petting his shoulders and entreating Johann once more in French. He didn't sound like an enemy doctor intent on hacking men into reusable pieces. In fact, Johann hadn't heard anyone speak with this much tenderness since he'd left his mother.

It was a little drugging. He decided he would gladly fight for Guillory's army, if it meant this man would croon to him at the end of every battle.

The pretty man explained the mechanical arm, with slow French and pantomime. Johann got the idea the man had installed it, or designed it, or something, because he was intensely proud and could explain how to work it even without a shared language. "*Nerf,*" he kept saying, tracing a line from Johann's elbow to his brain. He said *nerf* as he touched Johann's left eye too, putting Johann's right hand up there to feel the strange metal socket placed over the hollow where his mangled eye should have been.

He had Johann sit up, which was when Johann saw his legs.

The Frenchman hushed him once more when he cried out at the sight of his lower half—his right leg was *entirely* machine, steel and copper skeleton rising almost to his hip. His left leg was natural to his calf, where he had something which looked much like the foot version of his left arm. It was more intricate than the right side by far.

He had no legs. No feet. He was more clockwork than man.

Though Johann wanted to panic, it was difficult to remain upset with his doctor soothing him in what tonight had to be the prettiest language on Earth. The man hugged Johann's shoulders and spoke quietly into his ear, his lips gently brushing the skin and wresting Johann's attention away from his artificial limbs.

"*Tout ira bien, mon chéri. Croyez-moi. Je vous soignerai.*"

Johann shut his eyes, wondering how that worked when one was basically a copper lens. It did shut, though, when he told it to. In fact, all the clockwork parts seemed to respond to his most casual thought. *His,* not the Frenchman's. The question was, would it remain that way?

Would he care, if it meant this man would continue to be so kind to him? "I don't know what you're saying or what you've done to me, but..." He leaned helplessly into the man. "Please...don't stop talking. Or touching me."

With a soft French coo, the man prattled on, his tone even gentler and sweeter now. "*Je m'appelle Cornelius. Quel est votre nom?*"

Name, Johann's rusty brain offered up in translation. *He wants to know your name.* "Johann Berger. Of the Austrian Army's 51st regiment."

A shiver ran down his skin as the man—Cornelius—threaded fingers into Johann's hair. Johann decided he liked it, but it was strange. His mother always said the French had odd ways. He hadn't realized they were such *touchy* ways.

Probably he'd have run away to France when he'd first deserted the army, if he'd known.

"*Bienvenue, Johann Berger. Sur mon honneur, je jure que je vous protégerai.*"

Johann felt a kiss on his hairline, and he curled his mechanical hand instinctively at the touch.

As he lay in the embrace of the Frenchman, Johann recalled his mother. Her gentle hands on his face, her tears as she said goodbye. They'd both known it would be the last time they saw one another. Johann wondered if she had put him out of her heart the way he'd sealed off her and the rest of his family, his life in Stallenwald. It hurt too much to remember a time when life had been good.

In the Frenchman's arms, Johann broke the seal. He let himself feel the ache of loss, let himself acknowledge how much he missed love and light in his life. A sense of purpose that wasn't futile. A future filled with hope, not despair. It was a fever, no doubt, that let him turn the incomprehensible French coos into something to latch on to. He had no idea to what purpose this man meant to assign him now that he was a clockwork man, but in that moment he didn't care. However it happened, whether or not it was real, right now he felt safe and peaceful.

He'd been a son, a soldier, a pirate, a human sacrifice. If it meant he could keep feeling like this, he'd be whatever the Frenchman wanted him to be.

Chapter Two

Cornelius liked Johann.

He'd long maintained people in hospital revealed their true selves whether they liked it or not, and as a patient, Johann was gentle, friendly and eager to please. Conny had worried he'd end up with a grousing Austrian bruiser in his bed, but his patient was as far from this as a man could be. Cornelius couldn't imagine Johann Berger hurting anyone, though of course he must have, as a soldier. Here, however, he seemed happy, even grateful to be in Cornelius's care.

He also had a lovely smile, and though larger, rougher-looking men weren't usually Conny's type, he couldn't help but acknowledge his patient was attractive, in his own way.

For the first few weeks, the two of them existed in a quiet, charmed bubble. Cornelius kept Johann in his rooms, and by and large Johann mostly slept in between Cornelius's attempts to teach him how to manage his clockwork. To help those efforts along, Cornelius also taught Johann rudimentary French.

He told no one about his mystery patient, and at first the secret was ridiculously easy to keep. Maryann, the girl who ran the register in the shop and set up appointments for surgeries, was too busy flirting with customers to notice anything different about Cornelius's habits. Master Félix hated stairs and never went up to Conny's apartment unless he had to, so Cornelius gave him no reason to do so. The only trouble was convincing their maid Louise he didn't want his room disturbed for cleaning. She was almost ridiculously insistent she be allowed inside, but since no one but Félix could undo the locks he set on his doors and windows, she had little choice but to concede.

Cornelius's friends were a bit trickier, especially his closest friend, Valentin Durant.

While Val was away at a house party in Paris, keeping his friend in the dark was as simple as sending the occasional telegram, but once Valentin returned to Calais, he became annoyed his friend wouldn't come out drinking and whoring as he usually did. On the third day he was back in town, he convinced Louise to let him in the kitchen, then cornered Conny when he came down for a pair of sandwiches.

"What do you mean you don't feel like going out this evening? You haven't been out at all for weeks, from what everyone's been telling me. And none of them are fucking you, so they're agog to know who is."

"No one is fucking me. I'm working." Conny lifted the tray of sandwiches and tried to make his escape.

Val blocked him and gave a rough snort. "No one is fucking you? Darling. I've watched you arrested for inappropriate sexual display and fuck your way out of the arrest by servicing the police department and half the male inmates of the jail just for fun. You are never *not* fucking. Either you're ill, which is terrible, or you're lying to me, which is so very much worse."

"I have an unusually intense tinker project." Conny shooed Val out the door with a kiss. "I will tell you all about who I'm fucking once it's finished."

Val gave him a cutting glare as he hailed a cab, and Conny knew he had mere days before his friend renewed his efforts to find out what was going on.

Which meant he'd better be a lot quicker about teaching Johann French.

His patient was a remarkable student, which helped because Cornelius wasn't much of a teacher. When Conny went on nervous babbles in French so rapid-fire there was no way the man had any idea what Conny said, Johann listened so politely, so prettily, Cornelius had a hard time *not* talking to him constantly. About everything. And he couldn't seem to stop.

This was dangerous, because Val hadn't been exaggerating when he said Conny was always fucking someone, or thinking about fucking someone. And right now the only man Cornelius longed to take to bed was the beautiful brute of an Austrian listening patiently to him from the other side of the room.

He tried to keep things business between them, to remind himself as much as possible why an affair would be a terrible idea even if Johann *were* interested. "My father is the archduke," he explained to Johann one morning. "Guillory. The one who thinks he's going to conquer all of Europe, the one who, despite the existence of Emperor Éloi, is the real ruler of the French Empire. Which is why I need to be careful about anyone seeing you here. Well, I would need to be careful regardless of *who* I was, but being Francis's bastard makes everything more complicated."

Johann's eyes widened. "*Sie sind des Erzherzogs Sohn?*" He paused, then added, "*Unehelich?*"

Conny sat at the other end of Johann's bed—technically *his* bed, though he'd been camped on the pallet by the hearth since Johann's arrival—and crossed his ankles. "I have no idea, but goodness, everything that comes out of your mouth is deliciously guttural and raw."

Johann blinked at him, then smiled uncertainly, looking for all the world like a large, charming boy.

Groaning, Conny rubbed his thumb along his bottom lip and shifted to make room for his erection. "I should tell you, darling, I'm what my mother refers to as a nancy. We call it *mignon*, in French. I don't know what it is in German. None of the terms are nice, though, so I mostly say that I prefer the company of men to women in my bedroom. Which isn't to say this is all about seducing you. I'm not so coarse as that. Well—unless you *wanted* me."

Johann brightened and gestured around them. "Bedroom. This is bedroom, yes?"

"God help us both, it is indeed a bedroom." Conny sucked his lip into his mouth for a moment and let out a sigh. "I still have no idea what I'm going to do with you once you're healed and ready to return to the world. To be honest, it's causing all manner of problems, keeping everyone in the dark. Valentin, my closest friend, suspects I'm up to something. Eventually he'll make me confess. Which is why I need to find a way to explain to you that I'll be gone for a whole evening soon and that you must be quiet in my absence."

Johann settled against his cushions and listened intently.

Conny poked Johann's clockwork leg gently with the toe of his sock and let the pressure linger afterward, as if it had been an accident, which it of course had not been. He spoke slowly and clearly. "Leg, Johann? Does it hurt?"

Johann perked up again. "Is good," he replied as he touched his thigh where the clockwork appendage joined by magnets and plugs to his central nervous system. "No hurts." He smiled, pressing his hand against Conny's voyeuristic toe. "*Danke*. Thank you."

Conny colored under the praise and the touch. "It's nothing, really. You don't hurt because of the aether. Lovely side effect, the speedy healing. There's that fine line between when it heals, when it knocks you unconscious and when it kills you, but I promise I'm quite adept at managing those thresholds. I've done my best to put you completely to rights in all ways. I'm not fond of soldering clockwork parts to human skin, so I gave you sockets, which means we can easily swap you out if your clockwork parts get damaged. This also means if someone grabs your arm or your leg and pulls, they'll come off, and the disconnection without proper procedures will cause you pain." He bit his lip. "I really need to teach you French enough to explain that properly."

He still hadn't been able to even attempt to confess about the heart. Johann had noticed the scar and the flesh door, but who knew what was German for *mechanical heart.*

Johann smiled, his gaze falling on Cornelius's lip tucked between his teeth. Then he cleared his throat and straightened. "I must toilet, please."

"Oh. Certainly." Cornelius popped off the bed and ruffled the back of his hair nervously. "Do you—ah—want help?" He held out his arm.

Johann shook his head and reached for the metal cane propped by the bed. "*Nein. Ich muss lernen.*"

Even Conny could suss out that much German. "I must learn," he corrected.

Johann smiled. "Yes. I must learn. All things." Pushing the cane hard into the floor, he rose unsteadily on his clockwork feet.

Cornelius didn't steady him, but he walked with Johann across the room to the water closet. "You're doing fantastically well for having two artificial legs. I long to fuss with the nerve bundle at your hips, possibly give a clockwork translator for increased sensation. I need to review my neural anatomy before I attempt that, though. I *do* know how to rewire a spine, but I also know it's ridiculously impossible to get it exactly right. I'd hate to cut off all sensation entirely in an attempt to give you a boost. Oh. Here we are." He tugged at his ear and cast his gaze down at the floor. "I talk too much."

Johann stopped with the water closet door half open. "No." He waited until Cornelius looked up, and then he smiled. "I like you talk." He paused, frowned and corrected. "Your talking. When you talking."

Heart melting, Conny bussed a kiss on Johann's cheek. "You're a darling. Now go ahead and—"

A hard knocking on his bedroom door cut him off. "Cornelius, love? Make yourself decent, because I'm coming in."

All the blood drained from Cornelius's face. "Oh God. That's Valentin. *Hide*, Johann, hide."

"I hide," Johann echoed, and shut the water closet door behind him.

More knocking sounded on the door. "Conny? I hear you in there. I've come to collect you. You've been holed up in here far too long. The boys weep for the loss of you, and I'm getting bored drying their tears alone."

Cornelius did a quick sweep of the room to make sure nothing incriminating lay about. He'd been tweaking Johann's arm, so all those tools were on the table, but that wasn't anything Valentin would notice. Conny focused his attention on stacking sets of dishes so they looked like piles, not pairs. He'd decided he was almost in the clear when he spied the pallet by the hearth, and he unmade it with his heart in his throat.

Now Valentin was using his entire fist on the door. "*Cornelius Francis Stevens.*"

"Calm down, I'm *coming*," Conny called. Tossing his pillow onto the bed, he kicked the pile of sheets into the corner and headed for the door. Before he opened it, though, he messed up his hair and rubbed his eyes, trying to give himself the look of one who had been working too hard.

He barely had the latch pulled before Valentin burst into the room, dragging a cloud of scent behind him. He positioned himself in the center of Cornelius's workshop, propping his walking stick on the toe of his ivory suede boot as he took in the room with an eagle eye. "My God, this place is even more of a sty than normal. You haven't let the maid in? If you tell me you truly have been working on one of your bits of nonsense all this time, I swear I shall throw it in the bin."

"I *have* been working." Conny tried to think of what he could say he'd been working on, since he couldn't very well produce Johann from the water closet. "A project for Master Félix."

Valentin rolled his eyes and collapsed into an easy chair, pushing several scrolls of clockwork schematics aside as he did so. "*Tedious.* And no signs of sex at all. I thought this might have been another one of your slums with some dog from the docks. We all know how you love to dirty your knees for something rough. But it appears you have, inexplicably, been a nun." He opened his legs and palmed his crotch with a naughty wink. "You must be gagging for it, sweetheart. If you want to take the edge off with me, I won't mind."

He and Valentin hadn't done anything more suggestive with one another than dance since they were in university together, so he knew the offer wasn't serious, but the thought of Johann hearing Valentin's salacious tones through the water closet door made him blush and purse his lips. Yes, he was a terrible tart—but not with *Johann.*

"Enough." Conny waved a hand. "You've made your point. I'll come to the café tonight. But not for long, and I'm not taking anyone home. I have…a great deal of work to do."

"You're the bastard son of Guillory and a rich English actress, living off an allowance and tinkering with clockwork nonsense in a demented old master's shop. You have no *work* to do. Nothing you can't shunt aside for an evening."

Valentin's eyes narrowed. "Which means there's something here you don't want me to see."

Don't look at the water closet. Don't look at the water closet. "That's nonsense. I'm not in the mood for your games."

Valentin rose with a snort of disbelief and poked about the piles of clutter. "God bless, Conny, you've never been any kind of a liar." He sighed as he toppled a pile of laundry and kicked aside more schematics. "I've never seen you this panicked for me not to find out, though. Most intriguing. This is why I love you, darling. You never let me get bored."

"There's nothing to find. I've been a hermit, simple as that." He struggled for a whisper of truth to sell his lie. "I...haven't been myself since the night the corpse barge came through. It upset me, seeing so many men dead for such a stupid reason."

Valentin pursed his lips. "Yes, I hear that was terribly grisly. All those stinking Austrians, rotting in your backyard. You should have rung for me, my love. That isn't the sort of thing one should contemplate alone. I know I was in Paris, but I would have come home for you."

"I wanted...to work. So I've been working."

"Such a terrible affliction, this yen of yours to *work*. I blame your mother." He stopped still at the bed, poked the pillow with his stick, then crowed in triumph. "*Ha.* I knew it. You have a lover tucked away in here."

Cornelius's stomach lurched. "What? I do not."

With a smirk, Valentin held up one of Johann's long, dark and slightly curling hairs from the pillow. "You do. This hair says he's been here, and your zeal to remove me says he's here *right now*. I *knew* you hadn't lost your inner whore." His gaze shifted to the water closet, and he laughed. "But of course."

Cornelius climbed over the easy chair and pressed his body against the door before Valentin could get there. "*No.* You can't. Val, you *can't.*"

All humor left Valentin's expression. "Any lover who has you this terrified to introduce him to your friends is no one good at all."

"I'm not terrifi—" Conny bit off the lie and changed course. "It's not what you're thinking. I'm not ready, is all. For introductions."

Valentin's eyes went wide. "Don't tell me you're sleeping with a *woman*."

Conny pressed his hands against Valentin's chest and gazed pleadingly into his face. "Please—*please* let it go. You...you can meet him."

"Yes, as soon as you step aside."

"*No*." Conny curled his fingers into Val's shirt. "Tonight. You can meet him tonight. I'll...bring him. To the café."

"Why on earth can't I see him now? Is his cock pathetic? You know I've endured that before, and I won't hold it against you. Sometimes they make up with their hands what God has taken away from their root."

For the first week when Johann had been unconscious, Conny had used a catheter to relieve him. No, there was nothing pathetic about Johann's penis. "Please. *Please*, Val. I'll do anything you ask. Only give me until this evening."

He wasn't sure Val would agree, not until he got that tic in his jaw that said he didn't like it, but he'd endure it. "You're answering all my questions tonight. And so is he. This smells fishy, and I'll have the rotten out of it. I'll be watching the highway too—if you try to run him out of town, I'll know."

"I won't run anyone anywhere. We'll be there. I promise."

Val brushed kisses on either side of Conny's cheek, the greeting he normally would have given at the door. "Be well then, until tonight."

Conny stayed plastered against the water closet until Val's footsteps echoed on the stairs, at which point he tore across the room and bolted them inside. Then he pressed his face to the wood as he sank to his knees.

A minute later, he heard the water closet open before the *creak, creak* of gears announced Johann was crossing the room. He crouched beside Cornelius awkwardly, losing his balance briefly on his mechanical knee. He rested his clockwork hand on Conny's shoulders. "What happen? *Was is passiert?*"

"Everything. Everything has gone wrong." Conny covered his face with his hands. "Oh, why did I let him think you were my lover? I could almost make it work, but how can I keep you in the dark on that point when they behave the way they do? When they know how *I* normally behave?"

Johann said nothing, only kept up the comforting pressure on Conny's shoulders.

"What a cock-up. I'd even scandalize my mother this time." Conny bit his lip to stop a wave of tears. "But what was I to have done? Let you die? I couldn't. I should have, but I couldn't. I have to come up with a fiction. I have to hide as much of your clockwork as I can, and I must invent you a story of origin. I could tell them you were mute, if I could account for the fact that you don't understand French to the same degree you can't speak it. Because you'll be a scandal as soon as they hear your accent. I could lie and say you're from Berlin, but the least respectable German still knows French. They also don't have an arm full of Austrian Army tattoos. God help me, this is worse than if I showed up on the arm of a pirate—"

He stopped, lifting his head as the plan unfolded before him.

"*Yes.* That's it." He took Johann's face in his hands. "You're going out with me tonight, darling. You're going to pretend to be my Austrian pirate lover."

Johann stared at him, uncomprehending.

Cornelius sighed. "Right. I'll try to figure out how to explain."

Johann, still unaware of anything Conny said, smiled.

Conny let out a breath to resist kissing that hand. "Sometimes, Johann, I think you're an avenging angel, come to torture me for my wicked ways." Patting him on the head, Cornelius rose to his feet. "We'll start by making a few modifications to your clockwork."

* * * * *

Cornelius was upset about something, this much Johann understood. Everything else that happened that afternoon was a mystery to him.

As Cornelius unhooked Johann's right leg, he chattered away in French, making many gestures out the window toward the docks. He kept talking as he took the leg to his workbench and unscrewed the knee. Since Johann had no hope of understanding what Cornelius had to say, he focused on what his friend did. He took the mechanical leg apart for some reason—it wasn't broken, that Johann could tell, but sometimes Cornelius liked to fuss and fiddle with things simply because he could. This seemed a more involved procedure, though Johann couldn't work out why it was happening at all.

He gasped in shock when Cornelius sawed off the wooden leg of a small side table and attached it with a screw below the artificial knee.

"*Pirate*," Cornelius kept saying, as he attached what was essentially a peg leg onto Johann's otherwise beautiful, intricate clockwork limb.

Was Cornelius sending him away? He understood the visitor earlier this afternoon had upset his host, but he hadn't realized that encounter would be the reason he was sent away. He didn't want to overstay his welcome, but he wasn't sure he could properly care for his clockwork parts, and without them he had a single hand left of his formerly four functional limbs. He couldn't even properly crawl from one beggar's corner to another.

Had this visitor known of Johann's past, and that was why Cornelius was finished with him?

He was certainly sending him off well-kitted. All afternoon Cornelius had tinkered with Cornelius's clockwork parts—and then he'd hidden them all. Long black leather gloves covered Johann artificial hand, and what the glove couldn't manage, great leather cuffs did. Boots hid his left foot, and breeches tucked around his right knee disguised any hint of the clockwork knee and thigh. The peg leg had been roughly screwed into the delicate machinery.

Johann's amber eye was hidden behind a leather eyepatch. Most of Johann's body was covered in leather—leather vest, leather coat with long tails that brushed the floor, wide-brimmed leather hat. It had to have cost the earth to procure—and from where it came, Johann didn't know, only that Cornelius left without it and returned with a wheelbarrow full of parcels. It was well-gilded stuff too, full of filigree and ornament and rivets. Once he had Johann kitted out, he sat him down on the bed and stared intently into his eyes as he spoke slowly and carefully.

"You are pirate," he said, touching Johann's leather vest. "Sky pirate."

Johann's heart sank. "You take me to ship?"

"*Non, un faux pirate.*"

Johann shook his head in confusion. "*Je ne comprends pas.*"

Cornelius bit his lip, and as always the nervous tic tugged at Johann's heart. He would miss that lip-biting more than anything else.

Cornelius stood and paced, murmuring to himself. Eventually he stopped and took Johann's hat and eyepatch away, and put them on himself. "*Grr, je suis un pirate.*" He hunched down as he said this, playing out a rather bad caricature of story-time pirates. He swiped several random tools from his workbench, still growling at random. Then he winked, smiled and put down the tools as he shook his head. "*Non, je ne suis pas une pirate. Je suis inventeur.*" He mimed fixing the lower half of Johann's leg. "*Je ne suis pas une pirate. Je suis un faux pirate.*"

Johann did a rough translation. *I am not a pirate. I am a…something pirate.*

Cornelius pointed to his eyepatch. "*Ce n'est qu'un déguisement.*" He took the patch and hat off and put them back on Johann. He made his rather bad pirate face again. "*Voilà, maintenant vous êtes le pirate.*" He winked and shook his head. "*Non, vous êtes un soldat. Vous êtes un faux pirate.*"

Johann's eyes widened. *I'm not a pirate, I'm a soldier. But I'm…pretending?* "I am pretend pirate? No ship?"

Cornelius beamed. "*Non.* No ship."

Relief rolled off Johann like fog. Dare he press his luck? He had to know, though. "Johann…is stay with Cornelius?" He mimed picking up a bag and walking in place from his chair before nodding at the door. "I no go?"

Cornelius gasped. "*Non.*" He clutched Johann's hands tightly. "*Vous restez avec moi.*"

Johann was fairly sure Cornelius had just said he must stay with him. He let out a ragged sigh. "*Merci, Cornelius.*"

Cornelius drew their joined hands to his mouth and kissed each of Johann's sets of knuckles. Then he rose and brought Johann to his feet as well before handing him his cane. "Come. We go outside. Together." He tucked Johann's arm into his. "I will help you walk."

They walked together out the door to Cornelius's room, into a narrow hallway, then down a set of open stairs leading to a small kitchen, where a young lady was bent over a kettle of laundry. She scolded Cornelius in angry French, but she regarded Johann warily. As far as Johann could tell, she was demanding to know who Johann was and where he had come from.

Cornelius responded breezily, calling Johann *pirate* and repeatedly putting a hand on Johann's chest. It felt nice, and he was sorry when Cornelius stopped touching him and urged him out of the kitchen and through the workshop.

There was a tiny tinker shop in a larger village near Johann's back home, but it was nothing like the one he walked into now on Cornelius's arm. Shelves towered over him, stuffed full of clockwork. There were a few mechanical body parts here and there, but not many. Most were tools, household gadgets and several things Johann couldn't imagine a utility for, like a clockwork mouse.

A man stood at a workbench in the middle of the room, an old man with a long, shaggy white beard and thick spectacles—they had some kind of extended lens on them which reminded Johann of his false eye. When the old man saw Cornelius, he took off the spectacles and greeted him warmly. As he noticed Johann, his expression went still, an unreadable mask. "Who is this?"

"My pirate friend," Cornelius said, leaning on Johann's arm. "He's staying with me." Cornelius gestured from the old man to Johann. "Johann, this is Master Félix. Master Félix, Johann."

Félix began to rattle on in French, until Cornelius let him know Johann didn't speak much. "A foreign pirate?" Félix clucked his tongue. "You will get into trouble."

Cornelius winked and placed a hand on Johann's chest. "Trouble is so much fun," he said in a saucy voice that made something tingle in Johann's groin. Though that may have been because of the wink.

The tingling sensation lingered as Cornelius led Johann out of the shop. Johann still walked clumsily with his mechanical legs, but the wooden stump was even clumsier to maneuver, and he feared knocking over the delicate clockwork, equipment spilling over every available surface. He told himself fear made his insides feel funny, not the lingering memory of the way Cornelius had looked at him. The wink. The tone of his voice.

Johann had no idea what that had been about. Cornelius touched him all the time, but something about that touch, that look... *what* had that been for? And why did thinking of it make Johann feel like his one real knee would go out? Why did it make his guts tangle in a way that made him ache for Cornelius to look at him again?

Cornelius didn't look at him, though. In fact, as they descended the steps of the emporium to the street, Cornelius seemed especially subdued, almost blushing. He wore his velvet top hat and a natty jacket with a silk scarf wrapped around his throat, and he seemed to shrink into them both, until someone he knew greeted him, at which point he became flirty and touchy again.

Cornelius was very pretty, Johann thought. The fine clothes suited him.

Uncharacteristically, however, Cornelius didn't chatter, not even a little bit. Something was wrong, but Johann had no idea how to fix it. As they rounded the corner onto a main street, Johann stopped under a gaslight and put his good hand on Cornelius's shoulder.

Cornelius startled, jumpy as a cat. "What's wrong?"

That was what Johann was going to ask Cornelius. He indexed his French for a different query. "You are not happy. Sad. Afraid. Why?"

Cornelius bit his lip, but this time the tic made Johann ache for him. "We must pretend. For my friends."

Yes. Johann knew this part. "I am pirate. Pretend pirate."

"Not a soldier." Cornelius looked terrified. "You must *not* say you are a soldier."

Ah, at last Johann understood Cornelius's terror. "Austrian soldier, not good here." He rubbed the stubble on his chin. "I talk German. Bad French."

Cornelius launched into incomprehensible French, saw Johann's blank expression and stopped with a sigh. "No speaking. *Little* speaking."

Don't talk much. That would be easy. "I do what you say."

Cornelius touched Johann's face. "*Vous êtes un trésor.*"

I am a...something. Johann frowned as he tried to work it out, then froze as Cornelius's lips brushed his cheek.

It wasn't really a kiss—nothing more than the usual dry French buss. But it rekindled that strange sensation, made Johann unconsciously follow Cornelius's mouth as it moved away.

In the flickering, hissing gaslight, their gazes met and held. Cornelius's lashes were outlined, Johann realized, with kohl. Johann stared at the eyeliner, that strange sensation in his belly curdling until, to his astonishment, it made his cock swell ever so slightly in his trousers.

With a gasp, Johann drew back. He blinked rapidly, as if whatever was happening to him was some kind of grit in his good eye.

Blushing, his smile fading, Cornelius turned away. "Come. We go to the café."

Johann followed, not entirely certain of what had just happened, but eager to move on from it, whatever it had been.

Chapter Three

The café was terribly French.

Johann knew enough about the city to understand this was one of Calais's many *petits cafés littéraires*, with tall windows, cozy booths, and bright young men and women standing on tables, shouting philosophy while delicate chandeliers dangled overhead. A handful of women were present, prostitutes by the look of them, though Johann admitted he wasn't well-versed in distinguishing that sort of thing. He'd always been nervous around whores, because they were so pushy and grew more aggressive when they discovered he was shy. He refrained from looking at the women here entirely, hoping to avoid any confrontations.

Cornelius kept hold of Johann's arm, transforming as they entered the room. He was all bright smiles and winks, and his voice took on the same flirty quality that had so dismantled Johann at the emporium. Everyone who came to greet Cornelius hugged and kissed him, and many kissed the tinker's cheeks several times before relinquishing him to the next acquaintance. Johann couldn't catch much of what they said, but it seemed to be largely revolving around, "Where have you been?" and other concerns over Cornelius's absence.

Finally someone said, looking at Johann, "Who is *this?*"

Cornelius introduced Johann, touching him a great deal, stroking his arm and his chest and leaning into his side. It was clear Cornelius was incredibly nervous but working hard to hide that fact. Johann wanted to help him, but he knew opening his mouth and letting them hear his Austrian accent would alarm the room.

A young man pushed his way to the front, and even before he spoke,

Johann suspected this was the one who'd burst into Cornelius's room earlier in the day. Valentin Durant, Cornelius introduced him as. The man bowed prettily, never letting his gaze leave Johann.

This was the man to impress. This was the one who needed to believe the lie. So Johann did his best to project *pirate* and continued saying nothing.

A few gentlemen in the crush surrounding them asked Johann questions— *where did you come from?*—but Cornelius always answered in his rapid-fire French, deftly keeping them away. Johann began to think perhaps this could work, him standing quietly and Cornelius doing all the speaking.

Then one of the women pushed her way to the front and put her hand on Johann's chest and spoke. In a man's voice.

Part of Johann's brain registered something hadn't been quite the usual even before she'd spoken, but there was no mistaking she had a man's voice. She was a man, in a dress.

He'd never seen such a thing in his life. Johann stared at her, having absolutely no idea in the world what was going on.

Cornelius pushed the woman back with a saucy scolding and curled himself protectively against Johann's chest, putting a proprietary hand on his hip. "*Il est à moi!*"

He's mine.

Johann's cock, which hadn't entirely recovered from the earlier episode, surged back to life.

Panicking, Johann tried to keep Cornelius from becoming aware of his condition, but Cornelius had already turned around. Drawing close to Johann's side, he pulled down the brim of his hat and whispered into his ear, "I'm sorry. Please forgive me. I'm so sorry."

Then he placed a soft, lingering kiss right on Johann's lips.

The crowd crowed and clapped, but Cornelius didn't smile and laugh with them. Under the brim of Johann's hat, he looked intensely sad and terrified. "So sorry." He plastered on a smile and took on the flirty voice again as he addressed the crowd of young men watching them.

The young men who had all just watched Cornelius kiss him. And had cheered it on.

Kissed him like a lover. The thought made Johann's head spin. He couldn't imagine such a thing in his village. True, he'd seen some men coupling in the camps—not often, because if an officer caught them, they would be dead—but he had always chalked that up to the desolation of war. There were no women present, after all. Here in the café, though, it seemed to be only men and the men-as-women, and everyone was flirting with everyone else. Several men sat in the laps of other men or leaned against them like lovers. It dawned on him that everyone in the café were men who could love men. Who wanted to.

And I arrived with Cornelius, who has just kissed me.

The café abruptly did not have enough air. Johann pushed to his feet, ready to bolt out of the building.

Immediately, Cornelius stood before him. He took Johann's face in his slender hands and drew his head down to whisper once more in his ear. "*Restez calme.* It is all right. *Faites comme si.*"

Johann exhaled in a shudder. "*Sie...haben mich geküsst.*" He touched his lips in an attempt to translate.

His cock was still hard. Harder, even, than it had been before. *He* might be unnerved by this turn of events, but his body seemed right at home.

Cornelius touched Johann's lips too, which helped nothing in the department of Johann's trousers. "Valentin. He watches."

But why does that mean we have to kiss?

And why do I wish you would do it again?

Johann couldn't work out for the life of him why he and Cornelius had to pretend to be lovers. Male lovers? It was indecent. It was scandalous.

Or rather, it should have been.

Johann was absolutely certain the priest in his village would say this was a sin. The mayor would turn red in the face. Decidedly his mother wouldn't like it. His sergeant commander, either. Except evidently no one here cared what any of those people or their French counterparts would say. They appeared quite happy to be in each other's arms. Johann did not understand the men-women, but…well, they seemed very happy too. Happier than he had ever remembered being, so who was he to say it was wrong for them to wear dresses and paint? They all carried on in full view of the windows, hugging and kissing and flirting and drinking from delicate, expensive cups. No one came in to arrest them. No one clutched their breast in horror.

Johann did his best to write the whole thing off as *Frankreich, mein Gott*, but there was one stubborn problem with that dismissal, and that was his own misbehaving cock. It *liked* flirty Cornelius. It very much appreciated every brush of Cornelius's bottom on his thigh, where he could feel how round and firm and yet still soft Cornelius's derrière was. It wasn't entirely sure what to do with the men-women, but it didn't mind them half as much as Johann's terrified mind did.

Johann's cock loved Cornelius's kisses. The tender ones, the flirty ones along his jaw—but more than anything, it treasured the one time Cornelius had sucked, ever so gently, on the pulse in his neck. The crowd applauded and made lewd sounds—but then, as after every kiss, Cornelius gave Johann that pained expression and another apology when no one else was watching.

No one tried to get Johann to speak further, not even Valentin, who had become distracted by a charming Moor and a bottle of wine. People spoke *at* Johann, mostly encouraging more kisses, and if Johann waggled his eyebrow and nipped at Cornelius's shoulder, they cheered and left him alone.

Pretend to be Cornelius's lover. It seemed he could do this far too easily for comfort.

When the café closed, the men spilled into the streets, heading across the way to a raucous tavern with women and men both leaning out of upstairs windows, catcalling to the herd. Johann girded himself for the transfer, but to his surprise, Cornelius led him away. When their companions complained, Cornelius shook his finger at them. "No, I'm going home."

Everyone leered and applauded, making it clear they knew exactly what was going to happen when Cornelius and Johann got back to the apartment.

They drifted toward a side street, Cornelius still wrapped around Johann, but the instant they were out of view, Cornelius broke away. *Now* he chattered in French. Panicked, almost tearful pleadings, too fast and incoherent for Johann to catch more than the occasional fleeting word which out of context meant nothing. Except *sorry*. Over and over again, Cornelius apologized. And before long, he began to cry.

Johann clomped over on his peg leg and gripped Cornelius firmly by the shoulders. "*Nicht weinen.*" He wished he knew how to say *don't cry* in French. He trailed a fingertip beside a descending tear. "What is this? How do you say this? Water from eyes?"

"Tears," Cornelius croaked in a jagged whisper. His gaze, still full of sorrow and fear, still streaked with his weeping, never left Johann's.

Johann didn't look away either. "No tears." He grazed Cornelius's cheek with the knuckles of his flesh hand. "We pretend. No tears."

Cornelius's eyes spilled over once more, but some of his uneasiness melted away. "You are a fine man, Johann."

Johann kissed Cornelius's hand, then let it fall to his side. "Home?"

They walked in silence through the alleys back to the tinker shop. They didn't hold hands, but Cornelius kept close as Johann navigated his false leg and his cane. As they ascended the stairs and Cornelius fussed with the complicated lock to his rooms, Johann had a quick consultation with himself.

If Cornelius kissed him again, alone in the room…well, it wasn't as if there weren't a ledger full of other sins he could get arrested for in Calais. Clearly taking a male lover wasn't as scandalous as being an Austrian soldier. Anyway, he enjoyed Cornelius's gentle touches. He kissed well too, far better than Johann. Certainly it was unconventional, but that was the whole of his life now. He would do this. If Cornelius gave even the smallest sign he wanted more amorous play, Johann would find a way to indicate he was, in fact, willing to do more than pretend.

Except Cornelius made no further efforts to kiss him. In the room, he locked the door, sat Johann on the bed and undid his pirate disguise. No kisses, no flirts, only meticulously checked Johann's artificial joints and attached his usual calf and foot on his right leg. He smiled an awkward, uncertain smile, then busied himself with remaking his pallet bed before the hearth.

Johann watched him for a moment, then went to the water closet and relieved himself. He glanced Cornelius's way as he exited, hoping perhaps to catch an invitation, *something*—but Cornelius had his eyes shut tight.

Johann went to bed as silently as he could, wrapping his blanket around his torso. He told himself it was stupid to be disappointed he wasn't getting kissed again, and did his best to go to sleep.

* * * * *

Cornelius couldn't understand why the café hadn't repulsed Johann, but he didn't question the reaction. He didn't bring the episode up in conversation, either, and he didn't take him back to the café.

In fact, in the month following their initial outing, Cornelius avoided discussing or thinking of many things with many people. He allowed Louise to clean the room once more, but when she gave pointed looks at the hulking pirate practicing his walking along the side of the bed, Cornelius pretended to not understand what could possibly be wrong with this arrangement. Master Félix asked a few questions about Johann, then largely forgot his existence until the faux-pirate walked in front of him. He'd predict Johann would bring trouble, then return to whatever project had him captivated at the moment.

By early May, Conny couldn't avoid his father's increasingly insistent demands he visit the magistrate, and so one bright and sunny Tuesday afternoon he secured Johann with instructions to stay in the room and speak to no one, then hired a carriage to the other side of town.

The magistrate, Baptiste Tremblay, was a measly mouse of a man, and he was firmly in the archduke's pocket. Most city officials were, since they were installed by political favor, but Conny had always resented having such a simpering mewl as a minder. This visit was worse, since it wasn't simply Conny and Tremblay having awkward conversation over sherry. The tinker Cornelius had been avoiding the night he found Johann was also visiting the magistrate. Worse, once he'd introduced the two of them, Tremblay left them alone in the salon to have their discussion.

Dr. Martin Savoy didn't look like a tinker. His clothes were too neat and too plain, and the wrong style. He wore a high-necked jacket mirroring an officer's uniform, a style popular only with the most elite, politically minded set in Paris, which no tinker Cornelius had ever met would consider wearing. Some of their kind were tidy, yes, but Savoy was drawn with four pins. Tinkers would never set so much store by fashion, and they'd never waste their money on gold piping. If they wanted sparkle on their clothing, they'd use copper filament. Even his spectacles were wrong—small and round, the glass slightly tinted but highly reflective, making him appear to have no eyes. Possibly he dressed so because he was, as Tremblay had whispered in the hall, also a physician, and therefore he moved in higher social circles than a mere surgeon. But even if Savoy had been in proper plain trousers, he would have left Conny feeling uneasy. He regarded Conny like an old billy goat who didn't much care if Cornelius wanted to be mounted.

Savoy sat still and focused on Tremblay's sofa, holding a cup of tea before him as he regarded Conny with a discomfiting smile. "Your father speaks very highly of you. He says you will soon surpass your master in your skill at both clockwork prosthetics and clockwork surgery."

Conny sipped at his sherry and smiled thinly. "How kind of my father to notice my skill. I hope someday I will excel enough he might deign to praise me in person."

"Your father is well aware of your talents." The physician's reptilian smile curled into something Conny assumed was meant to be flirtatious but made him want to retch. "He isn't the only one noticing you, either, my little rabbit."

"Attracting attention has never been an issue for me." Conny crossed his legs and dusted lint from his shirtsleeve as he reclined in his chair.

"Your father would like you to work with me in Paris. I should like this as well."

Conny, who had been sipping his sherry, nearly choked on his laughter. "How wonderful for you both. And how tragic, as I have no intention of leaving Calais."

Savoy's smile became brittle. "I'm afraid it isn't a request, child. Though don't think of it as a command. Think of it as an opportunity."

Conny set the sherry aside, and his nonchalant façade as well. "If Archduke Guillory wishes to incarcerate me, he will need to send someone more adept than an unwashed bear to flash his lapel and drool onto my sleeve. Should either of you think you can by any means cajole me into helping your war effort, you are both so stupid I could cry."

Unfortunately this candor didn't erase Savoy's leer. "Such spirit. *Mmm.*" He sipped his tea in a manner that managed to make Conny's skin crawl, then set the cup on the table between his sofa and Conny's chair. "Enough of what will be. Tell me instead about working with Félix Dubois. They say he has many inventive clockwork prosthetics, some which are downright miraculous."

"Master Félix is a genius, yes. He is currently attempting a clockwork liver, and his mechanical spine was sold for a handsome sum to the King of Sweden, who wanted it for his young son afflicted with palsy. Every day another letter comes from a university begging him to teach, or a factory offering an emperor's ransom for his skills. But he wishes only to remain in Calais. Which is where I shall stay also."

"A liver? That would be something to see, certainly." Savoy laced his fingers together and leaned forward, his greasy smile back in full force. "Has he shown you any other organs? A stomach? A lung?"

"Of course. Lungs are entirely commonplace. Stomachs less so, but there have been a few."

"And what of a clockwork heart?"

Conny should have seen it coming. But he'd been too busy being revolted by Savoy, and when the question came out of nowhere, he wasn't ready. He startled, then quickly tried to steel himself, worrying it was too late. He did his best to channel his mother, hoping at least some of her acting ability was genetic. "Are you making a joke? Of course he doesn't have a clockwork heart. We don't have the technology for such a thing."

"We're closer than you think. And the rumors are wild that Dubois has cracked the code. That he keeps it hidden and moves it from place to place so it can't be discovered."

This was, of course, exactly the truth of what Master Félix had been doing. "Good God, you make it sound as if he is some kind of spy."

"How interesting you should bring that up. Because the rumors say he is that too. A spy for England."

A spy? Félix? Normally Cornelius would laugh, but given everything that had happened, he wasn't certain what to put his faith in anymore. What he did know was he wasn't sitting in this horrid lizard's company any longer. Conny stood, retrieving his jacket from the arm of the chair. "Charming as it is to listen to your fairy tales, I believe I must be going. I'm sure I'll never see you again, so I wish you the best of luck in finding a color of suit coat more flattering to your skin. *Bonne continuation.*"

He breezed out of the room before Savoy could force him to endure a response, managing to save his shudder for the privacy of the hallway. Much as he would have loved to vacate the house entirely, politeness dictated he find the magistrate first and bid him goodbye before taking his leave. Maddeningly, his host was indisposed, and Conny had to wait in the study for his chance at a brief audience.

He poked about idly, running his fingers down the spines of some books on a shelf while keeping one eye on the door, hoping Tremblay would appear, worried Savoy would instead. There was no hope in finding something to read to fill the time, as the magistrate only kept dull books of record in here, saving the better titles for his library. Still, Conny amused himself by poking around behind the dry leather tomes, hoping to discover an illicit hidden gem. Maybe something erotic or at least mildly titillating? After several searches to no avail, he began to read the report volumes out of sheer boredom, and this was when he found the dictionary.

It was tucked inside some dry book of law, and it tumbled to the floor when Conny removed the volume which housed it. *Dictionnaire Français-Allemand,* the title read, and Cornelius delighted to see this was precisely what it was. An old, battered thing with pages missing and all manner of notes scribbled in the margins and sometimes across whole words, but it was a *dictionary,* a means by which Cornelius could communicate more easily with Johann.

Conny tucked the slim volume into his pocket and took it home with him.

Johann was as excited as Cornelius at the discovery, and they spent the better part of the evening expanding each other's vocabularies. Conny rather enjoyed learning some of Johann's language too. Over the next few days, it helped improve Johann's progress by leaps and bounds. When Cornelius went out or performed surgery with Master Félix, Johann practiced writing and reading aloud, and when they worked together, Cornelius corrected Johann's pronunciation, trying to teach him a native French accent. He assumed Johann would have more questions once he had more language capability, but the only one he did ask took Cornelius entirely by surprise.

"Conny." Johann pointed to one of Master Félix's old journals they were using for reading practice. "This says *conne,* but others call you this too."

"An abbreviation for Cornelius, yes."

Johann frowned. "But is bad. *Conne* means..." He trailed off, blushing.

Conny lifted the corner of his mouth. "It means idiot, bitch, and it's feminine? Yes. The first night Valentin met me, he didn't like me, and he christened me with it. He thought it was funny, because my name is English, and my natural French nickname is such a terrible insult. My mother wasn't thinking things through, I'm afraid, when she Anglicized my father's middle name. But I've never been proud, and alas, sometimes the description is terribly apt."

Johann's frown deepened. "Pardon me, but I do not understand."

Such a *dear,* adorable man. Conny sighed and winked. "I don't mind the name."

Johann seemed mildly relieved. "Is good?"

"Is quite good. You may use the name as well, if you like."

"I call you…Conny?"

What had been an innocent exchange became immediately charged. Conny was long used to a state of constant arousal around Johann, but in that moment he went past longing into his increasingly common delusion that perhaps Johann fancied him too.

Clearing his throat, he popped to his feet. "Let's take a stroll, shall we?"

They took a great many strolls, the two of them, more and more often as Conny became increasingly desperate to escape the close confines of his bedroom with a handsome man he could not under any circumstances allow himself to seduce. Johann seemed to enjoy going out, sometimes speaking to strangers now that he knew enough French to get by. He liked to do the ordering at the market as well.

Once, while strolling down a crowded street with his protégé, Conny saw Savoy lurking on the other side of the street, observing them. Cornelius pretended not to notice, but he worried the rest of the day he'd return to the shop only to find the horrid little physician waiting for him, following through on his promise to bring trouble into Cornelius's already amply complicated life.

Alas, it was not Savoy waiting to turn the world on its head. When Conny and Johann returned to his apartment, they discovered the door unlocked and Valentin waiting for them inside.

He was holding the French-German dictionary.

Chapter Four

"What the devil is this?" Val waved the book at Cornelius, loosening one of the pages. "*Why* do you have this book?"

"It isn't mine. I borrowed it from the magistrate." Cornelius rescued the book and tucked the page back inside. "How did you get into my rooms? I know I remembered to set the locks."

"The door was open when I arrived. All the doors were, though no one answered when I called. Don't change the subject. I want to talk about this *book*." Valentin glared at Johann. "You need that dictionary because he's Austrian, don't you? Don't think I haven't noticed his bad French and that funny accent. I thought maybe he was a stupid thug from some border town, but it's worse than that, isn't it?"

"I don't know where he's from. It's not the sort of thing we discuss." That was the truth. Both of them carefully circumnavigated all talk of their past.

Johann said nothing, as was his custom, taking his lead in this fiction from Cornelius. But he watched Valentin from his post at the door.

Valentin aimed an angry finger at Conny. "You've been with him a month since I found out, and you'd been reclusive for two weeks before that, so I'm assuming he's been living with you for two months. What in the *world* have you been doing? Don't tell me teaching him French."

Yes, mostly. That, and perfecting Johann's gait and tweaking his clockwork. There was also that one time he'd gently drugged Johann so he could check on his heart, but he wasn't proud of that.

Of course, Cornelius could say none of this to Valentin. "What do you *think* I've been doing in my rooms with a handsome, lusty sky pirate?"

"No, you *haven't* been fucking him. You put on a good act that first night, but not since. You don't touch him overmuch. You don't take him out except what you feel you must to pacify us. Yet he absorbs all your time, causes you to shirk all but your most unavoidable obligations. And now I discover you're teaching him French. Because he can only speak *German*. With an *Austrian* dialect." Valentin closed the distance between them. "You will tell me, Cornelius, right now, what is going on. Or God help me, I'll write to your father."

Cornelius couldn't stop the gasp of terror that escaped him, or the shiver of pleasure he felt when Johann moved to stand behind him, placing a reassuring hand on Conny's shoulder.

Johann glared at Valentin. "I am a sky pirate. I was injured and lost on the shore. No more ship. Cornelius helps me. Keeps away soldiers. He is good lover. Good friend. What friend are you, making him frightened?"

Cornelius blushed to the roots of his hair, stunned speechless.

Valentin sneered. "You're not his lover. And you're not a pirate. Wearing an eyepatch doesn't make you a pirate." He looked up and down his nose at Johann. "I can't even tell how old you are. You seem to be somewhere between awkward young lug and old man."

"I am eighteen," Johann said.

Cornelius stared at Johann with his mouth open. "You're...*eighteen?*" Good Lord, he was younger than Cornelius! Conny had thought he was at least in his late twenties. Eighteen—he was barely of age.

Johann shrugged apologetically. "I am big. Everyone thinks I am older. Has always been."

"He's lying to you, obviously." Valentin faced Johann down now, righteous indignation at full fury.

Johann faced him calmly, but without hesitation. "I do not lie to Cornelius. You, maybe. You are—" He frowned, clearly mentally indexing. "*Ein Tyrann.* A not-friend."

Tyrant, it seemed, was a universal word. Cornelius enjoyed the way this wounded and disarmed Valentin, but pity quickly overruled him. "He's not a tyrant. Not really. He's overprotective and arrogant, but he's my oldest friend, and he loves me." He frowned at Valentin. "Though that was a very low blow, to threaten to go to my father."

Valentin's cheeks stained as he lifted his chin. "I don't like this man. He's going to bring you trouble." He glared again at Johann. "Why did you leave your ship?"

"Lost ship. I was in fight. Hurt. They left."

"And they didn't come find you?"

Johann snorted. "Pirates do not."

It made sense, Cornelius thought. Except Johann looked oddly angry when he said that, as if he was upset by being left. As if he *had* been a pirate and *had* been abandoned.

Valentin lifted his chin higher. "How did you become a pirate? There aren't any airships in Austria. It's a horribly backward country. Because I *know* you're Austrian."

"Yes, I am from *Österreich*. A small, simple village in the west, in the mountains. No airships. No food. I went into army at fourteen for stipend to family."

Valentin recoiled in horror as Cornelius winced. "You're an *Austrian soldier?*"

"Yes, but I ran away. Become pirate. Better life. Better money for family."

He spoke with such conviction, Cornelius almost believed it to be true.

Valentin clearly did not. "So what did you do as a fourteen-year-old pirate?"

"Sixteen. I was in the army two years. When I am pirate, I carry things. Cook. Cut people who say no boarding."

Valentin's countenance slipped from irritation to confusion. "Boarding? In an airship?"

"Yes." He mimed swinging a rope over his head and tossing it in front of him. "Big rope, hook. I slide."

"You *threw a rope* at a ship held aloft only by gas? You could kill everyone aboard."

Johann's grin was wicked. "If cargo is good, we do."

Valentin turned back to Cornelius. "You condone this? You, and your bleeding heart that cannot stand to see so much as a sparrow downed?"

No, Cornelius didn't. He bit his lip as he regarded Johann, hoping he was simply that good a liar with an imagination tainted by the horrors of war.

Johann's expression gentled. His hand, which had fallen from Cornelius's shoulder, returned. "I throw with care. I never miss."

"This is exactly what I mean." Valentin gestured between them. "You don't know anything about him, Cornelius. What is going on?"

Cornelius didn't know what to say. He had no truth to bend around, because he still didn't know why he was so obsessed with Johann, not enough to tell Valentin, not enough to understand it himself. Had Johann *actually* been a pirate? Why had he not said so before? He kept his gaze away from Valentin, wishing he knew a way out of this conversation.

"He is a good lover," Johann said, out of nowhere.

Cornelius stiffened, and Valentin snorted. "He is. But you don't look like lovers to me."

"Is not good to show love loud." Johann gestured to the window facing the street. "People are angry. Arrest."

Valentin rolled his eyes. "Please. We pay the police regularly. In any event, they'd never dare arrest Conny. Not unless they knew it was part of one of his games."

Conny wanted to object to this depiction of his sexual debauchery, or at least Val pointing it out, but Johann spoke first. "People arrest *Österreicher*. Hate me, like you do."

Valentin pursed his lips. "Fine. Kiss him now."

Cornelius's entire body blushed, flashing between cold terror and anticipation. "*Valentin.*"

"Stop playing prude. You're France's greatest exhibitionist. With enough cocaine and absinthe, you've let men fuck you over tables. I've watched your public performance enough I can recognize you in an orgy by the dimple in your left ass cheek. *You* can't object to a kiss in front of me. He can hardly either, as he did as much that first night." Valentin looked at Johann and pointed at Cornelius. "Kiss him. Prove you're lovers."

Johann quite noticeably did not blush or shy away. He turned to Cornelius, waiting for permission.

Cornelius couldn't give it. He'd worked hard to avoid this. He'd grown fond of Johann as a friend, a companion—true, they had difficulty communicating still, but the man was so easy to be around. Every time Cornelius had to leave him, all he thought about was when he'd be able to see that rough, smiling face. He hadn't felt this way about anyone, ever, whether or not they'd slept together. Johann was patient and kind, and his smile could undo kinks in Cornelius's weary soul. Conny swallowed hard and shut his eyes, unable to face the possibility of Johann being so repulsed by having to feign playing lovers once more that he might insist on leaving.

Soft lips brushed Cornelius's own and made him open his eyes.

Johann hovered over Cornelius's mouth, staring back at him. He didn't look upset. He didn't look repulsed. He didn't exactly look aroused, either. Only concerned.

That was the crux of the matter, Cornelius realized. He wanted Johann to want him too. Because yes, Cornelius wanted to kiss Johann. More every day. And though Valentin was right, he loved easily and often, there was something different about Johann. He wanted to kiss him, to make love to him, but he would rather have Johann as a friend and companion than a lover. If kissing Johann to pacify Valentin's paranoia lost Cornelius their friendship, it would shatter him. He didn't know why. He couldn't explain how this had happened when he barely knew the man, when he couldn't even be certain the man actually wanted him that way. He only knew he wanted.

With Johann's kiss still burning his lips, Cornelius was ready to admit he very nearly *needed*.

Johann ran the gloved fingers of his artificial hand down Cornelius's cheek.

Then, gripping Cornelius firmly by the waist, he bent his head and kissed him.

Cornelius's hands drifted, wrapped themselves around Johann's neck, slid to his face. His heart fluttered at his throat, and desire tangled with the nerves in his belly. He was charmed, disarmed by the realization Johann didn't know how to kiss. It was more than hesitation over kissing a man. He clearly hadn't done much kissing of anyone.

He's eighteen. Guilt threatened Cornelius, but then Johann's lips parted and his tongue haltingly grazed Cornelius's bottom lip.

Cornelius opened his mouth and invited Johann's tongue to play.

He gasped as Johann did just that, and when Cornelius pressed his body against Johann's and felt the evidence of his arousal, a thrill ran down his spine. True, any man got aroused by the right touch, but it was still Cornelius doing the touching, even if only for pretend, and he yearned enough for Johann that he didn't care what it took.

Johann *was* a bit large in stature, and though that didn't always excite him, it did in this case. Conny's imagination helpfully outlined sexual scenarios where Johann's strength could be an asset. How his clockwork could be made erotic. He forgot to guard himself, and he responded to the kiss as if it were real, as if they truly were lovers. In fact, he was in the process of shifting them to the edge of the table so he could sit on it and open his legs for Johann when a prim knock sounded on the door.

Johann pulled back, and Cornelius clung to him to steady himself, still lost in the kiss. When Valentin cleared his throat, Cornelius glanced at him blearily, surprised to find him there.

"Monsieur Stevens?" Louise knocked again. "A letter was delivered for you. Also, Master Félix is upset."

Cornelius smoothed a hand nervously over his hair, a vain attempt to bring himself back to earth. "I'll be right there," he called weakly to Louise. He glanced at Johann, at Valentin, feeling he should say something, not knowing even remotely what that something should be.

A shout from downstairs made him give up. Biting his lip, he pushed off the table, knowing he had to see to Félix.

"You would like help?" Johann asked, calm, concerned—not in any way looking as rattled as Cornelius felt.

Perhaps he was pretending after all.

Pursing his lips, Cornelius frowned at Valentin. "Are you convinced? Or will you wait until I come back, so you can watch me suck him off?"

Valentin glowered. "I want to speak to you this evening. The two of us, alone. Unless you have no more need for our friendship, with your pirate lover."

With a sigh, Cornelius kissed Valentin's cheeks. "You are too dramatic. Where shall I meet you?"

"At The Alison. I'll reserve the back room." He kissed Cornelius back and squeezed his arm. "Thank you."

Cornelius started toward the door, pausing when he realized Valentin wasn't following him. He would harangue Johann as soon as they were alone. Cornelius should stop it. Except he didn't know how.

Johann winked. "Go. Is good."

Yes, but was it really? Cornelius realized when they two were next alone, *they* would have to have an awkward conversation. Unless of course Johann was already gone, horrified by Conny's display or chased off by Val.

Pressing his hand against his suddenly splitting head, Cornelius stumbled out of the room and into the hall, certain the letter Louise possessed and whatever had Félix up in arms couldn't be half as bad as anything he was leaving behind.

As the door closed behind Cornelius, Johann and Valentin regarded one another. For a long time they said nothing, but eventually Valentin's irritation spilled over into words.

"I'll give you five hundred francs to go away."

Johann said nothing.

Valentin developed a tic in his cheek. "Eight hundred. A thousand. What is your price to leave him alone?"

Johann made no reply.

Valentin's nostrils flared as he closed the distance between them. "I don't know what's going on here, but you're not telling me the truth. That much I do understand. You should know this—if you hurt him, if you so much as break his heart, I'll kill you."

Johann kept his expression mild. "I feel this also. Do not hurt Cornelius."

Valentin made a very French noise through his nose, but said nothing more. Eventually he stormed out of the room, slamming the door behind him.

Alone at last, Johann shut his eyes and let the mask fall away from his face as he allowed himself to acknowledge the weight of what had happened. Of what he had done. What Cornelius had, quite clearly, been happy to have him do.

The kiss. The kisses. The touching, the holding.

The wanting. To kiss Cornelius more. To be his lover not for pretend. To make love to him for real.

It had not been bad. It had not even been merely tolerable. It had been as if someone had lit a flame inside Johann, a torch he hadn't known he carried. In fact, Johann didn't know when he'd yearned for something more.

He decided he would not wait a month to see if it happened again. When Cornelius returned, he would find a way to explain himself. That he wanted to do more than simply kiss. He didn't fully understand what else taking a male lover would entail, but he was ready to admit he was willing to embark on that adventure.

He was also fairly sure none of these things would be in the dictionary.

He wondered, too, if he should find a way to explain some of his past to Cornelius. About how he truly had been a pirate, how what he'd told Valentin had been the truth, with only the part about the army discovering him once more being omitted from the tale. He would tell Cornelius, yes. But he decided he would kiss him first. In case the kisses could help soften the blow, to keep those explanations from making Cornelius want to send Johann away.

Because that was the only thing Johann wanted now: to stay with Cornelius. With or without the kisses. For as long as Cornelius would let him remain by his side.

* * * * *

Cornelius found Master Félix in the vault where the tinker's most expensive, valuable clockwork prosthetics were kept, which also housed the additionally locked unit where the clockwork heart had been stored. The vault that was now in complete and utter shambles, every bit of priceless clockwork shattered and strewn across the floor.

Cornelius put a hand to his chest. "Were we burgled?"

Félix blinked up at Cornelius, despondent through his thick handmade clockwork glasses. "Yes. God help us, *yes*, child—someone has stolen the heart."

Cornelius did his best to look surprised. And innocent. "Are you certain?"

"Nearly. The door was blown open when I returned, and they forced open the lock on the heart's special case as well."

Cornelius paused. "So you found it like this? Everything strewn across the floor?"

"You think *I* would treat the contents of my vault this way?" He motioned impatiently to Cornelius. "Come. Help me put things to rights."

"But who would do this?" Cornelius asked Félix as he replaced a battery pack made with gold and silver diodes. The connectors in that one device were worth hundreds of francs for the metal alone. Yet whoever had come here hadn't taken it. Which yes, meant they wanted only one thing.

Of course, they could not possibly have found it.

"I have no idea who would be so beastly as to perform this atrocity." Félix paused as he put a gold-plated differential into a bin. "Well…I do have some ideas. But nothing solid enough to go on."

"We should tell the magistrate." Cornelius hoped his blush was easily mistaken for high emotions over the destruction, not his traitorous biology giving him away. He told himself there was no way to trace the theft to himself, not of the heart or the other pieces. He'd tarnished Johann's clockwork so it looked aged and worn, the way a real pirate's stolen clockwork would appear, and he'd rebuilt every bit he'd taken for his own use.

All but the heart.

Félix snorted. "I'm not telling the magistrate about this theft when he's at the top of my list of suspects."

"*What?*" Cornelius put down the broken clockwork finger he'd been holding. "You think…the *magistrate* could have ordered this?"

Félix hushed him and scurried to the door, closing them in. It wasn't an action advised for laymen, but a master tinker and his apprentice could certainly undo their own locks. Even after they were sealed in, however, Félix spoke in hushed tones. "Yes, I think he easily could have done so. He's kept strange company of late. Rumors are wild he is in cahoots with an Austrian spy."

Cornelius's eyes went wide. "I was with him the other day, but I saw no spy. A friend of my father's was there, however. Insisting I go work for him in Paris, at my father's decree."

"Savoy? He's nothing but a popinjay. The magistrate, however, is more than he seems. That flustered imbecile posture is nothing more than an act. And I fear now he and whoever he works for has penetrated my most secure space with relative ease." Félix grimaced. "I should have moved it then, but I wasn't ready. Frankly, I've put it out of my mind as much as possible, unwilling to address the problem of its security. And now look what has happened. I should have been more cautious, especially after the attack on the western shore two months ago. I had too much faith in my locks."

The attack which had brought Johann into Conny's life was somehow connected to this? "What do you mean?"

"The rumor is that it was a suicide mission meant to distract our soldiers while something nefarious happened on the eastern side of town. English airships, Austrian soldiers. I'm certain now they must have been after the heart."

The barge of dead soldiers with Johann dying on top drifted all too easily into Cornelius's mind. That had been a suicide mission? Had Johann known? Had he meant to die?

What on earth had Cornelius done, bringing such a dangerous man back to life?

He's not dangerous. He's Johann.

The thought was pretty and sentimental, emotions Cornelius began to realize he could ill afford. Johann rattled off a story about pirates so neatly, it seemed entirely true. Who was it, exactly, lurking in Cornelius's bedroom? Who had just kissed him so sweetly?

Was the magistrate not the only one conspiring with an Austrian spy?

Félix sighed and went back to sifting through the wreckage on the floor. "There is no logic to the Austrians capturing Calais—well, unless the rumors are true and the Austrians and English are forming an alliance once more. But even so, they could never hold it. So if they are here, they want something specific. That someone has stolen my clockwork heart bodes ill. Though I am confused as to why it would take two months for that to happen, if it truly was the Austrians. There haven't been any more burglaries since that night."

"Why would the Austrians want the heart? They don't have clockwork technology beyond the basics."

Félix looked over his glasses at Cornelius. "The heart is worth learning clockwork for. Everyone has wanted it ever since I made it all those years ago. I should never have made it. All I wanted was to help the sick and dying. If only I'd been less naive, it might have occurred to me that even the noblest of inventions will be used by evil men for war."

Cornelius paused. "War? How could the heart be a weapon?"

"Think it through, boy. What is a heart but a pump? An *engine*. The engine of our bodies, the host of our souls. What would a government do with a thousand clockwork hearts? Especially a government that needed to win a war? An entity with heaps and piles of broken men, who would do anything to have a heart making them strong and whole once more?"

Cornelius stared at Félix. "Oh, no. *No.*"

"They would make an army. Every dying man would be an opportunity to keep a trained soldier. With some of the experimental human clockwork going on in Marseille, they might even be able to animate corpses. All they lack is the engine. *My* engine." He shut his eyes and wiped his brow. Then he looked

Cornelius dead in the eye. "You didn't tell anyone about the heart, did you?"

The question was so direct, so unexpected, Cornelius stammered. "I— No, sir. I told no one."

I only stole it and put it inside a stranger, who might be one of the men searching for it.

Félix patted his shoulder. "I'm sorry, but I had to ask. I shouldn't have told you about the heart at all. I shouldn't have *kept* it. I should have destroyed it years ago. Thank God I never gave in to greed and sold it to anyone. Any fool carrying that infernal device would be nothing more than a target."

Cornelius's hands shook as he resumed his tidying. "Could you make another? Do you remember how?"

"Not without the schematics, which burned in a fire shortly after I completed it. I suppose I could copy it if I had it in my hands. *You* could too, possibly. But any other tinker? They don't have the skills, or the experience. This was my conceit. I thought only I could use it. It was safe to keep because of this. But what if I'm wrong? What if even now they are making others and creating a monstrous army?" He tossed a bit of filigree into Cornelius's bucket. "I think I must concede they came for the heart and took it. Why else would they leave so much treasure behind?"

No, if they'd come for the heart, they'd have taken it and left. This carnage came from *not* finding the heart. Somewhere, a spy was reporting the failure, and receiving new commands. Would they kidnap Félix next? Cornelius?

Would they figure out the strange visitor upstairs carried the treasure they sought? Would they cut him open and take it while Cornelius looked on?

Would Johann, the suicidal soldier, present himself for surgery if he knew what he carried?

"When did this happen?" Cornelius asked. "When was the break-in?"

"Earlier, when we were all out. All the doors were wide open when I returned. You were still walking with your pirate. I would have suspected him right off, young man, but there's no question he was with you the whole time. Maryann was clerking, but she'd closed the shop for lunch, and she swears up and down she set the locks. Louise was at market, and I was sent on a goose chase to meet a buyer who never showed. I'm certain now it was all a ruse to get me out of the house."

Cold seeped into Cornelius. "Valentin was here when I returned. In my rooms."

Félix waved this away impatiently. "That dandy couldn't organize an afternoon tea. Besides, he's too busy being jealous of you and your pirate lover to bother about clockwork hearts."

"Valentin doesn't feel that way about me."

"So you say." Félix tapped his glasses. "I may need these, but I still see."

Cornelius refused to think about that now. He put the bucket aside and reached for a cloth on the shelf to wipe grease from his fingers. "Louise said there was a letter for me and made it sound urgent."

"Oh yes, I quite forgot about it, with all the excitement." He withdrew an envelope from his jacket and passed it over to Cornelius. "It came via courier, so I assume it's from your mother. I didn't open it."

It *was* from his mother—he knew it by the bright blue seal with EG embossed in the stamp Cornelius had customized for her. "Would you mind if I read it now, or should I wait until we finish?"

"Go on. This will take all day, and she never writes unless it's important."

Cornelius tucked the letter under his arm while he worked the lock, but he began to open it as he walked down the hall. Usually he read his mother's letters with a glass of sherry in the library, but he didn't feel like the indulgence today. After the first paragraph, however, he put it away and didn't open it again until he had a snifter of brandy in his hand.

May 29, 1910
Derbyshire
Dearest Cornelius,

I pray this letter finds you in time. Please read it with a cup of tea and all your focus, for it is the most important letter I will ever send to you. Its contents are tricky to understand and require you to be brave and clever, as I know you can be. I have reason to believe you are in grave danger. You must leave Calais, for I've heard whispers the Austrian Army intends to kidnap you and hold you for ransom.

I cannot go into details in this letter as to how I know, but I implore you to trust me. This is vitally important. I would never play you false. I have arranged passage for you to London with the same ship that brought you this letter. They can hide you so well you won't know yourself. And you must tell no one where you are, not even friends. Do not doubt your carriers, though. Trust them as you would trust me or your father. You must stay away from France and remain in England until it is safe. I only wish I could say the war is over and nothing like this would be needed and you and I could be together. Pray God that day comes soon.

Go to the dock tonight and seek the seafaring ship whose name you will remember from our childhood game. You will find the clue easily, I hope. I love you always, my darling tinker boy, and hope to see you again soon.

Thinking of you always,

Mama

Cornelius drained his brandy and half of another snifter as he read the letter several times. Someone wanted to kidnap him? *Why?* His father loved him, after a fashion, and did his duty with a steady and generous allowance, but he wouldn't pay overmuch for a ransom, and he'd give exactly nothing if this were a political play, for the archduke loved war and power far, far more than he loved any actual human beings.

Except...what if they didn't want Conny for ransom? What if the thieves hadn't been looking *only* for the heart? What if they wanted the device...and someone who could make the pattern?

With shaking hands, he put his mother's letter back into the envelope and tucked it into his pocket. He didn't know what to do. He wanted to ask Félix, but his mother's letter said he shouldn't tell anyone what was going on.

Should he try and find this ship? What if they caught him?

What in the world should he do with Johann while he searched? Bring him along?

What if Johann was part of the plot?

It made no sense—Johann had been left for dead. But of course, he could have been back in contact with his superiors. *Look what's happened—the fool's repaired me and is falling in love with me while he teaches me French. I'll let you know when everyone's out of the house, and you can get the heart. I'll bring him along after.*

Except Johann had the heart. And didn't know it.

If Johann were truly part of a plot, why would he wait so long? What made today the day to search? Johann could have drugged Cornelius and sneaked away at any moment. This wasn't the first time the house had been empty, either— *plenty* of times Johann had been left alone and could have let anyone in.

Yes, that works out tidily. Have you finished arranging it so the most likely suspect isn't a traitor, simply because you wish him not to be?

Groaning, Cornelius finished off the brandy and paced the library. The thought of leaving Calais made him ill. He hated sea travel—even crossing the channel made him vomit. Slogging all the way to Derbyshire in the belly of some smelly fishing boat would have him retching so badly he wouldn't be able to walk by the end. She couldn't smuggle him out in a dirigible? If she were that far inland, air travel was so much more logical.

And wasn't he a brat, fussing over how he was being rescued?

Except...this whole affair made little *sense.* The letter was so odd. She didn't sound like herself in almost any sentence. *Please read this with tea?* He didn't drink tea, which she well knew. And why was she in Derbyshire? A new paramour? Except why was she lounging in the country if Cornelius was in danger?

The ransom was equally ridiculous. His father wouldn't ransom him from the Austrian Army. Cornelius had no value, unless the Austrians truly did want him for his tinkering ability. Except Félix would be as good as himself, for that. And his mother, fickle as she might be, adored Félix. He'd been her contact, back in her spying days. When espionage was mostly keeping score, not life and death. In any event, she wouldn't rescue Cornelius without bringing Félix along as well.

Which meant perhaps he should show this to Félix after all.

He walked quietly through the shop. Technically they were meant to be open, but Félix had locked the front door tight after the burglary, and the place was empty. Maryann had been sent home, and Louise as well. Dust danced in the afternoon sunlight, giving the illusion of glitter on the many brass and gilded parts on display. Cornelius stared, letting the hypnotic sight occupy his nervous mind while the better part of him sorted out what logic could be found in his situation.

The letter didn't make sense. She didn't sound like herself. Not exactly. The situation made no sense. Her rescue was off as well. He didn't know any childhood game that might be a clue to what the ship name would be.

Valentin couldn't possibly be involved. Félix was right, sorting through the vault with a set of tongs would overwhelm him. He hated clockwork. He hated politics more.

Johann, however, remained an absolute mystery. Cornelius could neither damn nor exonerate him.

Cornelius needed to sort out his pirate-soldier. He needed to put aside his attraction and ask hard questions and make certain he received decent answers. He had to make certain he could trust him.

Then Cornelius had to decide if he should ignore it all and keep shutting out the world, escape to his mother in London...or escape somewhere else entirely.

Except if he couldn't trust letters from his mother, couldn't count on protection from his father—where in the *world* was he meant to escape *to?*

Chapter Five

When Cornelius entered the room, Johann put down his book with a frown. "You are unhappy."

Cornelius rubbed his arms, but the cold he felt had nothing to do with temperature. He paced before the window for a moment, then leaned against the sill and focused his attention on Johann. "I need to ask you some questions. I need you to answer me honestly."

Grimacing, Johann put his hands on the desk and nodded. "Yes. I answer everything."

Excellent. Now what did Cornelius ask? *Are you here to steal the heart?* Obviously not. He tried to think of how his mother would handle it. She could smile and get anyone to reveal anything. But Conny didn't feel like smiling, and he wasn't good at playing like Elizabeth. He was as terrible an actor as she was a tinker. So he searched for an opening query that wouldn't give too much away but would hopefully give him a decent foothold to start.

"How did you make up all that information about sky pirates and hooks?" The question, once out, released a host of others behind it. "I didn't even know any of that. Is it true? What if Valentin had known you were lying?"

At first he thought he must have used too many unfamiliar words because Johann didn't say anything, but just as Conny was about to attempt to clarify, Johann spoke. "I was a pirate." He cast a sad glance at Cornelius. "Not pretend. It is as you said, almost exactly. Except you didn't find me when they leave me. The Austrian Army did."

Cornelius sank into a chair, mesmerized. "You...truly were a pirate? A sky pirate?"

Johann nodded. "When I was sixteen. The army is bad. When I die in the army, they send my family no money. I become pirate, I maybe live longer. Make more money. Send it home." He shut his eyes, looking decades older than eighteen.

That would make an excellent question also. "How old are you, really?"

"Eighteen."

Cornelius's shoulders slumped. "Truly?"

Johann frowned. "This is bad?"

Cornelius blushed. "I'm twenty-four. Twenty-five next month."

Johann blinked. "You look young. More young than twenty-five."

"*You* look thirty. But I suppose that comes with war." He rubbed his chin, acutely aware now of how little facial hair he had to the thick stubble Johann could grow by midafternoon. "Were you truly recruited at fourteen? That seems so young."

"Younger is better, they say." He made screwing motions around his head, but his gaze was cold and almost angry. "Fix our heads. Make us think like army."

"Did it work on you?"

Johann's nostrils flared, and his jaw visibly tightened for several seconds before he replied. "War is wrong. War kills children and mothers and innocents." He gestured to the window. "People here are kind. They want war? No. People in my village? No. People in castles? Yes. War is not for people. War is for—" he stopped and fished through the dictionary, "—politician." He huffed. "It is almost the same word in German."

Cornelius scooted his chair closer. "What happened the night I found you? I've never asked, but…I need to know. Why were you on the barge? Why were you the only one alive?"

Johann settled a little, more tired and sad than angry now. "They send—" He stopped to think. "They want us dead. They tell us try to win, but everyone know we will die." He checked the dictionary again. "Distraction. We were distraction. Your army kill us like animals very fast. Except me, I am not dead during distraction, only very hurt." He touched his nose. "Pretend. I hear stories about French. Take our bodies, make us soldiers with clockwork parts. So I think, better to die with brothers than be monster. They put me on barge with the dead. But then I wake with clockwork anyway."

Cornelius put a hand on his arm. "I'm so sorry. I would never give you to any army. I detest war too."

Johann patted his hand. "Is good. You are good doctor."

Cornelius blushed. "I'm just a tinker. Tinker-surgeon, yes, but I'm no physician. Not by a long way."

"You are the best doctor I ever have." Johann let go of Cornelius. "That is what happened. You set me free from Army and fixed my broken body. I thank you. I owe you much. I will answer all questions and do anything you ask."

It would be so easy for Cornelius to melt into him and fall under Johann's spell. He tried to resist. "Do you know why they sent you on a suicide mission? What were you a distraction for?"

"Something on other side of town. Airships have troops looking for weapon to destroy."

Cornelius frowned. "Destroy? Not steal?"

"Destroy. They say so many times. Bad weapon, kill many Austrians." He shrugged, as if to say he didn't really believe them.

This did not fit, though, with Félix's report, or Conny's mother's letter. He worried the edge of his sleeve. "But you don't know what weapon they spoke of?"

Johann shook his head. "They tell us nothing."

"Why didn't they try to steal the weapon?"

"I don't think they can use. I hear them talk when they don't know I listen. They sound afraid. This weapon is bad. They say…" He consulted the dictionary again. "Corpse. Corpse who walk. This is weapon. But it sound like story."

Yes, it did—the same story Félix had just told him. Cornelius felt sick. Any country making an army of the dead would commit a crime beyond all other crimes.

The secret to doing so lies in Johann's chest. And he knows nothing about it.

Probably.

This time Cornelius took both of Johann's hands. Conny's heart, all too human and vulnerable, pinched inside his chest. "Things have happened today. Serious things. I...I believe I am in danger."

Johann sat up straighter, looking ready to go to battle. "Where is danger?"

Cornelius tried to smile, but oddly it made him feel like he would cry. He steadied himself with a breath. "I need... I cannot tell who I can trust right now." He pulled a hand away to clap it over his mouth as he closed his eyes, sending a few of the tears out.

"Hush." Johann brushed the tears away with his good hand. "No tears. I will keep you safe. I am strong. Good at walking now. I know weapons. Swords. Knives. I can fight. I will protect you."

Cornelius forced his eyes open and choked the words out of his throat. "Can...I trust you?"

They seemed the stupidest words in the world, because of course a spy would lie, but Cornelius was not a spy. He was a sentimental tinker, and he wanted the man wiping away his tears to be real more than he wanted anything in the world.

Johann took both of Cornelius's hands again, drawing them to his mouth and kissing them with a reverence that sent shivers down Cornelius's spine. "You saved my life. It is for you now. I serve you. Protect you. I am not enemy. I will not hurt. I only help." He squeezed Cornelius's fingers gently. "What is danger?"

Cornelius was so tired, so overwhelmed, he wanted to weep, to hide in his bed, or better yet in his workshop and pretend none of this was happening. But he couldn't. He let out a breath. "I think...I need to leave Calais. Tonight."

"Where will you go?"

Cornelius bit his lip. "I...don't know. My mother sent me a letter telling me to come to England, but it is so strange. Something about it feels wrong. I know it's from her, but...I don't know."

"I can read this letter?"

"Oh—I'm sorry, no. It's in English. She's an actress, in London."

Johann's sideways smile did devilish things to Cornelius's insides. "I speak English."

Cornelius's mouth fell open. "You—you *what?*"

"I know English." He switched over to it, and his accent was almost gone, his words clearer. "I learned it with the pirates. They were English, and Chinese. But Chinese is very difficult to learn. I do know some curses, but that's it."

Cornelius slouched in his chair, his hand to his mouth. "All this time. We could have been speaking all this time." He cleared his throat. "So you read English as well?"

"Yes. I make some mistakes, but not so many as French. But I spoke it for nearly two years, so it makes sense. May I see the letter, or is it private?"

Cornelius passed it over as if in a dream. "I feel like such a fool. I didn't even think to ask if you spoke other languages."

"Yes, stupid Austrians don't often know anything but German." When Cornelius blushed, he winked at him. "I'm teasing you."

He was so much more…eloquent in English. This time Cornelius's blush had a bit to do with embarrassment but mostly was a side effect of his arousal. He'd become so accustomed to Johann being quiet, his conversation halting and rough. The realization that he could blossom into a wit with the simple switch of a language was like discovering a door leading to a house within a house.

He passed over the letter and watched Johann read it, his lips moving occasionally as he did so. "I don't think the Austrian Army would kidnap you. They have money, from the Turks and Italians, for aether."

"Yes—and I don't think my father would pay a ransom anyway."

"What is the childhood game?"

"I don't know. We didn't play games. I can't recall a single one, in fact." He shifted in his seat, taking a side of the letter so he could read it too. "My mother is an actress, but she used to be a spy as well. I wondered if maybe the letter is in code. But I'm wretched with codes. And all games, to be honest."

Johann rubbed his finger along the paper. "I can go to the docks and search the ships. I might not find anything, but it's better than if you go." He nodded to the clock on the wall. "You must meet Valentin for dinner." He paused. "Is... he safe?"

"I think so." Cornelius gave a mirthless laugh. "I don't know that anyone is safe anymore, to be honest."

Johann closed his hand over Cornelius's. "I am safe. I swear on my mother's name. Bertha." He ran a finger down Cornelius's cheek. "She would like you."

Without meaning to, Cornelius leaned into that finger, and all the yearning he'd been holding back rushed in with a vengeance. Johann's gaze darkened, and the finger tracing Cornelius's face became a hand cradling his cheek.

"Now I will ask you a question," Johann said, his voice rough.

Cornelius swallowed, unable to stop staring at Johann's stubble-surrounded lips. "Y-yes?"

"You keep telling Valentin and Félix we are lovers. You kiss me, but only in front of others. You tell me we're pretending." His thumb brushed Cornelius's chin. "Are we...pretending?"

There was no saliva left in Cornelius's mouth. "I...didn't think you...took men. As...lovers."

Johann's gaze didn't waver. "I haven't had any lovers. And no men have ever kissed me before."

"And...now that...one has?" He could barely get the words out of his mouth. Each one felt like sending life out of his lungs. *Please do not reject me. Not you, Johann, not now.* "What...what do you think of the...notion?"

He didn't smile, but his eyes danced like a devil's. "I don't know. I haven't had a kiss that wasn't pretend."

Cornelius's exhale was an anguished sigh. "Johann, *please—*"

And then he could say no more, because Johann's lips were on his.

Cornelius started to lean in, open his lips, then paused, still too nervous. It was an almost timid kiss. What if Johann were teasing? What—?

Johann's lips parted, his breath tingling Cornelius's mouth. This time Conny's sigh was surrender, and he opened too, taking Johann inside.

He wanted to climb into Johann's lap, to turn the kiss carnal, to beg

Johann to press him into the floor, or the table, or the bed. But he could not make himself move, could only do what Johann led him to. Sweet, slow kisses that made *him* feel eighteen. The most he dared do was lure Johann's tongue into play.

Johann went, willingly, clumsily, with the eager awkwardness of inexperience. It made Cornelius weak in the knees. It made the knots in his belly untangle, the confusion and danger fade away, because all that mattered was this man, this kiss.

The bell tower chimed in the distance, not quite breaking the spell, but reminding them there was more to the world than not-pretend kisses. Cornelius broke away gently, resting his forehead against Johann's, nuzzling his nose.

"So," he said at last, his heart beating like a butterfly at his throat. "That... was acceptable?"

Johann brushed a chaste kiss across Cornelius's mouth. "Yes."

"I don't think I can stay in Calais. Even if I don't go on this ship." He caught the fingers of Johann's false hand, threading his through. "Would... would you come with me?"

Johann squeezed back. "Of course."

Cornelius let out a shaky breath and shut his eyes. "Good. Because...I'm terrified."

"I will keep you safe."

After kissing Johann's nose, Cornelius sat up. "I need to pack some things. And I must meet Valentin. Even if only for a few moments."

"Take all the time you need. Unless you think he can't be trusted?"

Cornelius didn't know if it was because he was a fool, or because Valentin was, but he couldn't imagine any scenario where his friend became his enemy. "I don't think he's dangerous."

"I don't, either. He warned me not to hurt you, and I think he meant it." He nodded, a decision made. "You should see him, at least to say goodbye. But don't hurry. We should go at night. Harder to notice us then, and I can erase our tracks. I can inspect the ships while you visit." He touched his peg leg. "I think

I should wear the other one. I move better."

"Of course." Cornelius rose to get it. "I need to pack supplies so I can repair you as well. And maybe a few other gadgets to make things easier." He handed the leg to Johann. "Should—should I tell Félix?"

Johann frowned as he unscrewed the peg leg. "Less is better, sometimes. If he doesn't know where you are, he can't tell anyone. If he doesn't even know you're leaving, he seems more genuine. They will hurt him less, if they interrogate him."

Cornelius clapped a hand over his mouth and sat down hard on a chair.

Partly legless, Johann hobbled over and kissed his hair, squeezing his shoulder. "We will go tonight. Perhaps they won't ask him any questions."

"But *where* will we go? I don't know how to live on the run."

"I do. I promise to take care of you." He kissed Johann's cheek and sat back down to put his proper leg in place. "Pack your bag. Tell me how to help."

Cornelius rose unsteadily, staring blearily around the room. It was full, floor to ceiling, with his most precious collections: his books, his inventions, his gadgets, his tools. He would need three great carts to carry it all away. The idea of selecting down to a knapsack made him ill.

Reminding himself the thought of dying or watching Johann die as they tore him open to steal his heart would make him far sicker, he steeled his resolve, picked up a leather satchel and began making difficult choices.

* * * * *

Johann thought about Cornelius all the way to the docks. Specifically, he thought about *kissing* Cornelius.

It had been good, he thought. Johann wasn't the most skilled at lovemaking, but kisses, it turned out, were kisses. And either Cornelius was being very polite, or he'd found Johann adequate enough. The handy thing about kissing a man was his mouth didn't have to tell you he thought you were worth kissing. His trousers would do it for you.

Johann still found it a bit odd, to think he'd just kissed a man not for a pretense, but because he'd wanted to. It felt good. Right, even. He'd planned to die on that barge of corpses. He hadn't intended to be reborn in the arms of a man, but there were definitely worse ways to live. He wasn't certain others would agree with the acceptability of this kind of thinking, but Johann was highly disillusioned with what others expected him to do, especially since most of those expectations involved his misery or death.

Cornelius had given Johann back his life. Now he intended to make sure Cornelius had every means to keep on living too.

The sea docks at Calais would never die out, but they would forever now be the dingy cousin of the elegant, efficient sky docks farther along the pier. Sea travel was for fishermen, the poor, and any cargo so mundane even the insurance adjusters didn't mind paying out a loss when the poorly maintained ships spoiled the cargo with their leaky holds, or something so heavy and awkward the cost of spending the aether was too prohibitive. Johann could understand, theoretically, a situation where a fine gentleman needing quick passage out of country would go by sea ship instead of airship. But having helped more than a few fugitives during his time on *The Brass Farthing*, he knew anyone taking that route had to be very poor and very desperate, and very badly connected. The heavy wax seal and expensive stationery said Cornelius's mother was rich, and if she was a well-known actress and former spy, she would be awash in connections. This left only desperate.

This made Johann highly suspicious.

Eight ships lay in the sea harbor, and another three larger vessels weighed anchor farther off shore, bobbing gently in the fog. Johann paced the pier casually, lifting his patch so he didn't trip whenever he glanced sideways to catch the names painted on the ships' prows. None of them put him in mind of a childhood game of any kind. He did his best to memorize them anyway, in case one rang a bell for Cornelius. He made one more pass, checking to see if any crew appeared hopeful a handsome young tinker might wander up looking for passage. No one particularly stood out—they were all bored and watchful, and they narrowed their eyes at Johann, all but begging him to start something.

Johann tipped his hat at them and headed on down the pier.

He wanted to go back to The Alison, where he'd left Cornelius with Valentin, but he'd promised he wouldn't return until nine, and he had another hour to burn. He decided he might as well see if he could secure a more pleasant passage out of Calais. Cornelius hadn't seemed particular about where they went, so that meant he could hire anyone who felt suitable. They couldn't hire a regular passenger ship, obviously. Even using an alias wouldn't be enough to hide them, and on one of those they were at the mercy of the captain. On a cargo ship, only the dockmaster on the receiving end would complain about a ship being bribed off course, and every air captain knew about blaming turbulence.

There were far too many airships for Johann to know more than a few on sight, and of course none of the illegitimate businessmen would lay into port where overeager customs officers could ask bothersome questions about manifests. Johann gave the legitimate cargo ships a good study, but they were too small, too full or too fussy for his taste. No one looked particularly bribable.

He continued even farther down the pier to the north dock, down the cliff to Hangman's Landing.

He wasn't sure if anyone had ever been actually hanged at that dock, but knowing the sort who hung out there, it was even odds on truth or someone's romantic fancy. Whether it was the high altitude or the brandy, airship pirates were, in Johann's experience, caricatures of themselves. Oh, yes, all the leather vests and hats and goggles were necessary to keep out the cold and wet, but there was absolutely no need for so many rivets and buckles, and what in the world all the decorative gears were for, no one would ever know. The excessive use of brass did make things look nice, but to Johann's practical Austrian soul, it all seemed ridiculous.

On the upside, every single ship in the dock would turn themselves inside out to take a skilled tinker on board. If they didn't have one of their own at the moment—airship pirates were also notoriously high-strung—they might even *pay* Cornelius to take a ride.

At Hangman's Landing, Johann knew every ship in port. He arrived during the span of hours the customs officials took bribes to be somewhere other than the landing, so the air harbor was full to bursting. Several of the ships were works of art, a few of them known for their cunning crew and skill at thieving. But it was the ship on the far end that stole Johann's breath, and he stood and stared at her moorings for nearly five minutes, drinking her in again.

The Brass Farthing was here. And he absolutely could not make up his mind if that was a sign he should attempt to hire her or run away from the docks altogether.

A hand fell on his shoulder, a too-rough "friendly" slap becoming a rather painful pinch on the back of his neck. "Well, look what the cat dragged in."

Johann set his teeth to stop his mouth, but he couldn't do anything about his nostrils flaring.

Captain George Crawley let go of Johann with a less-than-playful shove that almost knocked him into the water. "Six months, and here you are, all toffed up and full of swagger. You imagine that's all it takes, a fancy coat, and I'll take you back, because I'm such a friendly chap?"

No, Johann was fairly sure he'd have to beg on his knees just to keep Crawley from poisoning all the other captains against him. Trouble was, he hadn't quite worked out how to kneel with the clockwork. He swallowed his anger and did his best to make nice. "I'm looking for passage for a friend. And myself. Tonight. We can pay."

"You can pay all day long, my love. The only trip I'll help you with is off the end of the pier."

Crawley looked too thin, and not remotely as fine as Johann knew he wished to appear. "You left me. I was drunk and beaten bloody—and then the army found me. *My* army."

Crawley rolled his eyes. "So sad for you. And yet *I* was the one who lingered long enough for you that we stayed past bribing time. I lost five thousand dollars' worth of aether that day. All because you picked a fight over a girl."

"I didn't pick a fight." He didn't even remember any girls in the tavern.

"Men hit me, and I hit back. Except there were ten of them and one of me. And I'd had a bit of beer."

"Yes, well, the end result of your little adventure was that I lost everything but my ship, and I only got that back last week by sheer luck. This is my first voyage after getting her refitted, and it cost me blood. I have enough crew to not get laughed out of the sky and nothing more, and only Heng from the original crew. I owe you, Johann Berger, and I shall happily pay you back by making certain you never get a ride out of Calais on anything more exotic than a teacup."

Johann grabbed Crawley as he started to turn away. "Do you have a tinker on your ship?"

Crawley pulled himself free with a snort. "If you want to rub my nose in my misfortune, I can burn you in *every* port I visit."

"The man who needs passage is a tinker. A tinker-surgeon. The most skilled I've ever seen." Before Crawley could do more than give him a dubious look, Johann pulled off his left glove and lifted his eyepatch. "He did these, and both my legs as well."

Crawley's eyes nearly bugged out of his head. "*Both* legs? That's not possible."

Johann lifted first one trouser leg, then the other. "The left begins mid-calf, but the right goes all the way up to my thigh. It's a bit like walking on stilts, but I'm getting the hang of it. He wanted me to look more like a pirate as a disguise—before he knew I had been one—so I have a wooden peg leg I use sometimes."

Crawley's expression turned half-wistful, half-incredulous. "And you aren't wearing it now?"

Johann ignored this for the sake of not insulting the man he was trying to woo. "He's not particular about where he goes, but away from the Empire wouldn't be a bad start. As I said, he can pay."

"*He* is welcome anytime, for as long as he likes. If he'll work while he flies, I'll give him a cut."

"He won't fly without me." *I hope.*

Crawley's lips flattened in annoyance. "I don't want you on my ship."

"I don't want to be on your ship either, but I have no other choice. He's in danger. He must leave, tonight."

"As I said, he's more than welcome." Crawley arched what was, in all likelihood, a plucked eyebrow. "Why exactly is it *you* must go with him? Are you married and expecting a child?" When Johann blushed and looked away, Crawley gasped. "You *arse*. We all flirt with you, and then you run off and fall for a tinker."

Johann blinked. Repeatedly. "You—*what?*"

"God in heaven, you're as green as when I left you. Yes, we flirted with you. You had a nice bum, and we wanted to fuck it."

Johann pressed the fingers of his good hand in two points on his forehead, holding back a headache. "Will you let us come, or do I go on to the next ship and offer his services instead?"

"If you do, I'll tell them—"

"You can tell them anything you like, you arrogant sot, but I'll offer them a tinker and show what he can do by lifting my sleeve and trouser leg, and they won't care if you tell them I'm Jack the Ripper. *They* will take me on to get *him*. And you bloody well know it."

Crawley folded his arms and glared at Johann. "I pull up five minutes before the bribery period is over. I won't wait for God, not after the last time."

"We'll be here before then." Johann held out his hand. In afterthought, he pulled it back and extended his clockwork hand instead.

Crawley took it carefully, shaking his head in awe as he felt his way around the artificial hand. "I can feel the intricacy of the clockwork through the leather. You're wearing three fortunes in the arm alone. Where did you *find* him? Who funds him?"

"He found me. And who funds him is his business, not mine."

Crawley let go of Johann's hand with a sigh. "Very well. We rise at ten bells."

With a dramatic swish of his heavily riveted, ratty leather tailcoat, he swung onto the ladder leading up to his ship, pausing for a moment as he swayed, staring out at the setting sun, likely imagining what a fine portrait he'd make at that particular moment.

Rolling his eyes, Johann turned with no drama at all and made his way back toward The Alison.

He hurried down the streets, glancing at his watch. He'd arrive a bit earlier than instructed, but he rationalized this because matters had altered—now they had passage out. He would interrupt their meal long enough to alert Cornelius to the plan, let Valentin glare at him, and then he'd order a meal for himself and eat it outside. They'd arrive at the *Farthing* with plenty of time to spare. Unless of course Cornelius decided one of the ship names did mean he should accept their passage, in which case Johann would use careful English to explain why he didn't think that was a good idea even if his mother herself waved at him from the deck. In fact, if she did, that would be perfect—he'd take them *all* aboard the *Farthing*.

It was a perfectly sound plan, one he was quite proud of.

Three steps into the tavern, someone grabbed him forcibly and shoved him into a chair. Before he could so much as shout in protest, his attacker straddled him and pressed both his shoulders into the wall. He went still as he perceived a pale, tousled, *beautiful* and intensely drunk Cornelius leering a mere inch from his face.

"*Bonjour.*" Cornelius grinned wider and breathed what could only be described as vaporous alcohol into Johann's face. Then Cornelius cupped Johann's balls, ran a thumb along his rapidly rising cock and shoved his tongue down Johann's throat.

Chapter Six

Johann knew one second of sanity, acknowledging this was not the time for kissing and he should absolutely disengage from the embrace to get Cornelius to the ship. He registered also that his lover reeked of strong alcohol—of licorice, in fact, meaning Cornelius had been drinking the devil absinthe, which he knew the French often liked to lace with cocaine. He knew also that this was a public tavern, and while France might be more accommodating than most places, there were still limits and standards of decorum to be observed.

Then Cornelius's deft fingers began to undo the buttons to Johann's trousers, and Johann could only groan, spread his legs wider, and grip Cornelius's shoulder and waist.

Cornelius took full advantage of that moan, dipping his tongue inside Johann's mouth at the same moment his fingers found their way through the trouser flap and past the fastenings of Johann's pants.

Johann had no defenses, and what little shame he could resurrect melted under the intensity and skill of Cornelius's touch. His cock filled Cornelius's questing hand, and his mouth opened eagerly under the onslaught. When Cornelius pushed his other hand beneath Johann's shirt, laying a cool palm against the scars on his abdomen, Johann's belly quivered, and his cock swelled in Conny's grip.

"*C'est ça,* darling, *oui. Laisse-moi te baiser.*" Cornelius trailed a wet mouth down Johann's chin and sucked on the cleft. "*Je te veux dans la bouche. Prends-moi par derrière, là sur la table, et fais-moi hurler de plaisir. Tu veux bien faire cela pour moi, mon doux Johann?*" He pumped Johann's cock with slow, wicked intent and laved the pulse of Johann's throat with his tongue. "*À Calais, est-ce que tu vas montrer ta belle bitte avant de me la forcer dans la gorge? Dans le cul?*"

Johann moaned into Conny's mouth and gripped his lover's arms as he fought to keep his hips from thrusting. He wasn't entirely sure what Conny had said—he'd called Johann darling, demanded to suck something, to be pushed onto a table…and someone was apparently meant to scream. Also something about mouths. And cocks.

It had never occurred to Johann to put a cock in his mouth, but he wanted Conny's *very* much right now. He wanted *everything* about Conny.

No one had ever kissed him like this. Touched him like this. Mastered him like this, taking away his quiet caution and making him feel, respond, *be*. He couldn't stop Cornelius, couldn't slow him down. He didn't want to. As Conny began to undress him, Johann felt everything but his clockwork parts give way, every muscle yielding to Cornelius's heated, lyrical whispers. The clockwork appendages became reminders of how much of Johann was crafted by Conny. Without Cornelius, Johann was barely functional, barely alive in every way. If it pleased him to make love to Johann in a public bar, then he would oblige.

The moment ended abruptly as Valentin pried Cornelius off of Johann and away to the side. Cornelius mewed and complained vehemently in lewd, surprisingly articulate and eloquent French given how inebriated he was, but Valentin held him fast.

"You cannot fuck him in the front booth of the tavern. Not at this hour." Valentin cut a glare at Johann, nodding at his groin without looking at it. "Do yourself up, *pirate*."

Blushing, Johann fumbled with his shirt and trousers as blood rushed back into his head, and with it, a bit of common sense. "We must go," he said to Cornelius in English. "I've secured passage for us on an airship. None of the sea ships had names sounding like games, but I remembered them in case—"

"What the *devil* are you saying?" Valentin's nostrils flared, and his chin tipped up so high he had to look down to glare at Johann. He had spoken in French. "You speak *English?*"

"Yes," Johann replied carefully, switching back to Valentin's language. "Better than French. Do you speak it also?"

"Of course I don't speak that mongrel tongue. And I won't have you whispering it in front of me when I can't understand."

Never mind that this had been the entire state of Johann's life, up until recently. "I must give Cornelius important information. I am better in English."

Valentin rolled his eyes as he fought a still-swearing Cornelius. "Good luck telling him anything. I haven't seen him this drunk in years."

And on the night Johann needed, desperately, for Cornelius to be sober. "Why did you let him drink so much?"

"He wouldn't slow down. I thought I had his measure, but I think he'd had more than a bit before he arrived, and knowing him, he skipped lunch, which means at best he had a bit of toast this morning. He has more alcohol than blood in his veins at the moment. And they always lace the absinthe here, so he's a fine mess."

Johann didn't understand all of that, but he comprehended enough to glean a general summary. "What did he tell you about the dangers he's facing?"

Valentin stilled. "Dangers?"

Cornelius swatted at Johann. "*Shh*. I didn't want to tell him," he said in English. His fiery mood turned abruptly sad and nervous. "I don't know what to tell him. I don't know what to do."

Johann caught Cornelius's hands. He continued in French despite hating to after the freedom of English so Val wouldn't interrupt him again. "I found the sea ships. They do not look good. No game names. Rough men." When Cornelius's eyes filled with tears, Johann drew a hand to his mouth and kissed the knuckles, shivering for a second in desire as he caught the musky whiff of his own cock. "I have passage on an airship. My airship, from my pirate days. But we must hurry."

"What airship is this? Why?" Valentin looked alarmed. "Conny, what's going on?"

"I don't know who I can tell," Cornelius whispered, then burst into tears.

"Do you have the letter from your mother?" Johann prompted him.

Cornelius patted his waistcoat clumsily, and when it became clear he was too drunk for something as complicated as reaching inside, Johann did it for him. This inspired him to clunk his head against Johann's as he attempted to nuzzle his face. "I want to kiss you. All this time, we could have been kissing. I want to make love to you now."

Johann fumbled the letter. "Let me get you to safety first," he murmured in English. "Then we can do anything you like."

Conny cooed and bit Johann's lip. "I want you to fuck me while people watch us. Is that all right? Will you hate me if you find out I'm a terrible slut?"

"I could never hate you," Johann whispered, pressing his lip close in case Cornelius wanted to bite it again.

"Stop speaking that language." Valentin glared at Johann as he pulled out the envelope. "What is this letter? Why are you talking about leaving? And what does he mean, all this time you could have been kissing? You *haven't* been? So I was right!"

Johann ignored him and opened the letter. "It is in English. I will read and say in French, but find patience."

"How can I trust you're telling the truth?"

Johann had endured enough of this. "You will trust me. Or you will find him taken, or dead."

Valentin fell into furious silence, and Johann did his best to translate from his second language into his third.

"'Dear Cornelius. I...wish letter is in time. Read it with tea and...thinking hard. It is an important letter.'"

"Read it with *tea*? What in the world does that mean?"

Johann stared at the letter. Yes, what *did* that mean? Cornelius had said the letter didn't make sense, and it seemed odd to list off such dire news but first suggest he have tea. Yes, he should calm down, but...it seemed odd.

"I detest tea," Cornelius murmured in French.

Like Cornelius dropping cogs into his clockwork hand and making it start again, all the little wheels fell into place in Johann's head. *His mother is a spy. He doesn't like tea. The letter makes no sense. No ship is right.* A barmaid passed him, and he put out a hand to stop her. "Please. Bring a pot of tea." He passed over several large coins Cornelius had given him earlier. "As quickly as possible."

She bobbed a curtsey and hurried away, and Valentin made several very French noises. "Are you so stupid you think you must literally drink tea as you read it?"

"The letter asks Cornelius to take a sea voyage. But the clue to find the ship makes no sense. Then there is the tea. Also, his mother was a spy." Johann rubbed the stubble on his jaw. "I think this is code. I think this is not the message."

Valentin appeared to be warring between disdain and intrigue. "A spy code? You use every third word, yes?"

Johann tried variations on skipped words, but nothing made sense. "I want to try the tea."

"Tea is disgusting." Cornelius slid free of Valentin and curled like a cat against Johann's side. "Darling, have a drink with me." He ran a finger down Johann's nose. "Not tea."

Johann willed himself to resist, but flirty Cornelius was almost as intoxicating as absinthe. "We must reach the docks by ten, or they will leave us."

"I don't want to leave Calais." Cornelius pressed an openmouthed kiss on the exposed skin at Johann's neck. "I want to take you home and make love to you."

He sucked lightly at Johann's neck, and Johann gripped his hair, though he couldn't seem to bring himself to pull Cornelius away.

Valentin crossed his arms over his chest. "Where is your peg leg?"

It was difficult to form his reply in French as Cornelius made love to his neck while re-unbuttoning his shirt and sliding a hand into the back of his trousers. "It...is clockwork."

"He gave you a clockwork leg?" This seemed to upset Valentin more than anything else. He glowered harder.

The barmaid returned with the tea, setting it on the table near them. "Here you are, sir."

Johann extricated himself from Cornelius as best he could and lifted the lid on the pot. It seemed steeped enough, though he wondered if he shouldn't let it go a bit longer, in case. But as he set the lid back on, Cornelius slipped a finger between his nether cheeks, and when Johann yelped and startled, he spilled the tea all over the letter, which he'd laid on the table.

As the liquid sloshed in thick droplets across the paper, most of the words faded, but a few of them remained.

Buzzing with triumph, Johann picked up the teapot and poured it liberally all over the letter. He hadn't even placed the pot back down before the old letter had vanished and a new one entirely remained.

Dearest Cornelius,

Danger, this letter is false. Hide yourself and tell no one where you are, not even friends. Do not trust your father. Stay away from France and England at all cost until the war is over. Pray God that day comes soon. I love you always, my darling tinker boy, and hope to see you again soon.

Thinking of you always, Mama

Valentin squinted helplessly at it. "What does it say?"

Before Johann could attempt to translate, Cornelius, abruptly sober, swiped the letter from the table and stared at it intently. Lowering it, he stared first at Johann, then at Valentin, his pain acute even through the haze of his inebriation. "I must leave Calais. Not by the sea ships. *Those* men mean to kidnap me. They forced my mother to write the first note, and she hid this one inside." He stared again at the letter, looking as if a new wound pierced deep. "She says I'm not to trust my father."

Valentin paled. "You cannot leave. Wherever would you go?"

"I have a ship waiting," Johann reminded them. "We must leave now and go to the pirate docks."

"You think *you* get to take him to safety?" Valentin puffed up, indignant. "*I* am his oldest friend. *I* will keep him safe."

Johann clenched his jaw, hating Valentin, despising having to fight through

French to express himself. "My ship is good. Many men will fight to keep him safe." He switched to English to soothe Cornelius. "They are eager to have a tinker. They'll give you anything you ask for. They'll pay *you* to come aboard. And as a member of the crew, they would protect you against any attackers." *Unless they decide to leave you dying on the docks for the army to find.*

But Johann would be there to ensure that didn't happen, not this time.

"Stop speaking English!" Valentin shouted.

Then everyone began shouting, and screaming, as five large, angry men burst into the tavern.

Johann pulled Cornelius beneath the table as he surveyed the scene with both a soldier and a pirate's gaze. He flipped up his patch so he could use his clockwork eye, which let him see so much better in the dark. Not five but *eight* men, all of them large and angry, wearing uniforms. They were searching for something.

For someone. They were searching, he knew in his bones, for Cornelius.

"We must go. Now." He scooped up the letter, stuffing it into his waistcoat before collecting Cornelius's heavy satchel from the floor. His *very* heavy satchel.

Valentin crouched beside them too, uncertain. "We don't know they're here for Cornelius."

As if they heard the name, which possibly they had, one of the men locked his gaze on Cornelius, pointed and shouted again. In German—but it was not good German. It was German, in fact, as bad as Johann's French. As the men moved into better light, Johann saw they were Austrian uniforms. Except the insignia was all wrong, and several crucial bits of dress were missing.

This situation, he realized, was bad, and it was about to get much, much worse.

Johann pushed Cornelius and the bag into Valentin's arms. "Take him out of here. Head to Hangman's Landing. Do you know it?"

"Yes, but—I can't fight these men!"

"I can." Johann rose, gaze fixed on the approaching faux-soldiers as he mapped out several different ways to fight them in his head. "Go. I will keep them away and come after."

He shoved them out of the booth and toward the rear of the tavern, then placed himself squarely between the attackers and his lover.

The leader shouted out garbled German, which probably sounded threatening to the room but came out clearly as *wet breakfast* to Johann.

He smiled a mirthless smile. "Breakfast is better warm and dry. You will never have him, and I will kill every man who tries."

After swiping the pistol from the man's belt beside him, he cocked it, aimed and shot the leader in the center of his chest.

In the chaos, he ran, but not directly for the back door. He took a long, winding route, overturning tables and chairs along the way, at one point stumbling onto a pot of oil, which he tossed on a table. After stealing a man's lit cigarette from his mouth, Johann threw it into the oil, which erupted in a fine blaze. This finished the job of sending the tavern fully into an uproar, and as he slipped along the wall toward the kitchen, Johann heard the frustrated shouts in bad German morphing occasionally into French as he made his way out of the tavern.

To his shock, however, as he exited, he saw Cornelius and Valentin hovering in a corner of the back room, not fleeing at all.

"He wouldn't leave you." Valentin's tone was both humble and frustrated.

Swearing in German, Johann grabbed them both and dragged them into the inn yard. They had mere seconds to escape before the men sought them here. Spying a horse loose in the chaos, he caught it and nodded to Valentin.

"Get on." He held out his good hand as a step. Valentin went, and Johann settled the satchel behind him. But when Johann tried to boost up Cornelius, he wouldn't go.

"I won't leave without you."

"*Conny,*" Valentin cried in despair.

Familiar shouts spurred Johann into action. "Hangman's Landing. Go, now," he told Valentin, and slapped the horse hard on the rump.

Then he picked up Cornelius, swung him around to his back and started to run.

He was a little unsteady at first, with his clockwork legs and the redistributed weight, but he adapted much quicker than he thought he would. Except for the extra strain on his human arm and his legs settling harder into the clockwork, carrying Cornelius didn't affect him at all. In fact, he found himself surprised at how fast he was moving. When he realized he'd just passed a carriage with horses trotting at a decent clip, he nearly stumbled in surprise.

"It's your legs," Cornelius said into his ear. "Clockwork works better than flesh and bone."

"But I'm not even the slightest bit winded. I've run over a half kilo at top speed, up and down hills and with extra weight on my back."

Cornelius clutched him tighter. "This might be the time to explain that you have more clockwork than simply your arm and legs and eye."

Johann slowed so he could glance over his shoulder at Cornelius. "What else is mechanical?"

"Some cogs and bellows to help a punctured lung. A bit of internal machinery that helps keep your metal limbs in better harmony with your flesh." He nuzzled Johann's ear sadly. "And...you have a clockwork heart. But you must never tell anyone about that."

The anxiety in Cornelius's tone made a shiver run down Johann's spine, one that resonated even more than the shock at finding out how mechanical he truly was. "Wh-why?"

"Because your heart is the weapon your army was trying to destroy. The one I think my father is trying to steal."

The world spun around Johann. He fought to make it stay right. "But... why did you save me at all?" *Why did you put a weapon inside me?*

"You were dying. I didn't want you to."

"*Why not?* You didn't know me."

"I don't know. Only that I couldn't bear to watch you die when I knew I could save you."

A thousand questions and fears rattled inside Johann. But he realized, no, he didn't feel any of this in his *heart*. A tightness in his chest, his throat—but as it had since he'd woken in Cornelius's bed, the left of center portion of his chest felt numb and strange. He'd thought the scar was Cornelius removing shrapnel, but now he knew better. If he concentrated, he could feel it pumping without fail, a powerful machine.

A weapon.

"Will it explode?"

"No." Cornelius brushed a kiss on his neck. "It is only a heart. An engine. But it will do whatever you ask of it. You may run as fast and hard as your legs can take you. It will power your every step without fail. And the bellows in your lung will give you all the air you require."

I am a monster. A terrible machine. "Can—can I die?"

"Oh yes. If your clockwork heart ceases to beat, you will live no more."

The world kept spinning, but Johann would not let anything keep him from taking Cornelius to safety. He wasn't sure yet what he thought of Cornelius's meddling, but this was not the moment for dramatics. They had to get to the *Farthing*. Once aboard, dramatics would be entirely appropriate, in many varied ways.

Show me what you can do, my monster heart.

He ran. His goal was more than simple escape now—he wanted to see what he could do. How fast? How hard? How far? The answer, it seemed, was as Cornelius said—as fast as he wanted. It was his legs that showed him the wall of limitation. But of course, so little of his legs were *his* legs. The span of his capability was rather impressively high.

This was amazing. This was a *miracle*. He was a monster, yes, but he was a monster who could move so fast, he felt any second he might begin to fly.

A warmth in his chest made him glance down—and slow. "Cornelius, something is wrong." There in the place where his heart was, a soft red glow emanated.

Cornelius pulled off Johann's hat and clapped it over the glow. "It's only a heat exchange. I have it in a casing. You'll be fine. But I'll keep it hidden."

He did, but Johann couldn't lose his sense of that heat, that bright red beacon burning inside him.

They moved so quickly, they arrived at the docks moments before Valentin on his horse.

"How—how did you do this?" Valentin slid off as Cornelius did, eyes wide. He pointed at Johann. "You ran! I came straight here, on a clear road, the fastest way, and I did not see you—"

Johann, not even a little bit winded, grabbed Valentin's shoulder with his clockwork hand and Cornelius with his right. "Come. We have no time to waste. Bring the satchel."

"But—where are we going? Why—?"

"Berger, what the *blazes* are you doing?" Crawley swung down from the *Farthing*, wearing a jaunty hat, a finer coat than he'd worn before and an outraged expression. "We said nothing of *three* passengers. Certainly there was *no* talk of a simpering French dandy."

Johann held up a hand at Crawley and turned to Valentin. "We must leave now. Will you go, or stay?"

"For fuck's sake," Crawley murmured.

Valentin's gaze darted between Crawley, Cornelius and Johann like a rabbit's. "I won't leave Cornelius."

Johann turned back to Crawley. "It is three. And we must leave immediately."

"It will *not* be three. I don't care how good this tinker is—"

Cornelius stepped in front of Johann, holding tight to his hand. "I am the best in France, save Félix Dubois," he said in almost perfect English.

Crawley paused. "That's quite a boast."

Johann saw a crack in the captain's resolve and pressed his advantage. "He is Dubois's apprentice."

Crawley said nothing.

Shouts from the cliff above the pier told Johann their pursuers had found them. There was no more time for finessing, only barging through. "We must leave now. *Now.*"

"Three years," Crawley said, still staring at Cornelius.

Johann's clockwork heart beat as regularly as it ever did, but that tightness in the center of his chest became acute. "*No.*"

"Three years' contract for the tinker." Crawley's tone was impassive and implacable. "That's the price for taking the three of you on."

Johann had never wanted to punch Crawley more, and he'd wanted to hit him very hard, many times. "I won't leave him with you."

"Then you may have a contract too." He cast a look of disdain at Valentin. "Not for the French weasel, however. He may ride only until he annoys me."

"Three years' contract for all three of us, and we have a deal," Cornelius said, extending his hand.

Johann pushed it down. "You don't know what you're agreeing to."

"Yes, I do." Now it was Cornelius who met Crawley's gaze without blinking. "We agree to stay on this ship for three years, under his command and his protection. For a wage. Mine will be four times whatever he has previously paid a tinker."

Crawley made a strangled noise, but Valentin outright yelped. "*Ils arrivent! Ils arrivent!*"

The men ran down the hill toward the pier, shouting and aiming their pistols. Swearing, Crawley shoved them toward the ship and called out to the ships—*rats ashore, mates, rats ashore!*—at which point every ship in the bay erupted with men and women, shouting and waving blades while others went about loading cannons.

Crawley hoisted them up the ladder one by one—first Valentin, then Cornelius, then Johann, following them up himself. As soon as Crawley's boot touched the rope, *The Brass Farthing*'s aether heaved, billowing bright into the dirigible's balloon, firing the propellers as the first mate unhooked the mooring and they cast away.

Chapter Seven

Sobriety came to Cornelius in dark, painful rushes—when he fled the tavern, when he realized Valentin meant to take him away from Johann, when he had to explain to Johann about his clockwork heart. When it was clear his choice was between death or indenture. Sadly, sobriety didn't feel swinging from a rope ladder on an airship rising into the night sky was a moment when clarity should descend. Or perhaps it was more that he could force a bit of sharpness to his mouth and mind, but too much alcohol in the blood would never make his fingers work properly.

Johann helped him, murmuring gentle words of encouragement in English and sometimes German as he moved Cornelius's hands up the ladder and used his knees as braces for Cornelius's fumbling feet. It was a noble effort, especially as Cornelius could tell Johann had significant trouble getting his mechanical feet into the rungs, but they managed, and by achingly marginal inches, they made their way onto the ship. When they came close enough to the edge, hands hoisted Cornelius into the gondola.

"*Non,*" Conny cried when they reached for Johann. "Not his left arm." He batted them away, his absinthe-soaked imagination all too able to visualize Johann and his separated appendage spiraling down into the water below. When Johann came close enough, Conny stabilized him above his left elbow as Johann hoisted himself aboard.

The English captain came up swiftly after, grumbling about inept, drunken landlubbers and stinking Frenchmen.

Cornelius swayed on his feet until Johann caught him up, murmuring reassurances into his ear, and Cornelius drank them in as he looked around the room. This was a gondola different than any he'd been in before, almost more as if a wooden ship had been grafted onto a balloon—which sometimes was exactly how privateer ships were built. They stood in the rear, in the enclosed portion of the carriage, with a mess and officer's cabin on one side, the grand captain's cabin on the other. A small storage area was visible on the right, probably for weapons, but then the wall of glass gave way to a small open deck, where two figures rushed about and another manned the wheel below the balloon. A second wheel was inside the glass-enclosed gondola, beside a narrow stair leading to the hold below. None of it was overly impressive.

"Who is this other one? I thought there were only meant to be two." This came from a man who appeared to be from a northern Asian country, most likely China by Conny's guess. He didn't look pleased to have new arrivals, and neither did the two women standing with arms folded beside him.

Like the captain, they were decked in leather armor and buckles greatly excessive beyond practical use, though the Asian man had a more Eastern flair to his style. The women continued in the theme of airship pirate decoration, but they were hugely distinct in their presentation. One woman, taller and darker of complexion, had cropped her hair shorter than most men and wore piercings in both ears, her nose and an eyebrow. Tattoos covered every available surface of her exposed skin below her neck, and her clothing was highly masculine. The other woman wore trousers as well, but her hair was longer, braided and tucked to one side. She'd gone out of her way to look feminine and slightly pretty whereas her companion used everything about her to telegraph aggression and rejection of the feminine ideal.

The captain mopped the back of his neck with the tail of his scarf. "Ladies and gentleman, may I introduce you to your three new crew members. Johann Berger, whom I've flown with before, his friend the master tinker, whose name I don't know, and their awkward French friend who will be of no use whatsoever."

Conny did his best to look grand and imposing. "My name is Cornelius. And my friend is Valentin."

"Capital." The captain pointed to himself, then the others. "I am Captain Crawley, and you may call me Captain, or Sir, or Your Worship. This is Heng, your quartermaster. You will call him Sir." He gestured to the short-haired woman. "Beside him is Olivia, our sailing master, and beside her is Molly, *The Brass Farthing*'s engineer." Crawley put his hands on his hips. "The three of you aren't simply getting a ride out of town. You'll be working every minute you're on this ship. Johann, you'll be a mate, same as you were before." He gestured to Cornelius. "You're obviously the tinker-surgeon." Crawley grinned nastily at Valentin. "You, sweet fop, will be our new jape."

Val, barely holding himself together, glanced at Conny and spoke in a tremulous voice in French. "What is he saying? Why is he looking at me like that?"

Heng shut his eyes and shook his head. He murmured something in Chinese, which made the rest of the pirates laugh.

Crawley switched to French as he addressed Val. "You're the jape, Frenchie. You're our odd-jobs man. You do the work no one else wants to do. You answer to everyone else. If someone has something they need doing, you do the job. You don't argue, you don't complain. You say *yes, sir* and *yes, ma'am* and work like a dog. If you last long enough for us to take on more crew, you'll be promoted to mate and someone else will be the jape."

For a tense moment, Conny feared Val would argue, but he only gave a surly nod and wrapped his arms around his belly.

Cornelius made a small bow. "How do you do. We're happy to be aboard."

Olivia raised her eyebrows. Molly snorted.

Heng looked dubious. "Master tinker? What's one of those doing on this piece of junk?"

"Getting his neck saved. And signing a contract." Crawley rubbed his hands together before gesturing to the officer's quarters. "If you'd be so kind as to follow me, gentlemen?"

The captain's office wasn't any nicer than the rest of the ship, though as he inspected things closer, Cornelius could tell it had once been quite grand. What he'd taken for tarnish on the rails was clearly places where filigree and ornament had been stripped away, likely to be sold. Many dark spots on the walls told stories of art and decoration that had hung long enough to withstand the stain of sun, but were absent now. The table serving as a desk was not grand, and the two chairs seated at it were wobbly and mismatched.

Crawley spread three scrolls across the table and laid out a broken fountain pen. He picked it up, initialed in a few places and wrote in wages. "I'm only giving you double, love."

Cornelius took the contract from his hands, and after a few lines of reading, he confiscated the pen as well. On his contract and the others', he crossed out several lines, added a few phrases of his own and adjusted everyone's percentages. He doubled once more the number Crawley had written for the post of tinker, signed at the bottom and handed it back. When Crawley started to sputter in rage, Cornelius interrupted him.

"Bring me the most complicated, necessary items you have in need of fixing."

While Crawley stood deciding if he would obey or not, Cornelius stumbled to Valentin, reclaimed his satchel and set it on the table. As he laid out tools he'd need to fix the chairs and the table, he couldn't stop himself from indexing the countless bits of equipment he'd had to leave behind, many which would be ever so helpful in this moment. Swallowing the lump in his throat, he steadied his hands as best he could and got to work.

He glanced up at Val, who appeared well beyond terrified. Perhaps giving him a task could help calm them both. "*Un café, Val?*"

"I can show him the coffee," Heng said, and caught Valentin by the elbow. "*Venez*, Frenchie."

Shortly after they left, Cornelius got the legs off the chair, and Crawley left too. Olivia and Molly stood off to the side, arms folded, but Johann crouched awkwardly on his mechanical legs. "May I help?"

Cornelius shook his head, more to clear it than anything else. "I need coffee." He bit his lip and added, "And a quarter wrench."

Johann became his assistant, passing him tools and parts, listening patiently when Cornelius had to explain what they looked like. Several times he had to reroute his plan because he was missing a part or a tool, but by the time Crawley returned with a ratty basket full of things sticking out of the sides, Conny had repaired the table and one of the chairs.

Crawley set the basket down. "I'm not giving you the shirt off my back because you fixed a table."

"I fixed the table and the chair so I had an adequate place to work." He plucked a broken spyglass from the basket. "I will require a room of at least this size and this level of brightness as my workshop. This space would be adequate, but I will need a great deal more shelving."

"I don't know who you are, lad, but—" He stopped as he watched Conny crack the spyglass open, pull out the lenses and spread them across a handkerchief.

When the coffee appeared beside Conny, he noted it absently, taking a few fortifying sips before diving back into his work. The spyglass was quite boring and not very good, so he improved it. When he finished, he handed it to Crawley without meeting his gaze. "Go and try it on the stars."

"It doesn't go that far—"

"*Go,* Captain." Conny pulled out an electric toaster and huffed. "*Appliances?*" He tossed it on the table and glared at Heng. "Bring me your compass."

"It isn't broken," Heng said.

"It isn't any good, either, is it?" Conny unscrewed the toaster with pursed lips. "*Toasters.* I could rebuild your engine in an hour, make your ship fly three times as fast in a long evening, if I had the right tools. *Bring me something that matters.*"

They did. They brought him the compass—out of balance, wobbling, which he repaired and improved, adding an aether-detecting sensor. They brought him a broken windlass, a grapnel, a lutchet and a steel length of martingale. Everything dull and unimpressive.

"Bring me something *more.*"

"That's all we have," they confessed.

With a Gallic sigh, Conny pulled open his satchel, grabbed a handful of parts and began to build.

He wasn't sure what it was meant to be at first, but when his weary, sodden mind seized on the animal he'd once seen in a traveling show, he couldn't help himself. He smiled as the monkey appeared out of the bits of wire and brass, and he gave it a golden set of gears for eyes. When it was finished, he wound it up and fitted an aether battery to its back, then sat back and watched it dance across the table.

The crew stared at him, open-mouthed.

"You are worth more for one day," Crawley croaked at last, "than the value of my entire ship."

Cornelius finished off the last of his coffee. "And yet I am grateful for your help. Twenty percent of the profits, plus eight for each of my companions, is all that I ask. At the end of the year, we can see if you still wish to retain me, at which point I might ask for a higher percentage again. As per the terms of the revised contracts."

He passed them over to Crawley, who fell over himself to sign.

* * * * *

As Johann led the others to the crew's quarters, his mind finally had quiet enough to panic.

The Brass Farthing had two sleeping chambers, one on the upper deck for the captain and quartermaster, and the smaller, darker one on the gun deck for the lesser officers' mates. Johann led Cornelius and Valentin down the narrow, open-slat stairs, past the aether cannons to the rack of bunks near the stern. At full capacity the ship had four officers and six mates, but even with the addition of the three of them they were at best a skeleton crew. Johann and his companions took up the center row of bunks with plenty of room on either side.

He could tell Cornelius wanted to talk to him, but Johann couldn't bear to. It had been one thing while they were convincing Crawley to let them stay aboard, but now that he had time to think about what had happened, there was too much to process. Being on the *Farthing* again. The soldiers pretending to be Austrian. The threat to Cornelius. Being with Cornelius as a lover. Running away with Cornelius—and Valentin.

Having a clockwork heart sewed into his chest, a heart the whole world wanted to use as a weapon.

It was too much. He couldn't speak of anything out loud. Not now. So when Cornelius put a hand on his arm and said his name with that sweet, worried voice, Johann didn't let himself give in to the urge to sink into his tinker's arms. "It's been a big day. We should sleep."

"We should *talk*. You seem upset."

Johann *was* upset. Which was why he didn't want to talk. "Tomorrow," he said to Cornelius, though he doubted morning would bring a different frame of mind.

He thought he'd lie awake, plagued by his thoughts, but the next thing he knew Heng was shouting down the hatch for them to wake. Johann rose with the rest of the crew, but Cornelius moaned in complaint and Valentin simply pulled his covers over his head. Johann felt a bit guilty not staying to help them out, but he knew Heng would make it worse for them if he did, so he simply went to mess with the others. He choked down gruel and coffee only slightly better than the army's, and rose to report to Olivia on the open deck as a bleary Cornelius and complaining Valentin stumbled to the table.

"You're leaving?" Cornelius frowned at Johann. "But I wanted to speak with you."

"I need to work." He tried to go, but Conny stepped into his way.

"I understand you're upset with me, but there are a few things we need to go over regardless."

Johann was trying to form a lie about how he wasn't upset with Conny when Olivia stepped between them, arms folded over her chest and a sneer of disdain on her face. "You can have your lover's quarrel later. Right now I need a mate on deck."

She grabbed Johann's left arm and tugged hard—and Johann doubled over as he cried out in pain, clutching the stub of his arm as Olivia stared in horror at the clockwork appendage in her hand.

Cornelius sprang to life, swearing in French as he reclaimed the clockwork and helped Johann to the floor. "Breathe, darling. You're not actually injured, but your nerve endings don't know that. Your brain is aware your arm was ripped off, but it can't understand that's simply a matter of circuitry, not blood and gore. It will throb until I can get you some aether, but once I reset the circuit it will all be well." After a kiss on Johann's forehead, Conny spoke harshly to Olivia. "As I was *trying* to explain, I hadn't engineered Johann's clockwork for hard labor or casual abuse. Normal people don't have their shoulders ripped out of their socket when going about their day, you see."

"I hardly tugged—"

"I'm a tinker-surgeon. I can calculate the amount of pressure my clockwork can take to the thousandth fraction of a newton. I can measure the strength of your grip after shaking your hand. You *tugged* his arm hard enough to punish him. Were his arm merely flesh and bone, your unannounced yank would have strained the ligaments of his shoulder a considerable amount. But since he is clockwork, you stressed a contact point of flesh and metal, and by design, the metal gave. Which means whatever else anyone had planned for either of us today, *now* I must spend hours repairing damage in addition to reinforcing his appendages." His lips brushed Johann's skin again. "Come, darling. Let's get you upstairs to my workshop so we can put you back together."

What Cornelius referred to as his workshop was actually the captain's drawing room, but everyone was so stupefied by the sight of Johann's plight, no one bothered to point out the mistake. Cornelius helped Johann up the stairs and onto the table. After demanding a vial of aether, he uncapped it, wafted it briefly beneath Johann's nose, and Johann floated away on a pretty pink cloud for several hours. When he drifted back to the *Farthing*, Cornelius was bent over his left side, squinting through half-moon glasses as he soldered fine wires on the clockwork arm.

He favored Johann with a flash of a smile before returning to his work. "Welcome back. I'm nearly finished with your upgrades." He wiped sweat away from his brow with a rueful smile. "Well, your *arm's* upgrades. Your legs in general aren't tugged about, and in any event I didn't bring enough copper wire to apply the change everywhere."

Johann blinked away bleariness enough to focus on Cornelius's work. "What have you done?"

He hadn't meant the question to be an accusation, but it hung in the air as one anyway. Cornelius's cheerful expression faded toward grim weariness. "The technical explanation of what I've done would require a few hours and some detailed drawings—which I'm happy to provide, if you wish. The short version is that I've altered the joint where your arm's flesh and metal meet."

The joint in question was completely exposed, the metal casing removed to allow Johann a disturbing view of his metal conductors. His flesh stub ached a bit, which made sense as tiny metal circles had been grafted to his skin.

Cornelius pressed the soldering iron to a wire, and a gentle shower of sparks rose as he spoke. "I dislike the army's clockwork joints, as they're known to cause aches and sometimes shooting pains if the soldier survives longer than ten years past the assignment of mechanical parts. But the advantage to their method is a tighter, more sure fit. It took me the better part of the morning, but I've worked out a kind of compromise, allowing preservation of your nerve endings but also locking the joint more tightly. As insurance, though, I'm going to add a leather sling to your wardrobe. It will allow your mechanical arm to be anchored to your shoulders, meaning if you receive a tug like that, your shoulders will pitch forward instead of your clockwork giving way. This is more how a flesh arm behaves, though you'll now have the advantage of being less likely to dislocate your shoulder because of the brace." He smiled again, but this time the gesture seemed quite forced. "Olivia is a fine leather craftswoman as it turns out. She's volunteered to produce my design as an apology for ripping off your arm."

Conny seemed to run out of conversation after that, and Johann watched him work in silence. The aether clung to him like cotton, softening the edges of the world. While he knew he was still upset with Cornelius, it didn't seem to matter at the moment. In fact, the more he watched Cornelius's deft fingers move across his arm, the more he observed Conny's habit of biting his lip while he focused, the more Johann thought about how good it had felt when they'd kissed and fondled one another at the café.

Then he caught Cornelius's glance at his naked chest, at the scars over the places where Johann's flesh organs had been replaced with ones of metal, and he remembered it all.

"Why did you make me a weapon?"

He winced as the question made Cornelius's hand tremble, the soldering iron slipping to send a message of heat along wiring attached to his nerves. Cornelius set the implement aside and folded his hands into his lap. "I didn't turn you into a weapon. I gave you a piece of machinery that saved your life. A pump allowing blood to circulate through your body."

"But you said this machine is what both armies want. That they will *make* it a weapon." He remembered the fear he'd felt when he'd first woken in Cornelius's chamber, that he'd been turned into an automaton. How easily and foolishly he'd let the pretty man convince him otherwise.

Cornelius caught the clockwork hand in his own, curling his fingers around the metal digits as he stared earnestly into Johann's face. "No one knows you have this heart but you and me. Félix believes it's been stolen. Whoever broke into the shop thinks someone else got to it first. There's no reason for anyone to suspect *you* carry the heart. No reason whatsoever."

Johann touched the scar with his right hand. "It glows red when I run. Through a leather waistcoat."

"If I add a shielding panel to your clothing, the problem is solved."

It annoyed Johann for Cornelius to be nonchalant over something so serious. He glowered and forced them back to the blunt truth of the matter. "Why did you give this to me? Why did you save me and give me this horrible thing? If it's this valuable, they won't stop looking for it. They'll find it. They'll find *me*. They'll make me their automaton. Which never would have happened if you'd left me to die as you should have."

Cornelius rose, hugging his arms tight over the midsection of his leather apron. He went to the large wall of windows, looking out over the clouds for several moments before speaking in a quiet, defeated tone. "I didn't know the heart was anything but a forgotten piece of machinery when I gave it to you. I only knew how angry I was with my father, my country. There was no reason to believe anyone would notice its absence."

"But now they have. Now *I* am what they seek."

"No." Cornelius turned to face Johann with fire in his gaze. "They're looking for a heart. They aren't giving you so much as a moment's consideration. Only a handful of people are aware I gave you *any* clockwork, and as far as they know, it's only limbs." He lifted his chin. "Frankly, they'd never believe I knew how to do such a complicated surgery. Everyone thinks I'm just a gentleman's bastard mucking about, that simply working with Félix couldn't make me as good as I am."

Johann shut his eyes and suppressed a sigh. He clenched his fists, conscious as always that one of his fists was flesh and one was clockwork. One was his, and one belonged to Cornelius.

All his life he'd belonged to other men. To his father. To the village elders. To the army commanders. To his sergeant. To Crawley. But with all of them, he'd been able to run away. He didn't want to run from Conny. But it bothered him that he *couldn't*. He'd been happy to belong to Conny, when he'd been able to give himself freely. That something so personal as his own heart didn't even belong to him any longer upset him more than he knew how to explain.

Was that why he didn't mind kissing Cornelius? Had the heart changed him, made him the type of man Cornelius preferred? Was he even Johann Berger any longer? It was the kind of superstitious nonsense he'd scoffed at his friends in the village for. He knew enough about machines to understand they didn't work that way.

And yet the dark thought lodged in the corner of his clockwork heart, refusing to budge, only gathering his fears and encouraging them to grow.

He dislodged his hand from Cornelius's own. "I need to get back to work."

He couldn't decide if he was relieved or dejected that Conny didn't stop him.

Chapter Eight

Several days after their arrival on the pirate airship, Cornelius could deny the truth no longer. Johann was angry, and Conny had no idea how to make him happy again.

Johann was a different kind of angry than Conny was accustomed to in a man, all stoic and frowning, without any rantings or accusations, only terse exchanges and tight-lipped assurances he was well, thank you. Nothing was wrong, he insisted. Never mind it was clear as the blue sky beyond the airship something was wrong, and it was equally clear Johann had no intention of telling Cornelius about his troubles.

He'd worried he'd been too vulgar in the café—truly, he'd been utterly tame, but he feared even this had repulsed Johann. This may or may not have been a compounding factor, but one thing *was* clear: Johann was upset about his heart. It didn't matter how many times Conny assured him no one else knew or would ever know, or how excellent he promised it would function. The disdain had spread to all his clockwork parts—anytime he needed a tune-up, he glowered sullenly until Conny turned him loose again.

The pirates found it funny. Crawley teased Conny about his lover's spat. Olivia suggested he use his screwdriver, usually while miming circular thrusts with her pelvis. Heng didn't laugh, only encouraged Conny to forget the Austrian and learn what the Chinese could do in bed, promising he knew erotic tricks the pedestrian West could never dream of.

Any other time, this would have tempted Conny or seemed like a good tactic to make his lover jealous. But the thought of Johann finding out and being angrier still kept Conny celibate and almost demure in his rebuff.

It helped nothing that life on a pirate ship left little room for soothing and cajoling an upset lover. Conny rose at the crack of dawn, worked like a dog until it was time for the evening meal, then did his best to stay awake until it wasn't embarrassingly early to go to bed. Johann worked harder, and only a little of it was his effort to get away from Cornelius.

Whereas Conny spent his days in his makeshift workroom repairing and redesigning items or on the deck attempting to improve the engine and steering, Johann was a workhorse. Once Conny had his clockwork better secured for ship work, Johann was the go-to sailor for hauling, pulling and anything that had to do with weight and effort. Occasionally their tasks brought them within proximity of one another, but even if Johann hadn't been closed off, more than perfunctory conversation would have been impossible.

At the end of each day, Conny was free, but Johann had arranged to be permanently on the evening watch, his shift ending at an hour so late Conny never had a prayer of staying awake long enough for conversation. Their repair/maintenance sessions didn't allow for much privacy, as Johann liked to time them when Crawley or Heng was in the room.

Conny wanted to force the issue, knowing objectively he needed to get Johann to talk to him. But his feelings were bruised, and he couldn't help wondering if some of Johann's accusations had merit. So he allowed things to simmer until weeks had gone by with the two of them barely speaking at all.

Valentin of course had no empathy for Johann or Conny or anyone else. He was too busy being scandalized over the barbarism of pirate life and the indignity of the tasks he was asked to perform as ship's jape. Eventually he made noise about going home. If the *Farthing* ever flew close enough to one of Valentin's family's chalets, Conny would urge Crawley to set his friend free. But so far they'd flown only around the coastlines and remote areas of the empire.

Twice now they'd been literal pirates, hijacking and raiding cargo airships, though until the *Farthing* was upgraded, she couldn't catch anything but the most pathetic ships, which meant they in turn had meager cargo. The crew at best broke even, though this was apparently an improvement over conditions since before the three of them had boarded in Calais.

One day the *Farthing* landed on a private island off the coast of France, and everyone but Conny and Valentin participated in a tense but lucrative raid for supplies, rations and a modest amount of treasure. Crawley and Heng beamed as they returned to the ship, slapping each other on the back and boasting of the party they'd have once they were airborne again. However, when Johann returned with sweat dripping down his neck and his face flushed, instinct told Cornelius something wasn't right. Since he hadn't had a chance to properly see to the clockwork heart since they'd boarded, he needed to begin there and work his way outward. Which meant, like it or not, Johann needed to be alone with him.

"Johann, I need to check your clockwork. Right away. I need your cabin, Captain." Conny's clipped tone made it clear this was a demand, not a request.

Crawley leered, mouth open for a joke, but he shut it and frowned when he saw Conny's face. "Is Johnny injured? Let me help."

"I'm fine," Johann bit off, and started to lumber away.

Cornelius caught him fast by his flesh arm as he addressed Crawley. "I must examine him, alone, in your quarters. We must not be interrupted." He realized he didn't have his tools and passed Johann's arm to the pirate captain. "Take him there, please. I need a few things, and I'll be along."

Johann fought to get free of them both. "I don't want you to touch me. I don't want *anyone* to touch me, *Schwein.*"

Conny started to argue, but then he got a better look at Johann, at his pale skin, more sweaty now than ever, and his glazed expression. *Oh no.* He ignored Johann and spoke only to Crawley. "Your cabin. *Immediately.* Bind him if you must, but *gently.* Do not let him strain if you can help it."

As Conny hurried to his workroom, Crawley, Heng and Olivia fought to wrestle Johann away, and by the time Conny re-emerged with his bag, Val and Molly had joined in. Johann struggled in the center of the room, flailing as they attempted to tie him to a chair.

Valentin huddled to the side, looking uneasy. "He is like a beast."

"One of his clockworks is making him ill." Conny managed to keep his voice even, but only just. *It's his heart. This can only be his heart.*

At this point Johann fought everyone, not just Cornelius, though when he caught sight of the tinker, his curses became more pointed and were punctuated with spittle. He'd regressed to German, which meant only Crawley, Molly and Heng knew what he said to any degree. Whatever they heard made them glance at one another with wide eyes.

Cornelius had no time to waste. "Out, all of you. I must have the room to work. I may have to operate."

"You can't think you can hold him down yourself." Molly dodged a swat from Johann's arm not yet tied down. "Also, he's plenty upset with you. Says you turned him into a monster and turned his heart to lead. Or something like that. My German's only so-so, though I think he sounds crazy in any language right now."

"I have aether to subdue him, and I work best alone when I operate." He glanced around the room at the pitcher of water and cake of soap beside the basin. "All I require is clean linen and your departure."

They helped him dose Johann and lay him out on a pallet, but even after the others had left, Crawley lingered, crouching beside Cornelius on the floor and grimacing at his sailor. "I'll give you whatever you need, including a pair of hands. I was a surgeon's mate in my early days. I know what the tools are and how to stay out of the way."

Welcome as assistance would be under any other circumstances, Conny didn't dare let the pirates know they carried treasure beyond their wildest imaginings inside their second-least-favorite sailor's chest. He shook his head. "Thank you, but I don't need assistance."

"Fair enough. If you change your mind, I'll be outside the door."

Once the captain left, Cornelius set the locks. He boiled his instruments in a copper bowl on the small potbellied stove in the corner, and while the water cooled enough for him to wash his hands in it, he stripped to his shirt, rucking up the sleeves and pinning them in place with the inside loop. He donned his surgical apron. He lined up the instruments on a towel beside Johann. He scrubbed his hands and forearms until his skin was beet red.

Then he picked up his scissors and cut carefully through the thin line of flesh that had grown over the door to the heart.

He hadn't allowed himself to dwell much on what could be wrong, but now that the clockwork heart lay whirring before him, he let the possibilities spin out. The gears worked well enough—nothing needed oiling, though he sluiced them all for good measure. Nothing in particular appeared broken. But something was amiss—he could smell it. First figuratively, and then when he leaned closer, literally.

Dirty. The heart was dirty. Not yet so much it impaired function, though that was on its way. Now it was only enough contamination to give Johann an infection. The scent of bacteria lingered behind the dirty clockwork, confirming his suspicions. It leached poison into Johann's blood and made him irritable and irrational. Made him sweaty, and a quick check of his temperature confirmed it also made him feverish. Caught earlier, the debris could have been easily dealt with. But Cornelius had pushed off the maintenance due to Johann's foul mood—the part of it having everything to do with Cornelius and nothing to do with his improperly maintained heart—and in the meantime, Johann had worked seven or eight times as hard as usual, creating more contamination. And infection.

He could not be seen to now, not with the heart inside him. It must be bathed in solution while the infection in Johann was treated, and then it must be reset. It required a Lazarus machine. It required a hospital, or better yet, Master Félix's laboratory. Under absolutely no circumstances could it be done on a pirate ship with minimal tools and one pair of hands.

In short, it couldn't be done.

Cornelius crouched beside the pallet, pressing his upper arm over his mouth and nose so he didn't contaminate his hands as he shut his eyes and did his best not to weep.

He told himself it would have ended here anyway. Johann had only ever been meant to die, and at best Conny had delayed that a bit. He'd given the man a significant extension, which was a minor miracle. He'd kept the heart safe too, which could quite conceivably save the world from chaos and destruction. He'd done his best. He couldn't ask anything more of himself. Because to go into any hospital would mean exposure, which would mean Johann's death, or worse, that he'd be turned into a clockwork soldier after all.

This was sound reason, all of it. And every last bit made Cornelius want to destroy the cabin in heart-wrenching fury. He would not accept logic or reason. He never did. There was a way. If he only had a Lazarus machine, he could do it right now. Inside of an hour.

He paced back and forth, murmuring as he searched desperately for an alternate plan. If he was clever and careful, perhaps he could get to Master Félix. If they changed course now, flew directly to Calais, they could make it. Of course, it would mean extra fuel. And getting Johann across town somehow. Without either of them getting attacked, or kidnapped, or killed.

And he'd have to convince the pirates, without letting them know why. Which they'd never agree to. Or he'd have to confess what Johann carried, which risked their turning him over for profit.

Which meant Johann would die. Likely not tonight, but sometime in the next few days. He'd go painfully, and he'd leave this earth hating Cornelius. Quite possibly with just cause.

Conny shut his eyes, swallowing his sobs as quietly as he could while tears ran down his cheeks.

He didn't hear the scratches on the door at first, not until a soft knock came as well. "Conny?"

Valentin. His emotions playing fast and loose with him now, Cornelius sobbed, audible enough for the sound to echo in the room. He didn't even straighten when the door opened, only remained where he was, hunched and powerless beside Johann's body. When Valentin put hands on his shoulders, Cornelius leaned into his friend. "H-how did you get in?"

"I begged a key from Heng. Besides, they were nervous about you locked in here alone with him." He stroked Cornelius's hair. "Darling, tell me what's wrong. Why are you crying?"

There seemed no point in hiding anything now. If Val betrayed him, it'd simply give Cornelius more reason to throw himself over the railing of the airship. He gestured to Johann's open chest. "He needs a Lazarus machine."

"Then we'll go to a hospital. There's no need for tears."

Cornelius shook his head. "He can't go. No one would know how to fix him but me or Master Félix. Anyone else would kill him to take the clockwork I've given him."

"*Conny.* You're too dramatic."

Cornelius shut his eyes. "I gave him the clockwork heart, Val."

"A clockwork heart? I've never heard of such a thing. Except that people have tried, and they're impossible."

"They're not impossible. There's only one, and Johann has it now. Master Félix made it years ago. No one else can replicate his work. He refused to use it, kept it locked away. Until I stole it and put it in Johann." His secrets, once spilled, tumbled out of him. "Someone's trying to steal it, possibly my own father. They don't know it's inside Johann. No one does. They'd kill him to take it, to use it to power soldiers. Except I'm killing him now. I didn't take care of him, and now he's dying."

"My God." Valentin let out a shaking breath. "Conny, what in the world have you done? *Why* did you do this?"

"I couldn't stand to see him die."

"Of course. To you, everything is so simple." He sighed. "Your mother is a world-class spy. Your father a ruthless leader. How that combination produced such a tender, impulsive creature, I'll never understand."

Tears would not stop running down Cornelius's cheeks. "He won't survive this. Not without a Lazarus machine. But if I tell the pirates, they'll steal the heart. It's worth all the money in the world."

Valentin huffed. "No, it isn't. Your father, or whoever seeks this machine, would kill anyone connected to it. It's not a gold mine. It's a death sentence. One they've already signed by taking you on. But don't worry. They'll help you, and Johann too." He stroked Cornelius's hair again. "I'll see to it."

Cornelius lifted his head to look at his friend in disbelief. "*You* will? But you hate Johann."

"Yes, but I love *you*." He kissed both of Cornelius's cheeks, then drew his handkerchief to dry Conny's face. "Come. No need to cry in your cottage. Pull yourself together. I'll bring in Heng and Crawley, and together we'll convince them."

Cornelius wasn't yet sure that was possible. But with no other choice on his horizon, he decided it was worth a try.

* * * * *

Crawley, Heng, Olivia and Molly stood around the pallet, turning their heads sideways and staring in slow-blinking shock at Johann's open chest. At first, they said nothing. Heng was the first to recover, though he couldn't look away as he spoke to Cornelius. "He's had this in him the whole time? A clockwork heart?"

Cornelius nodded. "Since he and I met, yes. His was irrevocably damaged when I found him. I stole the heart from Master Félix's vault and fitted it inside Johann. It works well, better than a flesh heart—until it isn't cared for properly."

Crawley couldn't stop shaking his head as he stared at Johann's whirring machinery. "Why can't I see the blood running through?"

"Oh, that's a separate system now, one I shouldn't have to tend to for years. But this engine here is the trouble." Cornelius gestured to the open cavity but was careful not to touch, as he'd contaminated his hands. "I need to remove the heart, clean and oil it, and extract the infected tissue. It won't take but an hour. Faster if I have Master Félix helping. But a Lazarus machine is required."

Heng rubbed his beard. "And this heart is why those goons were chasing you on the docks?"

"I doubt it. No one knows it's in him. That business seemed focused on me, and my mother."

Olivia raised an eyebrow. "The English spy?"

"Double agent, but for England, yes. She was meant to be retired, but I'm beginning to think that was another one of her lies. It's impossible to say if this is all part of her plot or if she's been compromised. She's involved, as the note was in her hand. But that's all I know."

"So they're already looking for you, but if they find out about Johnny's clockwork heart, they'll look even harder." Crawley drew a hand over his face. "I'd say I was sorry we signed you on, but you're the best tinker I've ever seen in my life, and Johann is a harder worker than ever." He nodded at Val, who stood beside Conny, looking ready to do battle as soon as he understood what people were saying. "Even Frenchie is pulling his weight, for the most part. Though I'm not sure how we save Johann, love. We'd never make it from the dock to the tinker's shop. Especially with a gurney."

Molly tapped her cheek. "What if we bypassed the dock entirely? Land on the roof in the dead of night. A few of us could run ahead, secure the location. Heng could arrange a distraction on the other side of town. Chimney smoke will give us decent cover for landing. If we get lucky, we might have some fog."

Cornelius's heart beat a little faster. "I could help with that. If we break into the alchemist shop on the south end of town, I can get the ingredients to make a smog bomb. That will alert the authorities, but if you provide a distraction farther away, they'll focus their attention there, not on the shop."

Valentin nudged Cornelius gently. "They are helping, yes?" he murmured in French.

"*Oui.*" Cornelius kissed his cheek. "They are. Thank you."

Crawley looked speculatively at Valentin, then spoke in French. "You know Calais. You can help provide a distraction so Cornelius can work."

Val nodded curtly. "I'll do whatever needs to be done to help Conny. Only don't try to leave me behind."

"I'll only leave you if you fail to meet us at the designated time."

"No." Conny lifted his chin. "You will bring him back. All of us. If you must leave for the rest of the crew's safety, you'll find a way to return for those left behind."

Crawley grunted before turning to Heng. "Fine. Set a course for Calais. We'll drop Valentin, Olivia and Heng on the south side. Get whatever the tinker needs for the bomb and secure a plan. We'll give you three hours, then swing back around to prepare for the night drop." He raised an eyebrow at Cornelius. "How much time does he have?"

Conny shrugged. "It's difficult to say. Days, likely, but of course until I lift the heart out and gauge the degree of infection, I won't know for sure."

"Then we'll work as swiftly as possible." Crawley rose and clapped his hands. "Get to it, sailors."

As the others filed out, Cornelius pulled Crawley aside. "A word, Captain." Crawley turned to face him. "What is it?"

His earnestness, even eagerness to help, was gratifying, but also unnerving. Cornelius decided to be blunt. "Why are you helping me so readily? I thought surely you would complain about going off course in the very least." He hesitated, then came out with the rest. "If you're thinking of turning us over to my father, he won't pay you. He'll take us and kill your entire crew afterward. He can't afford any witnesses, if he's scheming the way I suspect."

Crawley straightened, affronted. "For all you marked up that contract, you don't seem to have read it terribly closely. You and Johann are part of my crew. Your worthless fop of a friend as well. In addition to that, you and Johann add considerable value to my enterprise. Of course we'll do whatever we can to help him and keep you from the despair and therefore lack of productivity you'd clearly experience at his passing." His lips quirked in a smile. "That, and I suspect you'll want to make off with all manner of tools and supplies you keep carping about regretting having to leave in your workshop. The idea of you being able to tinker even *better* than you do now would be worth scaling a mountain for."

Cornelius hadn't even thought of his lost tools, but now a hot rush of pleasure filled him at the very possibility of their retrieval. "Master Félix will let us take other items as well, if we approach him correctly. Perhaps we could organize some kind of trade. He's always asking for parts from Italy. If he outfitted us with enough upgrades to sail south, we could bring him some of those directly and save him smuggler's fees."

"*Now* you're thinking like a pirate." Crawley chucked his chin, his smile sliding to wan. "Don't fret. We'll get your lover sorted. But then your first job is to straighten out the mess between you two, do you hear? He can be sore all he likes about his clockwork, but anything beats dead. A good lay ought to put you both to rights. Or at least provide distraction while the kinks work out on their own. I'll even lend you my cabin, though as a general rule we use the storeroom when we want to get each other off."

Cornelius blushed, unwilling to admit he had yet to do more than trade kisses and gropes with Johann. "Thank you." He took Crawley's hand and kissed the back of his knuckles. "You're a good captain, Crawley. And an incomparable man."

"Don't waste your breath buttering me up. Sew my sailor back together and ready yourself for a raid." He winked as he headed to the door. "Though once you kiss and make up, I'm not at all opposed to joining the two of you in my cabin. A little spice makes everything nice, as they say."

Cornelius wasn't sure he wanted to take the captain to a bed he shared with Johann. But the teasing remark did make him smile, lifting his spirits just a bit higher as he boiled more water to wash his hands and sew Johann up for transport.

Chapter Nine

Johann's dreams were strange.

He dreamed he was back in the Austrian Army, but he went this time as a clockwork man. All the soldiers were automatons, and they marched endlessly together through mud and cold, toward an unnamed front of an undisclosed war. Johann's dream clockwork ached, chafing at the points of contact in a way Cornelius's never did. But Cornelius was nowhere in this dream.

A general stood at the top of the hill, barking out orders in German. The sky rained steadily, soaking Johann to the bone, but the general stood beneath a tent, protected from the elements and further warmed by a brazier. "March on, march on," he shouted, pausing only to accept a plate of sausages or glass of wine from a servant. Meanwhile, *march* was all Johann and the other soldiers did. Endlessly. Obediently. Occasionally someone would drop dead, and a great mechanical arm would whisk them away before bringing another clockwork soldier to put in the fallen man's place. They weren't brought food or water or even told where they were going or why. Only that they should march on.

Johann noticed they weren't alone on the hill. French soldiers trudged on the other side—they were clockwork too, though their mechanical parts looked slightly different. There were less of these soldiers, and they moved more smoothly, but they proceeded much the same. Archduke Guillory himself stood on their side of the incline, his tent more grand than the Austrian general's. He urged his soldiers to march, between nibbles on turkey legs and mouthfuls of fruit and swigs of brandy. Occasionally he paused to motion to the Austrian general, passing him some food or whispering an exchange that made them both laugh. Then they both returned to their barked orders.

March on. March on. March on.

After what felt like days, Johann knew he couldn't continue. He did his best to fight, because he didn't know where the crane took the soldiers, but of course eventually he fell and it came for him too. Except as it hoisted him away from the hill toward a fiery factory, *The Brass Farthing* broke through the clouds, and Crawley addressed Johann from his perch on the rope ladder.

"Come on, lad. Fight."

For a moment the battlefield vanished. Johann flew through the air, the *Farthing* floating above him. Crawley wasn't on a ladder, but rather straddling a wide pallet upon which Johann lay. The captain clung to a set of ropes as they swung back and forth across a night sky.

Crawley stared hard at Johann a moment longer, then nodded to someone beyond Johann's line of sight. "He's still with us. Though I think it might be best we get him through the roof and onto that Lazarus as quickly as possible."

"I can see Master Félix waving to us from below."

Cornelius. Johann turned toward the sound of his voice, but the simple effort seemed beyond him. His chest hurt, and when he moved anything but his head, he ached all over.

Then Cornelius was there, crouching over him and touching Johann's face in concern. "Quiet now, darling. I'm going to put you to rights."

He lowered an aether mask over Johann's face, and the dream returned. The great crane plucked Johann out of the sky and swung him onto the battlefield again.

Johann marched with the others, but now he scanned the skies for the pirate ship. He saw nothing, not even the moon or stars, only the endless fog of war. He tasted saltpeter and ash. He smelled death and rot. He felt the ache of his clockwork as it ground on and on. From the top of the hill, the general and the archduke joked and laughed with one another, while below them sergeants commanded the soldiers.

I will not march.

"I will not march for you!"

Johann fought through the line, scaling the boulders separating the armies. He shouted at the general, at the archduke, at the world. He tore down their tents, sending them and their pampered servants and officers careening down the hillsides. He felt warmth seep through his chest, and when he looked down, his clockwork heart glowed proudly behind its flesh wall.

"Johann."

Looking up from the top of the windy hill, he saw the *Farthing* flying close once more, sluicing through the rain. Cornelius stood on the deck, motioning to Johann. But they were too far away for Johann to reach. "Fly closer," he called to the *Farthing*.

The *Farthing* remained where it was, however. If anything, it seemed to be moving the other direction.

"*No*." Johann ran toward the airship, down the hill to the battlefield, shoving soldiers from both sides aside as he tried to reach Cornelius's side. But the soldiers were too thick, and the *Farthing* kept moving farther away.

When Johann cried out again, he was back on the pallet, the world swaying crazily, the air full of smoke. He saw Cornelius and reached for him, tried to call his name. But he felt heavy and sick, and his body would not respond to his commands.

Cornelius clung to one of the ropes holding the pallet aloft. He looked worried as he spoke to Crawley. "Did they see us? What do we do if we're discovered? I need time to operate, but if they come in while I have him open—"

"Don't worry about such things. Trust Heng and Olivia to know their business. And Val too. I never thought we'd have use for a fop, but by God, Frenchie knows how to flounce about and keep the police occupied. He has an incredible knack for how far he can annoy them without getting tossed in jail."

"I'm so nervous." Cornelius wiped his eyes with his fingers, but tears stained his cheeks all the same. "I worry I let it go too long and I won't be able to save him."

"You'll make it work." Crawley glanced at Johann, then startled. "Christ, he's awake again. How does he do that? You've given him enough aether to kill a man."

"It's the heart, I think." Cornelius knelt beside Johann, touching his face as he studied him. "Darling, try to sleep. Don't fight it. Rest, and let me heal you."

The mask came back, and Johann tumbled once more onto the battlefield. This time he stood on the top of a cliff, and the *Farthing* sailed right for him. He could see Cornelius on the ladder, arm outstretched, his smile wide and welcoming, full of love.

Cannons fired below. The battlefield had shifted, and all their focus was on the *Farthing* now. One cannonball to the balloon and it would be over. They could easily move out of range—but that would take them away from Johann.

"Go back in the ship!" It made Johann ache to send Conny away, but he could not watch him die. "Go up the ladder, where you're safe."

Cornelius wouldn't leave. He stayed on the ladder, kept holding out his hand. "Come to me, darling. Come be safe *with* me. Let us be together, forever."

Johann wanted that more than he wanted anything in the world. "I can't reach you. You're too far away."

A cannon went off, making the earth shake, but Cornelius only grinned at Johann, unfazed. "Run to me, Johann. Run like the wind. You can outrun the bullets, the cannon shot. With your clockwork legs, you can leap from that cliff and land surefooted in the valley below. Leap, darling. Fly through the air, and come to me. Show them all how wonderful you are."

Johann ran. He leapt though the air, and just as Cornelius said, when he hit the ground, his legs didn't falter. They bore him forward, faster and faster though the night sky. The world lit up with artillery fire, but Johann moved through it all as if none of it mattered. It didn't. The only thing in the world he cared about was the man beckoning to him from the pirate ship waiting to take him home.

"Come to me, Johann," Cornelius called, smiling.

His clockwork heart whirring with happiness, Johann pushed a cannonball aside and flew into his lover's arms.

* * * * *

The entirety of the tinker shop was in shambles.

When Heng and Olivia had reported back to the *Farthing* with supplies for the bomb, they'd spoken of soldiers in the streets, of shuttered storefronts, of raided cafes. Secret police without insignia of any kind moved from building to building. But for Cornelius, seeing the tinker shop firsthand was heartbreaking. Every shelf had been ransacked, much of the clockwork on display broken or outright confiscated by the soldiers.

Master Félix welcomed the pirates' arrival, though he'd papered the upstairs windows in anticipation of their visit to block out their surgery lamps because he was closely watched. His condition for helping them wasn't the promise of supplies from Italy, either. *He* wanted to go to Italy. In return, the pirates were free to take what they liked from his shop.

Conny hadn't let Olivia or Heng explain why they were coming, though he himself came clean as soon as they'd lowered Johann through the skylight. To his surprise, Félix wasn't upset at all.

"I might have been upset if I'd found out before, but now I'm only relieved. If you hadn't taken it, lad, you and I and that heart would be locked in a castle somewhere right now, forced to replicate it and install it in the bodies of your father's favorite soldiers." He flicked a gnarled finger against the unconscious Johann's chest. "Besides, I'm curious to see how it's fared in its first trial."

Cornelius had wanted to know more about Félix's confirmation it was indeed his father behind the quest for the heart, but they didn't have time, not until they saw to Johann's heart.

They worked the surgery together, Félix cleaning the mechanism while Cornelius saw to the infection in Johann's body cavity. It was mild, which was a relief, but it also meant the greater issue was with the heart itself.

"It needs to be calibrated to the individual and the tasks undertaken." Félix pointed out a set of intricate, tiny gears. "When his greatest exertion was wandering about Calais and flirting with you, this setting was adequate. But if he's running faster than a horse and hauling rigging on an airship, he requires a different baseline setting. And more maintenance."

Cornelius grimaced at the obviousness of this diagnosis. "I feel ridiculous for not thinking of that."

"Seems to me you've had plenty of other business to occupy yourself with."

They were interrupted by Johann's cry, and preparations stopped while Cornelius yet again gave him gas to subdue him. Once that was seen to, they put Johann's pallet on the Lazarus machine, and Félix and Cornelius washed up and dressed for surgery.

With the two of them, it went quickly and easily, at least in so far as opening Johann up, hooking him to the Lazarus and removing his heart. Félix put it in a bath of alcohol and pored over it as Cornelius dealt with the infected tissue in Johann's chest cavity. In the middle of it, though, Johann briefly woke once more.

"How the devil does he keep doing that?" the captain asked as he pressed the mask to Johann's face at Cornelius's direction. "I know you said it's the clockwork heart, but *that* is currently sitting in a tray."

"It doesn't matter." Félix looked up from his work, his bald crown and thick white hair and beard making him look like a half-spent dandelion. "The boy is wired for the heart. It changes everything."

"Yes." Cornelius touched Johann's arm as he settled back into sleep. "Right now the Lazarus machine is replacing the clockwork heart's function—not a flesh heart, but the clockwork. His patterns have altered. The heart has become part of Johann, situating itself to him. Changing him. It's made Johann stronger. It's only a machine, but its superior functionality has allowed his body to put its efforts elsewhere instead of maintaining it. While this always happens with clockwork replacements, the level of improvement the heart has allowed is remarkable. *Johann* is remarkable. It's a testament to his genetics and to his life force what he's been able to do with his clockwork."

Crawley huffed. "Ah. Now I see why the army is so set on getting your heart, Conny."

"It isn't mine," Cornelius replied. "It isn't even Master Félix's any longer. It's Johann's heart. And I'll gut anyone who tries to take it from him."

They worked as quickly as they could to put Johann back together. Once the heart was cleaned and the infection dealt with, the rest of the surgery went smoothly. Félix said he wanted to take another, longer look at it when they were in Italy, but for the moment Johann was out of the woods and hale enough for a long journey. Molly escorted the sleeping Johann back to the ship, and once that was done, Cornelius and Félix helped Crawley disassemble the tinker shop.

They took the Lazarus machine in pieces—it hadn't been Conny's priority initially, but it was clear the device would be crucial in maintaining Johann, and so up it went. Conny had them empty out his room almost entirely of everything the police hadn't destroyed and some of what they had. They did the same for the surgery as well, and all of their supplies. Every vial and jar of medicine, every test tube and gas burner, his reference books—everything went up the hoist onto the *Farthing* that could be used or repaired.

Félix kept his personal acquisitions down to three small suitcases and a large trunk. When Crawley insisted they'd make room for his valuables, Félix only tapped the side of his head. "This is my most precious cargo. I can make any tool I need. In any event, I intend to drink a lot of wine and flirt with pretty Italian ladies and tinker in the Milani family's shed. I happily surrender grander pursuits to my apprentice."

Once the upstairs was cleared, they dug into the first floor. Félix and Cornelius directed Crawley to the most valuable and versatile bits of clockwork and supplies, but once that was done, the goal was to make off with as much as the *Farthing* could carry before the secret police arrived. Master Félix, less nimble on a ladder if they needed to flee in a hurry, retired to the ship and made himself busy improving the engine to more efficiently haul so much weight. Cornelius stayed below, assisting in selection and warning Crawley off items not worth the burden. The captain loved, he soon discovered, anything that looked flashy, filled with gears and wires. He often paused to effuse over this or that bit of junk which Crawley insisted would look a treat on the side of the ship or on their hat, or sewn into their lapel.

The party ended, however, when there came a timid knock at the kitchen door. Crawley drew his pistol, but Cornelius held up a hand to stay them when he heard a familiar timid call through the wood.

"It's Louise. Our maid. Félix said he let her go weeks ago. I wonder why she's come back."

Crawley glowered. "Could be a trap."

Cornelius doubted it—Louise was such a sweet girl. But given how much of his life had been compromised, he supposed he had to consider she'd been brought here under duress. "I have to answer, to make certain she's safe."

"Very well. But take care."

The captain hid behind the curtain to the pantry, pistol cocked and ready as Cornelius opened the door with the chain still in place. "Louise?"

"Oh! Master Cornelius." Louise's eyes filled with tears, and she pressed a gloved hand to the door, as if she could caress him through it. "I've been worried sick for you. Where have you been? Is Master Félix with you? He sent me away because of the soldiers, but I've been so afraid for him, for you both."

Aching for her, Cornelius reached for the chain, but Crawley stuck his head out from the pantry and whispered before he could. "What's a young woman like her doing out on such a night, with Heng and Olivia and Val making the fracas down the street? I smell fish, love."

It was a bit odd, yes, but the very idea of Louise being part of anything nefarious... Cornelius pulled the door as wide open on the chain as he could. "We're well, thank you, dear. But you should go home. It's not safe on the street. Come back in the morning, won't you, darling? We can catch up then."

"I will, of course, but let me kiss your cheek first, yes, and give you a hug? I've been so afraid for you, and your pirate friend."

Crawley had come fully out of the pantry now, shaking his head, clearly intending to shut the door. Cornelius cut a glance to him, wanting to tell him no, then realized that would give the captain away. "Tomorrow, please—hurry, Louise, I think I hear the police returning."

Her sweet, tender expression froze, then morphed into cold calculation in the space of a breath before she raised a pistol and aimed it at the chain.

Conny barely had time to yelp before Crawley yanked him out of the way. The chain broke as the door banged open to reveal Louise and a herd of soldiers.

"Where is Félix?" she demanded as the men took aim at Conny and the captain. "And where is the heart?"

Cornelius only blinked at her. "Louise? Why are you doing this?"

Louise rolled her eyes and folded her arms over her chest. "Your mother is a spy, but you can't see an agent when she's directly under your nose? Good God, what a worthless slut you are, after all. *Where is the heart?*"

Crawley had backed them into the wall, but when he inched them toward the doorway leading to the stairs, the soldiers cocked their rifles. The captain smiled at Louise as Cornelius continued to gape. "He can't spot a spy when she's kissing him on the cheek, and you think he knows where the clockwork heart is?"

Conny recovered enough to speak. "It was stolen, Louise. You *know* this."

"I know I searched high and low for it and came up empty." She aimed her pistol at Crawley's head. "I can't shoot the bastard without upsetting the archduke, but *you* are expendable. Tell me where the heart is, or I shoot your friend, Cornelius, and let these men haul you off to your father, who will extract information from you one way or another."

Cornelius blinked, frozen in terror. He had no idea what to do. He'd die before he gave Johann up to anyone, but he'd never considered letting someone else perish all because he wouldn't speak. Crawley, who was so kind to him, who had helped so much.

"Ignore them." Crawley had slipped behind Cornelius, pressing his front flush to Conny's back. "They can't shoot me without harming you." He chuckled softly. "And to be honest, we don't need to stall them much longer anyway."

Louise stiffened at this, but before she could give an order, the windows of the kitchen shattered. When the soldiers turned, ready to fight, Olivia and Heng burst through the door, and Val came in from the stairs, wide-eyed and aiming pistols badly with trembling hands. While the pirates and soldiers fought, Crawley whisked Conny out of the room and up to the skylight, where the ladder to the *Farthing* dangled.

"I can't believe Louise is a spy." Conny's hands shook as he tried to climb, and he glanced down at the shop, where shots and sounds of struggle echoed. "Will they be all right?"

"Your spy maid and her goons? No, I suspect most of them will be dead directly. Heng's much more vicious than he looks. And Olivia is exactly as lethal as she presents herself to be."

"Will our people make it back to the ship, I mean? Will Val accidentally shoot someone with those pistols?"

"I doubt Heng gave him anything loaded. But yes, we'll collect them all on the other side of town, once things have cleared. Heng appointed a meeting place on the west end. We'll wait for them there."

Crawley whistled, and the *Farthing* took off into the night with the two of them still dangling from the ladder. Cornelius startled when shots rang out, whizzing through the air beside him, but Crawley only spurred him upward, helping him along until they were both aboard.

"Take her into the clouds," he barked.

"Aye, Captain." Molly, at the wheel on the main deck, lowered her goggles and flew the *Farthing* away.

Chapter Ten

When Johann woke, he was in a strange bed, though it smelled familiar. It reminded him of Cornelius's bedroom at the tinker shop, and thinking of those days made his heart ache. *That* thought in turn reminded him he didn't have a heart that could ache, not any longer.

Except it did ache. A tug of longing lodged firmly in the center of his chest. *Perhaps that is my soul.* A comforting thought, because it meant he still had one.

What had happened, though? How had he come to be here? Where was *here*? He went quiet, shutting his eyes again, and listened. He heard the gentle whir of airship engines. Was he on the *Farthing*? A different airship?

Had he been taken prisoner? He shifted in the bed but found he wasn't chained down. He had all his clockwork on, and it seemed to have been well-oiled, possibly even improved in a few places. Though he tried to take all this as a good sign, he feared it meant he'd been impressed back into the Austrian Army, or worse, taken by the forces who'd tried to kidnap Cornelius. The only thing keeping him from panic was that smell.

Cornelius's bedclothes, that was what he smelled.

Cornelius himself appeared, hovering over Johann. Touching his face. Looking concerned. Relieved. But also sad.

"You're awake." Cornelius smoothed a hair away from Johann's clockwork eye, then seemed to remember himself and withdrew. This time his smile was a bit strained. "I hope you're feeling better."

Johann didn't remember feeling poorly. He flexed his hands, first his flesh one, then his clockwork one. "What happened? Where are we?"

"We're on the *Farthing*, in the captain's cabin. He lent it to you while you recover."

Recover? "I feel fine."

"That's because I have you well-dosed with aether." Cornelius settled on the edge of the bed, resting his hands in his lap. "Your clockwork heart required emergency surgery. We flew you to Calais, and Master Félix helped me with the repairs and the adjustments. Everything is working wonderfully now, and better yet, we know exactly how to keep you from having such difficulty in the future." He looked down as he continued in a demure voice. "Master Félix is coming with us. We're traveling to Italy, where he'll be staying. I've arranged with Captain Crawley to buy out your contract by extending mine, if you'd like to remain with Félix. He'll be able to see to your maintenance in my stead."

That same aching place as before yearned again, this time in a much more pointed, hollow manner. "You wish me to leave you?"

"I don't. But I understand if *you* wish to leave *me*."

Johann didn't wish to leave Cornelius, and he wasn't certain why Conny would think that. He lay still, breathing quietly as he tried to remember what had happened, and once again he was overwhelmed by the smell of lavender and spice. Conny's scent.

He frowned. "Why does Crawley's bed smell like you?"

Cornelius's blush stained high on his cheeks. "I...slept beside you last night." His thumbs twiddled nervously, and his voice trembled. "I'm very sorry I didn't tell you sooner about the heart. My excuse was you didn't know enough French, but of course that's faddle. I worried you'd be upset, which you were, when I had no choice but to confess. Briefly I feared you were a spy seeking the heart, though in hindsight that's utterly ridiculous. The truth is, without the clockwork heart, you wouldn't be alive. You would have died the night I found you on the barge. I worked like the devil to save you, and I nearly did, but then your heart gave out. I knew we had the mechanical one, sitting there going to waste, so I used it. I didn't think, only acted, which I acknowledge is my worst flaw. But the heart is nothing to fear. It's a machine. A pump made of metal, not flesh. No different than your leg or arm. I know everyone fancies the heart as the seat of the soul, but it truly isn't. It's nothing more than an organ, frail and mortal. I can't control you with it. No one can."

Johann remembered now why he'd been angry. He still was, a little, though lying there in the quiet, he admitted mostly he was scared. "You said the armies are after it."

"Yes. They want to put it in soldiers, I assume. Make copies of it."

"So *they* can control it?"

"No, they can't control people with clockwork hearts. But they already control the soldiers' minds, which is what would matter. If they resurrected corpses, it might be a different story, though such a thing isn't possible. It would require electricity at the very least, a subject I don't know much about."

Johann didn't know either. It made him feel slightly better, to hear no one could control him through the heart, though he admitted he should have figured that out on his own. His fear came from the army and what they might do to him, not from Cornelius. There was anger too, though, at how no matter what happened, he kept ending up someone's pawn.

But not a pawn of Cornelius. He understood that now. Cornelius only wanted to help him.

His stroked the tinker's knee timidly with his flesh hand. "I don't wish to leave you. And I'm glad you slept beside me, though I'm sorry I wasn't awake to notice."

Tears in his eyes, Cornelius caught Johann's hand, kissed the back of it and held the flesh to his lips. "I would never hurt you, darling. And I would never want you to stay with me if you didn't want to be here. But I *do* want you to stay, if you wish that also."

Johann rubbed his thumb along their joined hands. "I would like to kiss you again. And hold you." His shyness tried to stop him there, but the aether plowed over it like an airship skidding over choppy waves into port. "I want to hold you without your clothes on."

The shadows left Cornelius's eyes. "Without your clothes too, I hope."

Johann gestured derisively at himself. "I am all scars and fake parts. Too ugly."

"Not at all." Cornelius ran a hand down Johann's chest, trailing fingers across the exposed clockwork of his left arm. His tone was silky, and his French-accented English sent shivers across Johann's skin even as the light touch sparked thrills up the nerve endings attached to his clockwork. "Your scars give you character. Your flesh is firm and muscled from work." He threaded his fingers through Johann's clockwork ones, the tilt of his smile wicked. "Your clockwork is my finest art, but you wear it as no one else could. When I see it on you, I'm sometimes so aroused it's everything in me to hold back from pouncing on you and licking you head to toe."

Johann's cock, which was not in the least bit clockwork, grew stiff and eager in his drawers. "Lick me?"

Cornelius drew the clockwork hand as well as Johann's flesh one to his mouth, kissing each set of knuckles by turns. Then, his gaze locked with Johann's, his eyes sparkling, he ran his tongue over the same places.

Johann might not have nerve endings on the clockwork knuckles, but by God, Conny licking him there sent shivers down his spine all the same.

"I want to make love to you, Johann." Cornelius kissed his palm. "I want to bring you pleasure. Want to let you take pleasure with me."

Johann wanted that too. Except... "I don't know how."

"I do." Cornelius placed Johann's arms above his head. "Lie back, darling, and let me give you a demonstration."

Johann held still, his cock growing more rigid as Cornelius undid the buttons on his shirt and unlaced his drawers. His head spun too, a reminder he was under the influence of aether. "I will be embarrassing because of the aether. Too silly."

"That wouldn't bother me." Cornelius paused with his fingers tangled in Johann's chest hair, a wicked glint in his eye. "But...if you like, I could join you."

Cornelius took the black aether mask and affixed it over his face. His appearance was terrifying, the rubber nose expanding, his pretty eyes blinking through the glass eyepieces. When he pulled it away, he grinned like a boy. A naughty boy. He looked, Johann realized, much as he had the night at The Alison. When he'd pulled Johann's cock out of his pants in front of everyone.

Much as he was about to do again, now.

Johann pushed to his elbows as Cornelius undid his laces. Giggled with Conny when Johann's member tangled in the strings.

"Ooh, it's such a pretty cock." Cornelius rubbed his cheek against it, which made Johann's breath catch, but when Conny glanced up at him from down there, Johann caught the sheet in great fistfuls. Conny laughed. "I want to suck you, Johann."

Suck his cock, he meant. Johann pushed said organ into Conny's chin. "Yes. Do this. And speak more French. It makes me tingle."

Conny waggled his eyebrows and ran his tongue up the side of Johann's root. "*Baise-moi. Prends-moi par derrière. Défonce-moi.*" When Johann groaned, Cornelius laughed silkily. "Now you, Johann. Tell me to do it. To suck you. In German. All rough and rude, like you mean to make me do it for you if I didn't want it."

Johann didn't want to be rude, but he wanted to feel Cornelius's mouth on his organ more than he wanted anything in the world. "*Lutsch meinen Schwanz.*"

Conny purred. Then he lifted his head, made his mouth into an O and sucked the tip of Johann's cock inside.

Johann collapsed onto the bed, eyes rolling back in his head despite his efforts to watch what Cornelius was doing to him between whispered entreaties in French. His blood was full of sweet fire, and it all rushed to his groin. He kept thinking he would spend, but when he came close, Cornelius would move away. Soon he cursed Cornelius in his native tongue, demanding release.

When Johann finally thought he would come no matter what, Cornelius pulled off with a loud *pop* and kissed his way up Johann's trembling body. "I want to ride you, *chéri.* I want to feel your *Schwanz* deep inside me."

It *had* been deep inside Cornelius—his mouth—and it had been grand. Johann was about to mention this when Cornelius climbed off the bed and disrobed. He was beautiful—slender, but not small. *His* cock was pink, peeking out of its hood like a sausage. Johann thought he might like to touch it. Perhaps take it in *his* mouth. Before he could ask if he could do this, however, Cornelius produced a small jar from the table beside the bed, took some jelly and reached around to his own backside.

Johann's eyes went wide as he realized which *inside* Cornelius had meant. "It's forbidden," he whispered. It hurt too, he knew, because one of the other boys in the army had been caught by the older soldiers, and they used him there. He had cried, and it broke Johann's heart. He would not do this to Cornelius.

"It is a wonderful feeling." Cornelius straddled Johann's hips with his knees, still reaching behind himself, occasionally shutting his eyes and gasping. In pleasure, not pain.

Johann was still unconvinced. "I will not hurt you."

"No, darling. You'll spear me and make me squeal so loudly they'll hear us on the ground below."

With no other warning, he took hold of Johann's cock and sat down on it.

Johann arched his back and cried out. There was no thought of resisting, there was only this intense feeling. Tightness, heat, movement—*now* he would spend, without question. He didn't want this to end, though, so he fought it. Dug his fingernails into the meat of his right hand. Pressed the hard points of his clockwork digits into his left hip. But Cornelius looked so beautiful, riding him like a pony, stroking himself, all too quickly the tide took him, and he bucked, exploding into Cornelius.

Cornelius spent across Johann's belly, a great, warm blob of seed landing on Johann's heart, over the bandage beneath which lay his newly repaired clockwork. As he collapsed onto the bed beside him, Cornelius scooped up some of the rapidly cooling spunk with his fingers and pressed it to Johann's lips. Normally Johann would have faltered, but between the aether and the knowledge he had just committed sodomy and enjoyed it thoroughly, he didn't have it in him to refuse. Cornelius's spending tasted salty and bitter.

He wanted more.

Cornelius settled onto Johann's shoulder with a contented sigh. He wrapped his arms around Johann's torso, snuggling against the clockwork arm as if it were a feather pillow. "I'm so glad you're well, Johann. I'm sorry I didn't take better care of you."

Johann stroked his lover's hair, his body heavy from sex, his mind unburdened thanks to the aether. He didn't blame Cornelius for his lack of care. He remembered all too well his role in that, not letting him do his job. He thought too of what Cornelius had said, about how no clockwork could make him controlled by another man, only his mind.

This had been the state of his whole life, if he were honest. He hadn't needed any clockwork parts to be controlled by other men, ones who never had his best interests at heart. His whole life he'd given up his mind, and no one had given him anything but pain and suffering for his trouble.

Except for Cornelius. Who had never asked for his mind at all, had only helped him selflessly. Given generously. Loved easily.

I will give my mind to him, then. What I feared he'd taken, I'll give freely. I will follow him and obey him and let him lead me and keep me safe.

The decision felt good, and with that troublesome matter settled, Johann shut his eyes, snuggled deeper against Cornelius and went to sleep.

Chapter Eleven

The *Farthing* could travel forty knots at top speed and five hundred kilometers on a tank of aether, but only without a great deal of weight. They hadn't been at full fuel when they arrived at Calais, and when they added essentially the contents of a tinker shop, their capacity to travel diminished to twenty-five knots per hour with only two hours' worth of fuel left in the balloon, which they largely spent lingering on the edge of Calais as they waited for the others to catch up. Heng had scored them a lead on a bribable fueling station at Dunkirk, but until Master Félix and Cornelius improved the engine, the crew was in a race as to what would tank them: a lack of fuel, or the French Army catching up with them.

They landed the airship just outside of a small village in the middle of nowhere, half the crew spreading out for supplies while Molly and Johann helped the tinkers come up with a solution.

Cornelius had been tweaking the engine since he'd gone on board *The Brass Farthing*, but he'd been doing this missing almost every necessary tool and by repurposing material completely ill-suited for the task. Now he had every tool he could possibly dream of, more options for raw materials than most engine shops, and the unparalleled mind of his mentor. His greatest problem was remembering to hurry instead of amusing himself with endless possibility.

Molly generally saw to keeping him on task. As ship engineer, she knew her way around an engine, and she wasn't keen on, as she put it, Félix and Cornelius's fancy tinker business. "I thought you were *surgeons*, not engine-makers."

"Oh, every tinker is a dabbler." Félix squinted through his half-moon glasses at a set of gears as he tapped it with a wrench. "My first apprenticeship was to a tinker-builder. He once made me take a prototype aether train engine apart and put it back together, all by myself. Twice." He smiled wistfully. "Quite possibly the best three weeks of my life."

"Clockwork is clockwork." Cornelius wiped sweat from his brow with his wrist and pushed his goggles higher onto his head. "Whether it powers an airship or turns a wrist, it's a machine. It does what it's told and works with what it's given. It's more than building it well too. Give it quality fuel and treat it well, and it will work powerfully until its parts run out—and most of those can be replaced. Neglect it, give it shoddy support, and it will falter." He sighed and unscrewed the panel to a dirty set of gears. "Clockwork is so beautifully simple. It's people who are complicated."

He felt someone watching him, and when he turned, he saw it was Johann, looking thoughtful. He was shirtless in deference to the heat in the close chamber, his assigned task to haul and push and fetch whatever the tinkers needed. He didn't wear his eyepatch, either, so he was a beautiful display of clockwork and muscle and beauty. Heng had braided his hair into a dazzling array of thin strands to help keep it out of his way, and it hung about his stubbled chin in dark cords like the most beautifully woven cable. Had the two of them been alone, or even not pressed for time, Cornelius would have asked to be fucked. They'd made love several times now, and during those encounters Cornelius had discovered how aroused he became when Johann held him with both clockwork and flesh grips, and how the hard press of copper against his thigh as Johann fucked into him made his own bones turn to liquid.

When they broke for lunch, he couldn't handle it any longer. Leading Johann away from the others, he pressed him against a tree before falling to his knees and unlacing Johann's trousers. He wanted to feel Johann's clockwork leg against his hand as he stared, throat full of cock, at that amber eye.

Johann threaded shaking fingers into Cornelius's hair. "We need to be vigilant. We might need to flee at any moment."

Cornelius nuzzled Johann's balls, inhaling the musky scent of sweat, licking the wiry hair. "You be vigilant. I'll suck you until you're iron, and then you can make me face the ship while you pound into me from behind."

The dirty talk undid his lover, a trick Cornelius had learned during their brief time of fucking one another. He couldn't do much more than mewl now, as Johann fucked his mouth, but when Johann pushed him away, kneeling behind him as Cornelius made quick work of his trousers, Conny offered a litany of crude commentary, in French because it made Johann all the more desperate. He told his clockwork soldier to fuck him like a dog, to pull his anus wide and spit into it before spearing him with his fat meat. That was the only place where Johann resisted, however.

"It is not enough. You will hurt."

Bless Johann and his illusion Cornelius was a frail flower. "Yes, darling. It will burn and throb all afternoon. I won't be able to think of anything else but how beautifully you bugger me, and by the end of the day I'll be your dog, begging you to fuck me over the dinner table. Maybe that's what you'll do. Take me like your whore while the crew watches your cock pound me, while I beg you for more."

This pretty speech undid Johann so much he barely spat at all, working the tiniest bit of saliva into Cornelius before driving inside. Cornelius cried out, whimpered and demanded more, harder, faster. It went on forever too, because he'd wrung Johann out twice this morning. By the time Johann finished, Cornelius's backside and thighs throbbed with use. After he spent on the grass, he rose shakily and raised his trousers, only to feel Johann's spending leaking out of him.

He practically purred in happiness.

They had their lunch then, Cornelius lying on his side with his head on Johann's fleshy thigh. "I think we nearly have the engine sorted," he told his lover between bites of crusty bread. "If they find a fueling station, we should be able to get all the way to the border of the Austrian Empire." He closed his fingers over Johann's hand on his hip, tucking it tighter against his body. "We wanted to get enough to go all the way to Italy, but the Alps will take their toll. Molly says it will be a challenge to fuel again. I'm hoping Félix and I can trade tinker skills for aether over the border."

Johann's clockwork hand stroked Cornelius's hair. "Can you get to Stallenwald?"

Cornelius did some mental calculations. "I think so, yes. Oh—that's right, they have aether mines. The best in Europe, so I've been told. Father has long bemoaned that he can't conquer them. But how could we convince them to part with their store? They supply directly to the Austrian Army."

"The mines are run by my uncle. He will help us."

Cornelius sat up, looking Johann in the eye. "You're from Stallenwald?"

Johann nodded. "They've never had a tinker there. They will trade dearly for your skills."

"And you can see your family." Remembering Johann's hesitation over his clockwork, he touched his lover's chest. "Will they be angry with me for changing you?"

Johann's smile made warmth spread inside Cornelius. "No. They will be glad you saved me."

Cornelius smiled back. "Then Stallenwald is where we'll go." He pushed bread into Johann's mouth. "Eat your lunch, so we can get ready to travel."

Johann chewed the bread, but when he swallowed, his face had a different kind of hunger. "Would you truly do that—let me take you in front of the others?"

Cornelius's backside throbbed beautifully as he leaned in to kiss Johann's cheek and whisper in his ear. "Yes. Is...that exciting to you?"

"Yes."

He smiled as Johann nuzzled him. Conny knew his soldier-pirate well enough to understand that as much as the prospect of doing Cornelius in front of an audience excited him, he wasn't ready for such a lewd display.

Yet.

* * * * *

Johann didn't think his family would reject him for his clockwork. That didn't stop him from being more and more nervous as they drew closer to the Austrian border. They'd flown in from the north of Stallenwald, so they took in as few mountains as they could, and as they closed in on Johann's village, he busied himself with leading them over the top of the forest, keeping out of sight of the mining scouts while making sure they still had a place to land. He brought them down on the *Platz*, which he hoped still abutted his cousin Fredrick's smithy. It did, and Fredrick himself, beard rippling and hammer swinging, came out to see who the devil had landed on the city square.

Johann made sure he was the first off the ship without a weapon, his arms extended. "Fredrick," he called out as his cousin approached. He wore his patch, a jacket and gloves, though his leg clockwork was visible if one paid close attention to the way his boots were affixed. He hoped he still looked himself enough that his cousin recognized him. "It's me, Johann Berger. Your cousin. Jacob and Bertha's son."

Fredrick lowered the hammer, his eyes first narrowing in disbelief, then opening wide in shock. "Johann? But you've gone to war! How are you here? And on an airship?"

"It's a long story best told over drink." He gestured to *The Brass Farthing*. "While I tell it to you, my friends would love to offer some trades. Our cargo is so heavy, we need to lessen it. And we have two tinkers, one the best in France, who would love to work on anything anyone in town has to bring them. Free of charge for my home village."

Fredrick's laugh came from the bottom of his belly. "*Ja*, we will trade, and we can put the tinkers to work."

"We are also in need of fuel. I was hoping the *Bürgermeister* might help us make a deal with the mines."

"If your tinkers can fix the plumbing to his upstairs bathroom, he'll probably give you the moon. I'm sure something can work out either way, though."

Master Félix had wandered over to them, and he smiled through his white beard as he spoke in perfect German. "I can give the mayor plumbing in every room, and a device to send hot water wherever he likes it. As hot as he'd like."

Fredrick touched his nose. "Now, don't go too far, or his *wife* will run off with you, and then you won't get your fuel."

Félix and Fredrick went off together, chatting amicably and making plans as Crawley directed the others as they exited the airship. Johann ended up shepherding Valentin and Cornelius wherever he went. Cornelius knew a handful of words from their own exchanges, but in practical use he and Valentin were rendered utterly helpless in a village where Johann was the only native resident with multilingual ability.

Johann understood why Crawley had given him Valentin, but he wished he could have had a pardon of an hour. Because before he did anything else, he had a stop to make, and he didn't want the judgmental Frenchman along if he could help it. Since that wasn't an option, he went to his family's small house on the edge of town with his lover and his lover's pouting friend in tow.

He knocked on the door, all his lies about how he wasn't nervous fleeing as he admitted how much it would hurt if his mother saw how he'd changed and recoiled. It was she who answered his knock, and at first seeing her was worse than having her recoil, because it was clear she didn't recognize him.

He removed his hat and clutched it over his heart. "*Guten Morgen, Mutter.*"

She blinked at him a few times. Then she clapped her hands over her cheeks, her eyes wide and full of tears. "*Johann. Mein geliebter Sohne.*"

If she was repulsed by how much clockwork she felt when she embraced him, she hid it well. In fact, she crushed him tight to her body, pulling him down so she could bury her face in his neck. She ushered them all inside, but she never let go of Johann. She put him on a chair in the kitchen and sat before him, touching him all over as if it were the only way she could believe he was real.

"You came home. You came home." She touched the thread of his eyepatch with sadness. "You lost an eye. I'm sorry, darling. I'm so sorry."

"I lost many parts. So many I nearly died." It was starting to bother him she hadn't mentioned his clockwork. He held up his arm, gestured to his legs.

Then he nodded at Cornelius. "He gave me new arms, legs. Organs. Nursed me to health. Saved my life."

Stole my heart. In every way possible.

Johann's mother rose, hand over her breast as she approached Cornelius reverently. With a sob, she took his hands, kissing his fingers over and over. "Thank you. Thank you for giving me back my son. Thank you. Thank you."

Cornelius looked ready to cry too. "*Bitte.*"

They stayed the whole afternoon, far longer than Johann had planned, but he couldn't bring himself to leave. His mother made them stay in the kitchen while she cooked all his favorite foods, plied them with beer and news about every member of his family, his neighbors, and everyone in the village. Assured him she'd received the money he'd sent, and thanked him for it. She asked for his stories, of the war and of his time as a pirate.

She was in the middle of coaxing him into eating a fifth sausage and another bowl of kraut when the front door burst open and Johann's father came in.

He noticed the clockwork right away, and it seemed to punch him in the belly. But when he drew Johann into a tight embrace, none of that mattered. All Johann knew was that his father welcomed him home. Sat beside him at the table, listened intently to his stories. Welcomed his friends.

Took his hand, squeezed it hard with tears in his eyes, and said, "I'm proud of you, my son."

Valentin and Cornelius were largely quiet during the visit, but when Heng came by to ask for their help with something at the mayor's house, Johann thanked them for their patience. "It was good to see my family. It wasn't something I thought I'd ever do again."

Cornelius began to take Johann's hand, remembered where they were, and thought better of it, though he leaned against him briefly as a compromise. "It was a pleasure to watch the reunion. I only wish I had even half that love from either of my parents."

Johann glanced at Valentin, who looked pensive. "Where are your parents?" Johann asked in French.

Valentin startled out of his thoughts, then made a dismissive and very French wave of his hand. "A house party somewhere, no doubt. They go where they like. They're fond of Paris, but only the pretty parts."

"When we go to Paris," Cornelius explained, "we go to the Bohemian district. I find it quite pretty, myself."

Valentin rolled his eyes, but he smiled a little too. "Very well, my parents favor the *respectable* parts."

Cornelius snorted a laugh. "Oh, I can't abide those at all."

Johann laughed too, but privately he felt sorry for both of them. It had never occurred to him that other people's parents wouldn't welcome them home. He wondered if it was because Valentin and Cornelius were so open about their relationships with men. The thought left him cold. Would his parents have been so eager to embrace him if they'd known what he'd done with Conny?

He decided not to think about it any longer.

It felt good to work in the village. With his clockwork, he was stronger than any man there, and they soon had him doing all the lifting and carrying. It made him proud, because he'd been a young boy in this village, skinny and weak, watching strong men work and wishing he could be like them. It was more fun, though, to see how marvelous everyone found what Cornelius and Félix could do with a bit of wire and a wrench. They fixed the fountain on the *Platz*. They made the miller's stone grind faster and more efficiently. They fixed wheels and improved hitches and taught several men, including Johann's father, how to safely use electricity, and gave them enough rolls of copper wire to get started.

"I feel a bit bad," Conny confessed to him when they were alone. "I truly am quite oafish with electric tinkering. I only know the most rudimentary things, and Félix knows only what I've taught him. There's an entirely new breed of tinker up and coming who can make electric clockwork, but the two of us can at best badly wire a wall."

"What you have given them is beyond anything they have ever dreamed of receiving," Johann assured him.

This statement was very true, and the residents of Stallenwald were hugely grateful for what they had received. They heaped *The Brass Farthing* with food, wool and other goods, and above all filled the balloon to the brim with aether straight from the mountain. They prepared a feast for the pirates in the mayor's house, where the beer and wine flowed and food heaped so high they could never eat it all in a thousand days, let alone a single evening. They had a dance on the *Platz* afterward, all the young girls giggling and dancing with the male pirates, looking curiously at the ladies from the ship. The village men looked more than curiously at them, though Johann was fairly certain Molly and Olivia were more interested in each other than other men.

Johann's parents offered him space in their home for the evening, but he declined, going with Cornelius to the alcove they'd made of their part of the sleeping quarters on the *Farthing*. He'd promised to bring the entire crew by in the morning so his parents could have the pleasure and the bragging rights of giving the village heroes breakfast before their long journey. The night, though, he wanted to spend with Cornelius in his arms.

"You keep smiling." Cornelius smiled too as he ran fingers over Johann's chest, teasing the edge of the door to his clockwork heart. "I didn't know your chest could puff out so far."

Johann *was* proud. "My village has so little. The mountain belongs to the emperor, so we get no money for the aether, and it's all the resource we have. You and Félix have made Stallenwald the most modern village this side of Salzburg, with your improvements. We lose all our men to the mines or the war, and there isn't much to life here. They will speak of this day for one hundred years."

Cornelius settled onto Johann's shoulder with a sigh. "The world shouldn't be this way. The village should have so much more to talk about than the day some pirates encouraged them to illegally siphon aether and gave them rudimentary electricity. We've made so many wonderful advancements and discoveries. We have so many *more* to make. I hate that we waste so much money and so many lives in war."

Johann kissed him, first to soothe him and then simply because kissing him was such a pleasure. They made love quietly, then slept the sleep of kings until Heng woke them.

Throughout breakfast, Johann tried not to think about how this might be the last time he saw his family again. He told himself he'd been lucky to have this grand moment to play hero in his village, to hear his father tell him he was a good son, to eat his mother's wurst once more. Still, when he made his goodbyes, he was overwhelmed, unable to speak lest he let loose the torrent of emotion in his heart.

"No tears," his mother told him as she hugged him tight. "You came home to us once. You will come again."

It was a lovely sentiment, even if Johann knew it was little more than that. Still, when the *Farthing* rose into the sky and Johann stood on deck, waving down at the cheering villagers below, he kept his mother's words close to his heart, letting them help carry him into the clouds.

Chapter Twelve

Cornelius had never been to Naples.

He'd been to Genoa once when he was very young. His mother had performed onstage, then entertained several gentlemen in her suite, and Conny's nanny had sat with him on a balcony as he watched people go by. All he remembered from that visit was the sound of music on the street, the red cap of a man on a bicycle, and the way his nanny covered his ears whenever the sounds of sex from his mother's room were particularly obscene. He assumed Naples would be like his hazy memories of Genoa, only bigger.

It was, it turned out, *much* bigger, and shockingly, deliciously cosmopolitan. Naples was the international hub of the Mediterranean, a place where the parts of the world that managed to stay largely out of the conflicts between France and Austria did business with one another. There were a startling number of Americans on the streets, which Conny found terribly interesting, as he'd only ever met a handful of them in his life. Even the fancy ones were a bit rugged and straightforward. There were plenty of Spaniards too, refugees from Cornelius's father's invasions. The English were everywhere, because of course they were allied, loosely, with the Italians, partnered out of a mutual desire to not be ruled by France's iron fist or drafted into military service by the Austrians. There were some Turks as well, and North Africans—the whole world seemed to be happening in Naples.

And the technology! Félix said Naples had not only a street of tinkers, but a thriving district, so grand it had its own food shops and cafes.

"It's like its own little world." Félix's eyes glittered, and he smiled as he spoke. "In fact, the district's name, *ingegnopoli*, means tinker-town. Plenty of tinkers never leave *ingegnopoli*, living above their shops or somewhere in the district, though the wealthier ones have villas just outside of the city. Suppliers deliver whatever is required and often skulk about the streets hawking their wares, competing with each other to offer the best price."

Conny couldn't imagine such a life. "Is there a black market trade too, like in Calais?"

"No need for one. They have free trade with Africa and the Americas, which means their worst prices are ones we didn't dare to dream of in France. My contacts have told me that lately Arabs have been giving away barrels of their crude oil, offering it to any tinker willing to find a use for one of their most plentiful commodities." He smiled as if this were a funny joke. "I doubt they'll get anywhere. Who wants to play with tar when they have more work in aether than they can finish in a lifetime? Not to mention the new electronic tinkering. The Italians *love* their clockwork, both the practical and the luxurious applications. Body enhancements, daily life assistants, and of course whatever clockwork fashion fad has struck them at the moment."

Cornelius couldn't even begin to wrap his mind around all of it. It seemed as if he'd fallen into a dream.

The one downside to Naples was there was no pirate port, which meant *The Brass Farthing* had to be inspected stem to stern and assigned a tariff for its goods, which after Calais were plentiful. Captain Crawley balked at this until Félix assured him matters would be taken care of. Indeed, after the tinker had a lengthy discussion with the dockmaster, a city official made an at-best-cursory glance of the hold, assigned them a tepid docking fee and bid them have a pleasant stay. At least, this was what Heng reported him to have said. He, Crawley and Félix were the only ones who could speak Italian.

Félix arranged for a wagon to carry their things and the delegation of pirates accompanying him to his final destination. This group included Cornelius, Johann, Valentin, Crawley, Heng, Olivia and Molly.

"You're welcome to stay at Signor Rodrigo's as long as you like," Félix assured them as they rode together in a carriage behind their wagon. "He lives in a great villa on the Milani estate just outside of the city. He has more than enough room. And once I introduce you to him and explain our situation, you can park the airship there after you've done whatever trading you might like to do in town. His father gave me most of my training as a tinker, and we were friends while I worked in his father's shop. We've had dealings off and on over the years since then as well. He gives me supplies I need, and I repay him in other ways when I can." Félix settled into his cushion and pushed back the curtain to watch the beautiful Italian scenery go by after sparing a smile at Cornelius. "Wait until you see the Milani family tinker shop. Though I'll probably have to bring smelling salts for when you see his personal laboratory in their shed at the villa."

The tinker district was several kilometers from the docks, but once they arrived, Conny saw it was every bit as grand as Félix had hinted it would be. The buildings were all painted bright colors of varying shades, which Félix explained dictated what type of tinker shop it was. Red for tinker-surgeons, blue for tinker-engineers, green for tinker-mechanics, yellow for tinker-general. The new electronic tinkers had adopted a faint lavender tint, and there were only two Conny saw on the entire ride through the district. Between these brightly colored buildings were smaller terra cotta and tan buildings housing restaurants, cafés and even a few grocery stores. Everything was neat and tidy, and the streets bustled with customers and tinkers alike.

"This is the most wonderful place in the world!" Cornelius all but had his head out the carriage window, trying to take everything in. "Master Félix, how did you ever leave such a city?"

"Duty called me." Félix pointed at a large complex at the end of a street, a single building painted a stripe of every tinker-assignment color. "That's the Milani shop ahead. A different master tinker runs each section, but they all answer to Signor Rodrigo. Ah, and there he is, waving to us from the curb."

Rodrigo Milani was a giant of a man, broad-shouldered with a thick mustache smoothed with pomade and curled delicately at each end. He lifted great bushy eyebrows and called out joyously in Italian when Félix approached him, and the two exchanged three *faire la bise* before embracing and repeating the cheek kisses once more. Cornelius, once introduced, received a more respectable single air-kiss, and Johann and the pirates received only handshakes and smiles. The tinker-master did linger over Johann, praising his clockwork and smiling knowingly when he learned it was all Conny's craftsmanship. As Rodrigo gave them a tour of the shops, he put an arm around Cornelius's shoulders and led him eagerly from station to station.

"It's wonderful to finally make your acquaintance," Rodrigo told Cornelius in correct but roughly accented French. "Félix has told me so much about you over the years. He says you are the most promising apprentice he's ever had and one of the best tinkers in the world." He grinned, revealing several gold-capped, glinting teeth. "But you are ready for a new challenge, yes? You will fall in love with my city, and with my shops."

Conny did his best to explain to Signor Rodrigo that wasn't why they'd come to Naples, but he quickly learned it would be easier to go along with the assumption. Were he honest, the more he saw of the Milani family shop, the more Conny wished he *were* in the market for a new tinker-master. There was so much to see, so many different types of tinkering going on, but also so clearly a burgeoning demand for services. Even the clientele was upscale and knowledgeable.

Of course, even if he weren't indentured to a pirate, he was on the run from his father and only God knew who else. And if none of *that* had happened, he'd still be in Calais, tinkering to amuse himself between idylls with Val.

Rodrigo took them to his favorite café for lunch, then bustled them off to his villa, which was on a sprawling estate just outside the city on a hillside lined with olive trees. Rodrigo's wife, Letizia, greeted them upon their arrival, ushering them to their rooms where they were expected, apparently, to take a *riposo*.

"They want us to nap?" Johann asked as he sat on their bed. "Like children?"

Cornelius straddled his hips and touched his face. "Perhaps not so *very* like children."

They kissed languidly, nuzzling noses and taking teasing kisses from the other's lips—making quiet, careful love. Neither one of them was particularly interested in letting the others know what they did with one another, not today. God only knew what Italians thought of men sleeping with men. Or more to the point, what Rodrigo and Letizia thought of it. Had they been given a room to share because all the men except Félix were doubling up, or was this a nod to their relationship? It was impossible to know, and so they prepared to be discreet.

Cornelius had removed most of his clothes before getting into bed, and he shed the last of them until he was naked as he moved across Johann's body. He peeled away Johann's shirt and opened his trousers to make sliding against his lover that much more pleasurable for them both.

"I have so much I want to teach you. So much I want to do to you, to have you do to me." Conny dipped his head so he could trace the thick cords of Johann's neck with his tongue as his hands freed Johann's cock from the last vestiges of its confinement.

Johann's right hand skimmed Cornelius's back, his left hand pressing clockwork into Conny's hip. "How long will we stay here, do you think?"

"Difficult to say." Cornelius kissed his way down Johann's sternum. "You know Crawley better than I do. How long does he usually remain in port?"

"Long enough to secure another job. But we never traveled to Italy when I was on the *Farthing* the first time. Heng and Crawley had briefly been on other ships, but they never had the money to come this far when they flew their own vessel. So I don't know if they'll want to leave because they don't have the contacts to compete for work, or stay to see if they can negotiate some. To be honest, they might well spend a month redecorating the hull with all the tinker scrap you gave them. You know what they say about pirates and their ornaments. Likely Crawley will think himself in a better bargaining position if his ship is properly displayed." He drew a sharp breath, belly tightening as Cornelius kissed his way across it. "Oh, but I love it when you do that."

Cornelius was well aware how fond his lover was of a good teasing before he was sucked off. He ran his nose along the juncture between Johann's belly and groin, along a bare patch of taut muscle. "Lie back and rest, darling. You're meant to be napping."

Conny made his way lazily to Johann's cock, letting the velvet length poke him in the neck a bit before he took hold of his root and licked his way up and down. "You're rather like your mother's wurst, darling. Such lovely sausages the Bergers make."

Conny laughed at the way this made Johann startle—poor thing, so easily teased, so predictably Germanic. He wondered what his lover would think when he discovered the erotic treat in store for him today.

For several long, languid minutes Cornelius contented himself with sucking his lover's cock. Never enough to bring Johann release, not quite enough to put him in a frenzy. While he did this, he pushed Johann's legs until they bent at the knees, giving Conny access to the insides of those furry thighs. Of course, his right thigh was mostly clockwork, which only increased Conny's ardor. For quite some time he was content to suck and stroke.

But then, as he'd always intended to do, his right hand strayed to the joint of Conny's leg. Fondled his heavy, hairy balls. The thin, sensitive strip of skin behind them.

The tense, puckered bud behind that.

When Conny first brushed Johann's hole, his lover bucked and tried to resist, though as Cornelius immediately increased the intensity of his cock-sucking, Johann all too quickly surrendered to lust, accepting having his bunghole massaged as part of the price of seeing his cock so sweetly attended to. Massage it Conny did, gently at first, then with more and more pointed deliberation.

Yes, darling. Doesn't it feel good for me to touch you here?

At first, Johann seemed to agree. But when Conny nuzzled his face to that musky hole, pressing the flat of his tongue against the wrinkled flesh, Johann cried out and wriggled away.

"*Nein.*" His body shook, and he tried to shut his legs, but Conny was between them.

Conny took advantage of his position and resumed the massage on his target as he did his best to draw his prey back in. "Come, darling. It will feel wonderful, I promise. I'm only going to lick it and suck on it. Let me show you how wonderful it feels."

"It's unclean." But Johann's anus flexed against Conny's insistent touch, making it clear only Johann's mind had an objection to this activity.

"Darling, I've watched you bathe. You attend to every inch of yourself when you wash in that basin." His lover's anus flexed again, the bud not quite opening, but yearning to. Conny kissed the side of Johann's balls. "I promise you, it feels like heaven. Pull your knees back, love, and watch me lick your hole. Tug on my hair, push my head in closer. Make me lick you, Johann. Make me taste you."

He switched to French then, saying all he had just spoken but adding that he wanted to fuck Johann with his finger, to press inside that heat while he sucked Johann's brains out of his cock. It drove Johann wild. And eventually, to Conny's extreme delight, Johann pushed Cornelius's head down, putting him back in front of the object of his desire.

Now that he had Johann's cooperation, Conny took his time. He licked around Johann's anus, into the crack of his ass, massaged the tender, quivering flesh around the bud. He admired how hairy Johann was here as well. All around that bud, but of course not the rose itself.

I shall pluck you, sweet flower.

Conny ran the tip of his tongue in swirls around his target, until the bud quivered and begged for more attention. He pressed the flat of his tongue against it, thrust the center of that muscle as if he meant to fuck it, but of course could not from that position. He did this until Johann tugged on his hair, and then with a dark chuckle, he teased some more. Light flicks. Hard flicks. He painted a five-point star across Johann's rosebud. He drew the alphabet, complete with flourishes. All the while Johann pulled harder and harder at his hair, his thighs quivering around Conny's head.

When Johann began to swear at him in breathless, beautifully guttural

German, Cornelius smiled darkly and put his thumbs on either side of Johann's anus. Then he tugged his lover gently open and thrust his tongue inside.

He moaned as Johann simultaneously clenched around his tongue and clamped his thighs around Conny's head. Mewling, Conny wormed his tongue deeper before forming a seal around Johann's skin, sucking and fucking as he massaged circles with his thumbs.

He was so lost to what he was doing that when Johann yanked him away by his hair, he was on his back before he realized it had happened. Johann pinned him by the hair to the mattress, then attacked Conny's mouth ruthlessly, biting at his lips and thrusting his tongue before dragging his lips to Conny's ear.

"I want to fuck you. You wicked man who licks my ass. I want to fuck yours."

Yes. But not yet. "Open me. Dip your fingers in the grease beside the bed, and open me." He watched as Johann reached for the tin, then gave in to request what he craved the most. "No. Use your other hand."

He loved how Johann's gaze darkened as he raised his clockwork hand. "You want this inside you?"

Oh, yes, Conny wanted *that*, all of it, but he had to study a lot more about clockwork before he could engineer a hand for that task. Though it occurred to him he could give Johann a narrower, less articulated hand, or an entirely different appendage, just for lovemaking...

Swallowing a whimper, Conny nodded at the tin. "First one finger, then two, if you like. Coat them in the grease. Then yes. Put your clockwork inside me, Johann. Fuck me with it."

He worried Johann would hesitate, fussing about hurting him, but God bless, this time he eagerly complied with the order. When Johann's clockwork index finger slipped inside, Conny gasped and arched, partly from the thrill of knowing what this was inside him, mostly because the little knobs and articulations of the metal digit felt so very *intense* against his most sensitive space.

"*Du bist ein perverser Mann.*" Johann's roughly stubbled cheek rubbed against Conny's knee as he thrust. "I don't know it in French or English. Wicked.

Naughty. Twisted desires."

Conny tried to laugh, but he could only moan. "*Un pervers. Je suis un pervers.* I am perverted. And I am, darling." He forced his eyes open, though he could only manage halfway. "Are you sorry I've corrupted you?"

"*Non.*" Johann kissed Conny's knee as he thrust a second finger alongside the first. But when Conny's cries became too much for him, Johann withdrew his fingers and replaced them with his cock.

They came together with sudden fever, with enough noise anyone in the hall or, to be honest, a nearby room, would have no doubt two men were fucking nearby. When they were finished, they collapsed into the mattress together, Johann rolling off of Conny as if all his clockwork parts had turned to lead.

Johann nuzzled Conny's hair, and when Conny met him for a weary kiss, he found Johann gazing at him with heavy-lidded tenderness. For several moments they only gazed at one another, Johann looking as if he wanted very much to say something meaningful. But as if he'd lost his courage, he let out a sad sigh and lightly kissed Cornelius's lips.

"I would stay with you, always," he said in timid French.

Conny's heart melted, and he kissed Johann back. "I want that too." He traced a gentle touch down Johann's cheek. "And I think it's well past time I learned some German. More than the odd word and phrase."

Johann smiled a little shyly, but a little wickedly too. "I will teach you the dirty things first."

"Naturally." Conny ran his thumb over Johann's lips, gathered his courage and let his heart lead him. "Perhaps teach me some tender things too?"

Oh, risk was worth it and the moon, for the way it made Johann melt and capture Conny's fingers and press a long, lingering kiss against them. "Yes. The tender things too."

* * * * *

To his surprise, Johann *did* nap, though not terribly long. He woke with afternoon sun streaming onto his face and with Cornelius wrapped around his body. Johann would have lingered in bed, enjoying the decadent feeling of lying on a soft mattress in the sunshine with his lover close by, but he had to piss, and he reluctantly rose to find a chamber pot. Cornelius moaned softly, rolled into the place where Johann had been and continued sleeping.

There was no chamber pot, though Johann did find a water closet in the hallway, a fancier one than the one in Cornelius's apartment. Since he was up and dressed, he wandered the hallways instead of returning to his room, wondering if he could find the others.

A distant, familiar whirring of a tinker-enhanced aether engine lured Johann down the stairs and out a side door just in time to watch *The Brass Farthing* land on the grounds near a large shed. Crawley and the others were there—to Johann's surprise, Valentin was present, helping Olivia set the moorings.

She waved a greeting as Johann approached. "Ahoy, sailor. All rested from your nap?"

Johann ignored the sniggers this comment elicited and nodded at the *Farthing*. "Are we settling in, then?"

Heng emerged from the gondola with a shrug, wiping grease from his hands. "We could use the chance to better outfit the ship, and Crawley has it in mind to make some Italian contacts. Besides, we figured the tinkers wanted to play with you a bit." He gestured vaguely at Johann's chest.

While Heng's remark was likely true, Johann wasn't certain he wanted anyone but Conny seeing to his clockwork. He kept that to himself, however, squinting into the afternoon sun as he pondered how to best address the other issue on his mind.

"Do you think it's safe to stay here long?" The three of them stood near a crumbling stone wall off to the side. Olivia sat on it, Heng leaned on it, and Johann paced idly back and forth in front of it as he continued. "There's no way they aren't looking for us. Possibly both armies."

Heng sighed. "I admit, I was dismayed to hear Félix's association with this Italian tinker is long established. They'll certainly look here eventually."

"We're repainting the *Farthing*, and we have a few false names and identification numbers ready for the hull. This and the new decorations from Calais will help change our look. Though if we sold a bit of scrap, we could plate her and alter her look radically. Though of course that would take even more time." Olivia indicated the main house with a grim nod. "I'll be frank. I'm not sure if I trust this Rodrigo."

Johann wasn't sure he did either, but he could admit some of that was he thought he'd caught the tinker eyeing Conny with more than professional admiration. "If we're truly on the run from the armies, where do we go?"

"I wouldn't object to Morocco." Heng scratched the back of his head and waggled his eyebrows at Olivia. "I think you might like it quite a bit. A few places I know of, at the very least."

Olivia waved him idly away with a quiet smile. "I say we focus on smuggling in Germany and east Austria. We're faster now, and Cornelius can help us rig the ship for more cargo. There's no point in hiding out. I came on this ship to make my fortune, and we're better positioned to do this than we've ever been. Let's not waste the opportunity."

Johann liked this idea, but he worried wherever they hid, the armies would find them. "Perhaps you should convince Crawley to break our contracts. If Conny and I were on our own, we could move more quickly, and it would take the heat off the *Farthing* crew."

"You think Frenchie would let you leave him behind?" Heng put his hands behind his head and stared across the grounds to a grove of olive trees. "You'll be too easy pickings on land, and you're better with a team. What if your ticker clunks again? You'd die in his arms, and then what? Besides, Crawley won't ever hear of it."

The statement made Johann feel both comforted and uneasy. "I don't know why he's so determined to help."

Heng lowered his arms and gave Johann an incredulous look. "You're serious when you say that, aren't you?" He swore in Chinese, shaking his head as he turned to face Johann with hands on his hips. "It nearly killed him to leave you behind that night we lost you, and it *did* cost him his ship. He tried to play it in his head that you ran off, but to find out you ended up back in the army and in pieces on a tinker's table has undone him. He doesn't abandon crew, but he did you. He didn't want to put you back under contract because he didn't want to face that, but now that he has your ink? He's going to spend the rest of your charter proving himself. So stop trying to give him an out he doesn't want."

Johann had no idea what to say to all that, and as Molly called the quartermaster over, Johann stared after Heng, blinking.

Olivia patted him on his shoulder with a wry smile. "Come on. You look like someone who needs to be put to work, and I have some jobs for you."

This statement was no lie. They'd been sorting and cataloging the spoils from Calais since they left France, and they weren't even through the half of it. Johann followed Olivia into the crowded hold, where he worked for hours hauling crates, shifting piles and carting barrels of spare parts to the tarpaulin Molly had spread on the grass. As he often did, he lost himself in the work. It dawned on him this was the first time since he'd been separated from the pirates and rediscovered by the army that he'd worked in any kind of peace. He wasn't angry at Cornelius any longer, wasn't running from fake soldiers, wasn't fleeing a town or trying not to let his family see how deeply he felt for his *good friend.* It felt good to lose himself to his task. To work his muscles, to dampen his shirt with sweat.

It felt better, though, to watch Cornelius's gaze darken with sensual approval when he came outside after he finally woke from his *riposo.* To have that sly smile remind Johann of all the forbidden things they'd done together in bed, and all they would do yet again.

Perhaps it *would* be good to stay in Italy for a while.

Chapter Thirteen

For the first few days in Naples, Johann and Cornelius did what they could to keep their relationship a secret from their host and his wife. They were careful not to mess the sheets when they had sex, and tried to keep quiet. Since Conny couldn't help moaning, this meant Johann gagged him during their amorous encounters, and oh, but Conny loved it when Johann fucked him that way. All in all, they thought they were doing a fairly decent job keeping their affair a secret from their hosts.

Then one day Conny gave himself a tour of the villa and discovered all their discretion had been entirely unnecessary.

He'd thought he was exiting into a side garden, but he stumbled instead into a kind of bathhouse, and Rodrigo was inside. Through the steam Cornelius could see him, seated on a wooden bench wearing only a towel—or rather, with a towel draped casually over one thigh. The other leg, furry and meaty, was being kneaded by the right hand of a young man, who was naked and kneeling, his head bobbing enthusiastically over the Italian tinker's cock. Another young man, slightly larger than the kneeling one, sat beside Rodrigo, mewling into Rodrigo's mouth as the older man roughly pumped his cock and pinched his nipple.

Cornelius tried to back out quietly the way he'd come, but Rodrigo spotted him. Unconcerned, he stopped twisting the young man's nipple and waved him in. "Come, join us, Cornelius." He tugged on the hair of the boy still eagerly sucking his cock. "Aldo. Celio. *Date il benvenuto al mio ospite.*"

"*Wait.*" Cornelius held up his hands and backed farther into the hallway. "*Grazie*, truly, but I already have a lover."

Rodrigo raised an eyebrow. "*Sì*, your soldier friend, but this is of no consequence. I have a wife, and a mistress. Love of men is for sharing." He gestured to Cornelius's crotch. "You cannot tell me you disagree."

Under normal circumstances Cornelius would *not* disagree, this scene being one right out of his personal fantasies, but every instinct told him Johann wouldn't approve. "Please, Signor Rodrigo—I'm flattered, but I cannot."

With a resigned sigh, Rodrigo spoke brusquely to the young men in Italian. As he put his towel back in place around his hips, one man rushed to fetch a box of cigars and the other a bottle of wine and two wooden cups. "Then we will smoke and drink, and you will tell me all about the exquisite clockwork you've given your friend."

Cornelius hesitated as he accepted a cup of wine. How much of Johann's history should he reveal? He and Félix had given Johann another, more rigorous checkup in the *Farthing*'s new surgery, but Rodrigo had not been present. "He had been in the army, and he was gravely injured. His clockwork was necessary for his survival and remains so today."

Rodrigo hesitated, then spoke to the young men again. Once they left the room, closing the door behind them, he leaned forward with his elbow on his knee, a glint in his eye. "Tell me about the heart. You put it inside him, yes?" When Cornelius froze, he winked and waved a hand as if Conny were very funny. "Look at you. Such a babe in the woods, for all your mother is the greatest spy in Europe, to say nothing of your master."

Cornelius blinked. "Master Félix is a spy?"

He laughed. "Of course he's a spy. You think your mother would let you apprentice to any tinker? But we are all spies, practically, anymore."

Cornelius sat down heavily, clutching the wine like a lifeline. He couldn't accept that Master Félix was a spy. Yes, he'd been a contact, but a full-fledged *spy*? All he ever cared about was his clockwork. Though he'd always had a meeting with someone in Calais. Cornelius had assumed that was for clients.

Rodrigo must be lying. Trying to lure information out of him.

Rodrigo must be a spy too.

The Italian tinker drew a deep toke on the cigar, offering it to Cornelius before resting it on his knee after his refusal. "You don't have to be shy about the heart to me. My father helped design it."

Cornelius sipped his wine instead of answering. "I don't wish to discuss this further." *Not until I give Félix a stern talking-to.*

Rodrigo sighed, but he didn't seem particularly upset. *"Here* you are like your mother. Never wanting to give anything away. Very well. We will simply speak of clockwork in general, then. Let me tell you about the clockwork tibia I set for a dear grandmother the other day."

Rodrigo was full of stories about his work, and he lured several out of Cornelius as well, ones that didn't involve Johann. Cornelius was almost able to forget the man's wild accusations as he spoke at length about a replacement hand he'd made for a merchant who'd learned the hard way what a Turkish prince would take as punishment for touching things he'd warned the man to leave alone. They discussed techniques, materials, philosophy of design. They drained a bottle of wine and Rodrigo finished the entirety of his cigar before a knock sounded at the door. A female servant called out in Italian, and Rodrigo answered happily, rising. He spoke with her for a moment, then nodded at Conny.

"I must leave to attend to some business. Feel free to undress and enjoy the baths. If you like, you may bring your lover, or ring for the boys." He winked. "Though I do hope if you let them entertain you, you allow me to watch."

Conny did not ring for the boys or seek out Johann. As soon as Rodrigo left, Conny hunted down Félix and grilled him about Rodrigo's accusations.

"Is it true? Are you a spy?"

Félix sighed and sank back in his chair, gesturing for Conny to take a seat across from him. "Rodrigo has you in a lather, I see. Sit down, and let me settle you."

Conny sat stiffly. "So it's true. You *are* an agent."

"Yes, but you needn't look so alarmed. I don't work for your father. I work for your mother. I'm not entirely sure who she's serving at the moment—I don't ask. I only do what I can to aid her and protect you."

Conny's head spun. "What is my mother thinking? She told me she was through with this, but you say she's not just dabbling, she's in deeper than ever? And what do you mean, you're protecting me?"

"Your mother will retire from espionage when she's dead." Félix poured some tea from the pot he'd been brewing and gestured to a cupboard for Conny to fetch himself a cup as well. "Frankly, I'm glad for it. Whoever she's serving, I know it's with an aim to end this eternal war and return Europe to a more prosperous path. Your father's war is crippling the continent and England by extension. The Americans have stopped being backwater upstarts and are a force to contend with. Asia is thriving, rich off the smuggling trade. Russia continues to be complicated, but even *they* will outpace us soon. You've seen the difference between Naples and anywhere in Paris, and this is only the beginning. This war must end. Your father dreams of uniting the continent, but Europe needn't be ruled as a single empire to be influential."

"But how can France be stopped?"

Félix sipped his tea and shook his head. "There are some, I know, who dream of a neutral trade alliance, a union between individual nations of some sort. I've heard there's a secret union across nations and social classes working to make this a reality. Perhaps that's who your mother works for. I have my doubts about true prosperity happening for France in my lifetime, but what I long to see is an end to war. I want a rail line from Calais to Messina, to Vienna, Berlin, Madrid. I want to see if the madmen really can dig a rail tunnel beneath the English Channel between Dover and Calais. But none of this will happen if we cannot stop this war."

It was a lovely idea, to be sure. "How does the clockwork heart fit into all of this? And did Rodrigo's father truly help you build it?"

Félix waved this away with a huff. "Oh, he suggested a few valves and gave me some titanium gears. As for how the heart affects the war—well, you know what your father would love to do with it."

"But does he have the capability to turn corpses into soldiers?"

"I doubt it, but he'd long to learn." He sighed and ran his gnarled finger along the handle of his teacup. "Such a perfect bit of clockwork. Such art, such possibility. This is all my fault, for not moving it when I knew I needed to, for not destroying it. But I could no sooner dismantle you than it."

"Well, I'm quite glad you never managed." Conny set his tea down, letting all these thoughts swirl in his head. "What will you do now? Why did you come here?"

"I've come to do exactly what I told you. Relax in retirement in a warm climate with my wealthy friend and his luxurious workshop." He gestured in annoyance to the north. "Your father can play his games. I'm done with them. If he succeeds in conquering Italy, I'll emigrate to the Americas. *They* have embraced rail. And some madman has developed a steam-powered carriage. No rail, no horses. Did you know there's an airship traveling from Lisbon to New York? A huge balloon and the fastest aether engine in the world."

A journey to the Americas didn't sound appealing to Cornelius. He loved Europe. He'd make a terrible spy, but he believed in the same dream of Félix's network, and he *did* think the continent could generate a universal governing body. Imagine, being able to fly in the *Farthing* as legitimate privateers, hauling freight and exploring the world in the process.

Except Conny's heart grew heavy as the most obvious solution to their dilemma dawned. "If Johann were in the Americas, he would be safe."

Félix's countenance turned sad. "Dear naive boy. Your clockwork soldier will never be safe. Even if the war ends, men greedy for power will seek his heart for their own devious purposes."

"But what are we to do? Give up? Hide in a cave and hope no one finds us?"

Félix nodded at the window, where *The Brass Farthing* was visible through the curtains billowing in a warm afternoon breeze. "Don't hide, Conny. Fly. Outfit that ship with an engine to beat the Lisbon Flyer. Work for Rodrigo long enough to build your vessel the best aether cannons there are to be had, then make the weapons even better." He smiled, settling into his chair, still watching the ship. "Treasure that crew. They're a motley mix, but they're loyal and strong.

You will find, when the chips are down, their fellowship will be more valuable than all the aether in the Alps."

That much Conny had already learned, and he knew the depth of that truth. But Félix made a good point, about the cannons, and the engine. "I wonder if anyone in Naples has the schematics for that Lisbon Flyer?"

Félix winked. "I bet they do, young man. I bet they do."

* * * * *

Johann wasn't certain why Conny was suddenly so focused on his work, but there was no question he'd never seen his tinker with such zeal. Yes, Cornelius had spent time daily on the *Farthing*'s engine since Calais, but now he had a determination no one could shake. Though Johann didn't understand this abrupt obsession, he didn't mind.

What he didn't like was that this meant Conny spent a great deal of time in Rodrigo's private workshop…with Rodrigo.

Conny had told Johann about finding Rodrigo in the bathhouse and his invitation for Conny to have sex with Rodrigo's male paramours. Though Conny had turned him down, every time Johann saw the two of them together it was clear the Italian hadn't given up his quest. Johann didn't like it, but he assumed it would remain an annoyance only, something never to be lived out. And then one day Conny pulled him aside, looking guilty and embarrassed, and told Johann he *wanted* to go to the bathhouse.

"There's an aether cannon I want for the *Farthing*, the best that can be had, and Rodrigo is blackmailing me. He won't give it to me *unless* I go to the baths with him." He smiled. "I thought it might be fun, if we went together."

Johann was furious. "Go and have sex with him? For a cannon? We don't need it."

"Yes, we do. I already have the *Farthing* capable of outrunning any army ship, but I want her to be able to destroy her enemies as well." Conny ran a coy hand down Johann's clockwork arm. "I don't mind his bargain, to be honest. It's a bit thrilling to me, having sex in front of other people. And I wouldn't have sex with him, only with you." He glanced up at Johann, and the look alone gave him an erection. "Unless you wanted me to."

Those words, though, killed Johann's ardor. "Are you unsatisfied with me?" The thought made him hollow inside.

"No, of course not—but I won't lie to you. I like a bit of play. It's not about wanting other men. I wouldn't be with him in the way I am with you. And I wouldn't want to have sex with him alone." He bit his lip as he smiled. "Well, only if you'd *told* me to go off and let him fuck me. That would be terribly thrilling. To know you'd given me to him. To know you were listening from another room. Feeling that you'd given me away like property."

Johann would have found everything Cornelius described abhorrent— except the way Conny said it, his cock ached, and he imagined a door closing, listening to Conny cry out, knowing he was being fucked by another man. The thought was arousing...and confusing. "You would like this? To be treated like a thing?"

They were in their bedroom, sitting together on the bed. They were fully clothed, but suddenly Johann felt as if they were both naked. Especially as Cornelius sat still, getting the hooded look he adopted when he wanted them to go to bed together. "Haven't I shown you that I like such treatment during sex?" Conny's lips parted, his lips sliding into a wicked smile. "Go on, darling. Order me to do something shameful."

Johann felt hot and cold, and his head felt as if he'd been spinning in circles, like a child. Why did Conny want him to do this? Why did Conny want this?

Why did part of Johann want this too?

He shook his head, hard enough to make his head hurt, and he shut his eyes tight. "No. I will not do this. It's wrong."

"It's not wrong if we both want it."

"I don't want it."

He spoke the words with enough conviction to convince himself, and it worked, in that the stern voice reminding him of his father or his sergeant made him sit straighter and dredged up the old feelings of obedience. But it wasn't until he opened his eyes that it dawned on him when he spoke like that he wasn't the only one hearing the strident tone.

"Ah. Well." Conny's shoulders rounded, and he looked about the bed awkwardly, clearly embarrassed and humiliated. "Forgive me, then, for misunderstanding."

Johann wanted to soothe Cornelius, but he was so confused and upset all he could do was rise and leave the room, even as he acknowledged this would only serve to widen the breach between the two of them. His mood turned blacker with every step as he stomped around the grounds, which were quiet as the rest of the household took their *riposo*.

How could Cornelius want such things? How could he ask Johann to want them too? Why did he *want* to have sex with Rodrigo? Wasn't Johann enough? Was this something French Johann couldn't understand? Or was everyone like this in the world, except in Johann's simple village? Much as he hated to admit it, a great deal of evidence pointed to that. He'd always been the one to turn down the whores who followed the army. He was always shocked by whatever new twist Conny wanted to introduce into their lovemaking. He tended to enjoy himself quickly enough, but he could never shake the thought that they were doing something forbidden. He worried someone would catch him gazing fondly at his lover in public, though he couldn't articulate what it was he feared would happen if they were discovered. He didn't dread the obvious, which was that other men might beat him for his newly discovered predilections. He feared something more abstract, more sinister.

He feared discovering what he'd suspected since he was a child was true: there was something wrong with him as a person, and if that were discovered… well, he'd never been able to work out what would happen then. But it wouldn't be good, he knew that much.

The more Johann wandered about the villa's grounds, the more upset he became. Things had been so good, and now they seemed impossible. The root of it lay at Rodrigo's feet.

What kind of man made that kind of a demand on another? A powerful man, that's who. Like the officials from Vienna who came to the village and told everyone what they had to do, all to please the emperor.

What was Johann to do to counteract this? He was only a soldier. Only a fool from a tiny village. So simple he couldn't even begin to understand what Conny wanted. Maybe what he needed.

No one was in the hold when Johann stomped angrily through the *Farthing*, but Molly appeared before he had the barrel of grog cracked open. He tensed, certain she was about to tell him he couldn't drink the ship's supplies without permission, but she only studied him a moment, then dug through some crates until she produced a smaller barrel with a spigot.

"You look as if you could use something more than grog, love." She jerked her head to the far end of the hold. "Come on. We'll drink the captain's brandy and you can tell me all your troubles."

Johann told himself he wouldn't confess his problems to anyone, but he didn't have but two mugs of brandy in him before it all came tumbling out. How much he cared for Conny, how he worried he was unworthy of his handsome tinker. He told her about Rodrigo's mad demand, how he couldn't understand why Cornelius *wanted* to be passed over, as if it were some kind of a game.

"But it *is* a game, sweetheart." Molly smiled a crooked little smile and leaned back against the sack of flour she was using as a cushion. "This is one of the pleasures of fucking your own sex. There's no pretending it's for procreation or to seal an archaic union to remind the woman she's property. Sex for us is nothing but fun. Pleasure for pleasure's sake. What's wrong with that?"

A great deal was wrong with that, according to the pastor in Johann's church back in Stallenwald. But then, so was deserting the army—twice. So was consorting with thieves. Lying with men in any manner other than beside them in a soldiers' tent. "I have done many things those who raised me—and loved me—would say is wrong. But I don't think that means I can do anything wrong I wish." He paused, then added, "Does it?"

Molly smiled slowly, seeming almost sad. "I forget how young you are, sometimes, and how young I was once too. If it helps, I'll share with you the principle I use to guide myself. Because for a time I did exactly what you just suggested. I decided since I was breaking rules, I would break them all. But over time, I realized I had rules of my own. I didn't like to hurt innocent people if I could help it. I joined this ship because Crawley made it clear he prioritizes legitimate jobs over outright theft. He doesn't join the pirate gangs, which costs him dearly but affords him his pride. He steals from merchants, but as much as possible he steals from ones who are insured. The secret to a happy life is that we all need a code. Lawlessness doesn't suit the soul. If the code your family and your people present works for you, then you might as well follow it. But if you find you need something different, it's all right to make your own."

Johann considered this as he drank more brandy. "Do you and Olivia have sex with other women?"

"Heavens, yes." Molly rolled her eyes. "Sweetheart, we aren't a couple. We fuck each other because it's very rare for either of us to want to sleep with men, and we're convenient. Olivia wants *nothing* to do with men, but I'm simply particular."

"But would you want to be with only one woman, or one man, if you fell in love?"

The question hung in the air. Johann's cheeks heated, and he focused his gaze on his hands, unwilling to look Molly in the eye. When she touched his knee, he glanced up, uncertain.

Her smile was sweet, not mocking. "Are you saying you love Cornelius?"

Johann wasn't sure. He felt so much for Cornelius, and he wanted him more than he wanted anything in the world. He would do anything for him. Including, he realized, sleep with other men, if that was what it took to keep Conny happy. He'd given up his country, signed his life into another contract with Crawley, let him do wicked things in bed, spent every waking moment thinking about him and making sure he was well and safe—if that wasn't love, what was?

"Yes. I think I do."

"Then it might be best to tell him. To explain this is the reason why you don't want him with another man."

Johann wasn't entirely certain he *couldn't* stand for Conny to be with another man. He could not consent to Rodrigo, not as a barter. Even though Conny said it was a game, Johann didn't think so. But perhaps…perhaps he could explore with another man. Even Valentin would be preferable. Or Crawley, though Johann wasn't sure he could contain his jealousy.

"I don't know if I don't want him with another man. He said he likes this. I don't want to keep Conny from something he likes."

"That's a fair point. But this is a relationship, sweet boy. Giving and taking. Compromising. The trick is learning what you can compromise on, and what you can't, and the same goes for him."

"But what if those things contradict one another? What if he insists on being with other men, and I know I cannot compromise on this?"

"Then you must likely allow the relationship won't work. Which is sad, yes. But wouldn't it be better to learn this now, rather than later?"

Johann didn't know his answer to that question. As if she could sense he needed time to dwell on this subject in private, they didn't speak any more of Cornelius or love. They spoke of the ship, of how eager Molly was to see it fly with all the improvements Conny had made. Of Crawley's longing to sail to Portugal and make trade with the wealthy nation that managed to defy French takeover with help from its colonies in the Americas. Of traveling to Morocco and Tunisia, and Egypt. Johann listened to her speak with so much passion, and he relaxed.

When he left her, he took a long walk across the grounds and down a long lane lined with tall, oddly shaped trees. As he finally made his way back to the house, everyone was in bed, including Conny, though he wasn't asleep. A bottle of absinthe and two glasses told him his lover had been drinking, likely with Val. Indeed, when Conny turned to greet Johann as he arrived, his eyes were bloodshot, his body movements erratic and clumsy.

"Oh—you've come home. I didn't know if you would."

Conny was worried—very much so, it was clear—and Johann found this comforting. "Yes, I'm home." He removed his shoes and began to undo his shirt.

It pleased him to see how closely Conny watched him undress, how his gaze focused and narrowed, even under the power of so much drink. "Are you still angry with me?"

Here Johann paused with his necktie in his hand. "I was never angry with you. I'm sorry if that's what you thought."

Conny's body posture didn't ease much. "But you *were* angry."

Johann considered this. "Mostly I was confused and uncertain, because what you suggested shocked and upset me, and I needed to be alone to work out why."

Now Conny wilted. "I'm so sorry, darling. Please forget everything I said."

This also made Johann feel good, to discover Conny felt the same way as he did, that he was more concerned with keeping Johann happy than insisting they add partners to their bed. But he wasn't certain he wanted to extract that promise from his lover, or that his lover could honestly agree to this without longing for it later. He sat on the edge of the mattress and motioned for Conny to sit beside him. Conny sat on his left side, so he took his lover's right hand with his clockwork left.

"I'm not upset with what you said, not any longer. I'm not shocked at *you*, only the ideas you suggest. You must remember I come from a small, quiet village. You saw my home, the people I grew up with. I didn't see much during my time in the Austrian Army but boggy marches through trees and over mountains and sometimes the bleak hulls of ocean ships or dirigibles. It's true I became more worldly as I joined Crawley's crew, but not much. I'm not a bold man. Not like you."

Conny leaned into him. "But I *like* that about you, Johann."

"This is the cost of that temperament, then. The things you say sometimes, the things you ask me to do—they are so foreign to me, like another language I must learn. It's not that I don't want to. But sometimes I need time to comprehend it." He squeezed Conny's hand and spit out the rest. "I might enjoy playing with you and another man. But not Rodrigo. Not for a trade like that. It makes me uneasy, and…well, it makes me jealous. He's a rich, powerful man. I'm nothing like that, and I couldn't fight him if he decided to take you away from me for good."

Conny drew the clockwork fingers to his lips and kissed them passionately. "Darling, he could never take me from you. But I won't go to him at all, if he makes you jealous, and I'll find another way to get a cannon." He smiled as he said that, lifting his other hand to gently stroke Johann's cheek below his clockwork eye. "It pleases me that you feel jealous. In fact, I'd like nothing more for you to tell me forcefully how jealous Rodrigo's offer makes you." His gaze darkened, and his tongue stole out to wet his bottom lip as his thumb brushed along the scruff of Johann's chin. "Show me my place, darling. Show me your jealousy. Punish me with your body for even considering thinking of it."

It was clear this idea excited Conny, and as Johann watched his lover in an absinthe haze, he began to understand. This was playing. Conny didn't want Johann to be truly upset. Only to pretend. He still wasn't certain he knew how to join this game, however. "How do you want me to do this?"

"Be forceful." Conny stroked Johann's cheeks, his nose, the slope of his neck into his open collar. "Show me what you think of the idea. Because I could go to him now, darling. I could send a servant to tell him to meet me in the baths. He'd come. He wants to fuck me, and I think perhaps I want him to. That big man, pushing me to my knees? Making me taste his cock? Mmm. Perhaps I'll go right now."

For the briefest moment, the words hurt Johann—but then he noticed Conny *didn't* rise and call a servant. He wasn't looking at the door and licking his lips for Rodrigo. He was staring at Johann with naked lust and teasing the pelt of Johann's chest with drunken fingers.

You can play too, Johann encouraged himself. *You can trust he wants you and not the Italian.* He gripped Conny's shoulders hard, but not too hard. "You will go nowhere. Especially not to him. You will not go on your knees for him."

Conny pouted coquettishly, and the sight made Johann's whole body ache with want. "But I want to go on my knees. I want a big cock in my mouth."

Johann pushed Conny to the floor and dragged him between his knees. "Here is a cock for you." The words felt bold and made him blush, but the way Conny yielded encouraged him. "Take it out."

Conny fumbled with the fastenings of Johann's trousers, looking up at Johann with a wicked gaze. "I can't stop thinking of him, I'm afraid. Of what it would be like. I want someone to fuck my mouth so hard, darling. So hard I can't breathe. I want a man to pull my hair and call me dirty names. Rodrigo would do this, if I asked him."

For the briefest second, Johann thought he might want this too. Even Rodrigo, though the idea made him ache with jealousy. But his mind was still relaxed by the brandy, and it let him acknowledge that might be very pretty to see. Perhaps while he fucked Conny from behind...

He shook the image from his head and grabbed Conny's hair, determined to drive the thought away from them both. "If you want your mouth fucked, I will fuck it. I will pound your throat with my cock until you are too weak and sore to consider any other man."

The words felt so shocking, so terrible—but Conny didn't seem to think so. Mewling, he finished freeing Johann's cock, then took the tip inside. He looked up at Johann as he slid down the length, until Johann could *feel* the back of Conny's throat. Conny's lips strained, his throat convulsed lightly, and his eyes watered. His gaze was fixed on Johann, begging him to follow through with his promise.

Johann did. He kept a sliver of himself aware as guardian, so that he didn't hurt Conny more than he could take, but other than that, he let himself go. He pulled his hair, switched them around and fucked into Conny's mouth. He dragged him onto the bed and pushed Conny's head off the side so he could go deeper. He never let his gaze leave Conny's, and as the delicious darkness of the act consumed him, he gave Conny the rest of what he'd said he wanted.

"Dirty slut." He smiled as this made Conny cry out, the sound muffled by

Johann's cock. "You still want Rodrigo, don't you, even after I fuck your mouth like this. You want to let him use you, because you're such a dirty, slutty man. Nothing but a whore. You'd let every man in Naples use you. Nothing is enough for you." He pulled on Conny's hair, making his lover's eyes water more. "I won't let you. I might be shy, but I'll learn to be dirty enough for you. I'll lick you until you beg me. The way I know you want me to."

Conny tightened his grip on Johann's thighs and shut his eyes, looking blissful.

Johann slowed his thrusts as he went on, all his guards down. "I'll learn to do anything you wish. I'll use my clockwork fingers in you. I'll let you use your fingers in me." He shut his eyes too, let the rest roll out. "I'll learn to fuck you in front of other men. The crew. Strangers. Maybe even a man like Rodrigo." Conny moaned and shivered, and Johann burrowed his cock deep. "You want that very much, don't you? You *like* the idea of a powerful man seeing you so helpless." Johann stroked Conny's strained lips with his clockwork finger. "Perhaps we will do this. Perhaps we will let powerful men watch us fuck."

He wasn't sure he meant the words he said, but in hearing them, Conny went wild, pushing and clawing and now sucking desperately at Johann's cock. He drove Johann over the edge, until he spilled his seed so forcefully it made Conny choke. When Johann drew back, spittle and spending dripped out of the corners of Conny's swollen, trembling lips.

Johann kissed those lips as he pulled his lover onto the bed, turning him over and tipping his bottom into the air. "Now it is your turn, dirty boy. Tell me what you want."

Conny's legs trembled. "Stroke me. Fuck me. Make it slow and wicked until I can't stand it. Until I beg you to bring me release." He touched his cock. "But don't. Don't let me. Make me sob for it, Johann. Make me tell you how dirty I am." He fumbled for Johann's hand, holding it in a hesitant grip. "Would you truly use me like this with another man? Without thinking me terrible?"

"I would never think you terrible." He kissed Conny's pretty, upturned backside, his eager hole. "Yes," he whispered to it. "If you wish, I'll let others see you like this. Let them watch us. Perhaps, if I get brave, I'll let them lick you too."

It was difficult to say if this was what made Conny cry out so desperately, or if it was the way Johann pressed the flat side of his tongue against Conny's opening. He had done this twice now, kissing and licking Conny here, and while it still made him feel indecent, it also filled him with a rush of power. Tonight, his emotions riding high from his discussion with Molly, their arguments and now their confessions, he felt crazed inside, all those feelings pouring out of him and into his lovemaking. He licked Conny until he was a mess of tears and pleadings, and only then did he add a lubricated finger from his clockwork hand. Then another. Then another.

Then, ignoring the bitter taste of the lubricant, Johann began to lick his lover again.

This is how Conny came, with a finger inside him and Johann's tongue swirling all around that puckered entrance, Johann's other hand stroking him vigorously to release. Afterward, they collapsed into the bed together, both of them partially dressed, the air and bedclothes reeking of sweat and sex. Johann drew Conny close, holding him as tight as his exhausted arms could allow.

I love you, he thought as he lay in the quiet, safe in the villa from all the trouble he knew still pursued them. Molly was right, he needed to say the words aloud, to Cornelius. To let him know *why* he was so jealous—and so willing to try to overcome that feeling.

He needed to say them, soon. But not tonight, he decided as he drifted off to sleep. Not tonight.

Chapter Fourteen

After the fight and deliciously wicked bedroom reconciliation with Johann, Conny's life was essentially nothing but charm. It was a joy to work with Félix again, and the afternoons he spent in Rodrigo's shop in *ingegnopoli* were like being escorted into a tinker's heaven. He'd almost forgotten what it was like to lose himself in a project, to lift his head hours later and feel as if he were returning from the moon, he'd been so far away. Because of the district's wide dining offerings, he didn't even miss his beloved northern-French cuisine.

He learned new things every day, working at the Milani shop. While Conny had heard of wireless technology, in France it was limited to official use and severely restricted. In Italy, everyone had a transmitter, and Conny spent endless hours taking ones apart and putting them back together. Rodrigo had begun experimenting with putting transmitters *in* clockwork, which he'd said came in handy when thieves made off with his supplies. Conny couldn't help thinking there must be countless other ways this technology could be of use.

Johann seemed happy too, in his way. He loved work, the odd man, and was content to haul and carry and lift and pull when anyone required him. Conny would admit he often saved heavy jobs for his lover he could technically do himself, but it was so pleasing to see Johann flex his muscles and efficiently manipulate his clockwork, he could not help himself. Johann accompanied Conny into town when Cornelius went to the tinker shop, still clearly quietly jealous of Rodrigo and nervous of what he might do to Conny in Johann's absence. Rodrigo never pressed his advantage further than his lighthearted blackmail, though he flirted liberally. This suited Conny quite nicely, as those winks and innuendoes inflamed Johann so much he tended to fuck Conny in their private carriage ride home at the end of the day, and often again once they were back at the villa.

The pirates were content to fuss over the *Farthing* and imagine improvements for Conny to build. Crawley in particular was in heaven, polishing his Italian and learning Portuguese with Heng so they could find new trade and cargo opportunities. Molly and Olivia enjoyed tormenting the male staff at the villa and seducing the females into their bed, often together.

Poor Val, though.

Valentin had been initially better after his role in the escape of Calais, but now he was the member of their merry band who could never easily speak with anyone but Conny or Félix, unless they chose to speak to him in French. In the evenings Conny did his best to teach him English, and he'd seen Valentin poring over the French-German book Johann and he had used when they'd first begun their lessons, but Val had never been much of a student. Conny didn't think having so *many* languages flying about helped either Val's learning or his disposition.

A week into their stay at Naples, tired of seeing his friend so miserable, Conny tried once again to convince Val to let Crawley release him from his contract. "Even if you don't go home, we can find you somewhere you'll be happier. I hate seeing you like this."

"You think I would abandon you?" They were enjoying cigarettes—rarities heavily taxed at home but common as mud in Italy—and wine on a patio overlooking the grounds, and Val gestured angrily at the *Farthing* in the distance. "Or is this your way of telling me you don't need me, now that you have your brute of a lover and his pack of pirates?"

Conny tossed the cigarette into the ashtray and let his offense be illustrated by intense gesturing. "How can you think I would, or could, replace you? I'm only concerned about you."

"Oh, I see. You think I'm so self-centered I can't endure a little hardship." Val waved angrily back at Conny, his cigarette painting misty circles in the air as he did so. "You think you're the noble one and I'm the pouting one."

"Please. I've watched you spend hours in the mirror *perfecting* your pout."

"Very well. I don't want to be the pouting one *anymore*. And I'm not leaving the ship, or abandoning our cause." Val sighed and took a long drag of his cigarette, some of his misery seeping back in. "I don't understand political intrigue any more than I ever have, but I'm fairly certain my family is firmly beside your father as the authors of this terror. I'll endure humiliation and drudgery and being passed over by Crawley to help undo their schemes."

Conny wanted to applaud his friend's uncharacteristic sense of righteousness, and he told himself he would, but he couldn't relinquish the opportunity to press on that bit of gossip. "What do you mean, you were passed over by Crawley?"

Val's cheek's stained as he smoked furiously. "He won't take me to bed. He fucks Heng regularly, but never me. Yesterday I saw him leading two of Rodrigo's maids into his cabin, and this morning a footman. Any man or woman is fine, clearly, so long as they aren't me."

That he'd overlooked his friend's heart set on the airship captain told Conny it was *he* who'd been the self-centered one. "Darling, I'm so sorry. Clearly it's that the man has no taste, if he's that sloppy. Surely he's simply afraid of someone so refined."

Normally such a catty remark would have Val smiling, but he only slouched and gestured helplessly to himself. "What refinement? I look a mess. My clothes are in tatters, my hair is too long, and I haven't had a decent shave in weeks."

Conny smiled. "I think it's well past time we both had an afternoon off, don't you, darling? We'll spend some time in the baths, find a hairdresser and a proper tailor. Perhaps we can find a cozy establishment like The Alison where we can have a bit of absinthe and a flirt."

Val looked slightly mollified, though he clung to the edges of his pout a bit longer. "I suppose we must take your Johann along?"

How Conny loved hearing *your Johann*, even spoken so jealously. "Yes, but we'll dress him up properly, and won't we look dashing with our bodyguard?" He winked. "Come on, Val. We deserve some time away. Tell me you'll go."

Of course Val was nothing but eager to spend a day being spoiled in the city, and Conny immediately set out to organize the outing. Félix thought it was a brilliant idea, when Cornelius approached him. "I'll see Rodrigo about sending one of his men with you. Do you have particular shopping in mind?"

"No, just a good airing, I think. Val always likes pretty things, and I know he'd like better clothes, but essentially anything that makes it feel like old times would do."

"Very good. You'll need a translator, of course. I'll make sure Rodrigo sends a gentleman who knows French. Let me arrange that while you settle your absence with the captain. I can't imagine he'll object, but it will be good to make a proper request."

To Conny's surprise, however, Crawley *did* object, and strenuously so. "Do you have any idea how dangerous Naples is? No, I won't have two of my crew members waltzing around the city."

"It didn't seem that dangerous to me," Conny countered.

"It hasn't seemed dangerous to you because you've only ever traveled with Rodrigo's entourage and within the *ingegnopoli*. Naples is the center of Italy's organized crime, and it's a haven to all manner of petty thieves. You two practically have *I'm an easy mark* tattooed on your foreheads. Plus you're the biggest pair of nancies I've ever seen. You'll be mugged, killed and tossed into a canal within an hour."

Conny's cheeks heated. "Fine. We'd planned to take Johann anyway, in addition to Rodrigo's man. Johann is a soldier, and he's good in a fight."

"Oh good. Then *three* of my crew will be wandering around Naples." He threw up his hands with a heavy sigh. "Let me give some instructions to Heng, and I'll go with you."

Conny tried, with vigor, to dissuade him, but the only options Crawley would allow were to not go at all or to let him come along. And when Val found out the captain was accompanying them, he very nearly called the whole outing off.

"He's the whole reason I want to get away, and he's our *escort*? No."

Conny wouldn't relent. "We'll ignore him and make him keep his distance. I promise."

Val sniffed. "What about Johann? Is he still coming?"

"To be honest, if Naples is as rough as Crawley says, I wouldn't mind having him. You've seen him in a tight situation. Though I don't know how much he'll enjoy shopping. Maybe with him along, Crawley will be less obnoxious." He moved in for the kill before Val could execute a proper pout. "Darling, our entourage is there only to preserve our day of decadence. This shall be entirely about you and me having a brilliant, exceptional day out together."

Valentin scuffed his toe in the dirt in a show of indifference, though he did a poor job of hiding how much he enjoyed being cajoled. "Perhaps we can get Crawley drunk enough for me to have my way with him."

Cornelius's smile crept slowly across his face. "That's the spirit. He may be an English dog, not a Frenchman of refinement, but he's not immune to the web the two of us weave, when we're in a mood. You won't have to lower yourself to chasing him down. We'll make sure he comes to you."

It took almost a week to arrange their shopping adventure. Rodrigo's wife said the shops were better on certain days and gave them an ornate calendar peppered with official meetings, underground boss movements and political parades. For many of the open times, Johann was busy helping Heng install an ornate filigree on the balloon bracings, and Crawley was off having his meetings with tradesmen. To make matters worse, when Olivia and Molly heard there were shopping plans, they begged to come along.

"It will be fun to go along with the rest of you, and maybe we won't get so many whistles and suggestive comments if you hold on to our arms in the streets. Much as I hate to admit that will ease our way, it will." Olivia and Cornelius sat on the deck of the ship at the end of a leisurely day of ship improvement, sharing a bottle of wine between the two of them. She had her shirtsleeves rolled up and neckline unbuttoned in deference to the heat, and her bare feet rested on one of the rails as she leaned back on her stool against a barrel.

Cornelius refilled her glass and pulled a slim cigarette from the case in his vest pocket, offering one to her before lighting one up himself.

Olivia nodded thanks as she accepted Cornelius's lighter. She lit, inhaled and blew the smoke out, eyes sparkling as she waggled her eyebrows at Conny. "You and Johann seem to be getting on well. Are you exclusive to each other?"

Conny toyed idly with his cigarette. "We've talked a bit about inviting someone in, but that's all we've done. I'd thought about inviting Crawley, because he's not terrible to look at, but it'd break Val's heart. I wish we could find a tavern catering to our tastes so we could do a bit of shopping."

"I heard there's a place just outside the tinker district that might suit all of us. Perhaps after shopping we can spend an evening there." She took a deep drink of her wine, looking thoughtful. "I'll work on Heng. He's always horny, and he can convince Crawley to do almost anything."

And so the day Val and Conny finally were able to have their long-awaited afternoon of shopping and pampering, they went not alone, not with Johann and one of Rodrigo's men, but with Johann, *two* of Rodrigo's men, Crawley, Molly, Olivia and Heng. They traveled to the city in a small caravan of carriages, and when they walked down the streets, they were surrounded by their crew and their host's servants, chattering and fighting with one another in three languages. In short, people embodying the very culture they'd attempted to escape.

"Forget them," Conny insisted when Val began to turn morose. He linked their arms and dismissed their entourage with an airy gesture. "They are our servants, here to protect us and carry our things. Oh, look. What a lovely shop. Let's find some things to make them hold for us. Something boxy and awkward, yes?"

Of course, they had to take an Italian speaker with them to do this shopping, and Val stiffened when Crawley volunteered, but Conny cajoled his friend into enjoying himself, and soon they were both laughing and having a grand time as they tried on scarves and admired waistcoats and hats. They didn't buy anything outside of a few accessories, because Val hated ready-made clothing. Crawley came along with them when they found a tailor, and Johann went with Heng and the ladies to the dressmakers next door.

In the tailor shop, Val was in his element. He got very much in the spirit of ordering Crawley about, demanding he tell the tailor to fetch another bolt of fabric, a slightly different shade, another texture. As dismissive and almost brutal as Val became, Conny wondered if Crawley would balk. To his surprise, the captain never once complained.

They managed, in fact, to enjoy themselves despite their personal circus. It was good, too, the way having so many people about them allowed them the pleasure of forgetting to be careful. There was decidedly an unsavory element on the streets—twice Heng collared pickpockets after Conny's purse, and Conny became glad for their large group as he spied several clusters of large, ominous-looking men lurking in alleyways. None of them approached, however, and by the end of the day, Conny was happily exhausted.

When he asked Crawley when they planned to return to the villa, however, he was shocked to find the captain had rented them a suite of rooms in the city for the evening. They were to rest, enjoy an early dinner, then attend a party at the home of one of his new merchant contacts.

"He's an unsavory character, but in a way that suits us." He winked at Conny and Val from his side of the carriage. "He's more your sort than mine—I don't mind a lady in my bed for variety, but César has no use for a pair of breasts. His parties are legendarily decorous and scandalous. I heard tell the two of you are missing your wild times at your bohemian café and might enjoy seeing what the Italian version of the same might be like."

Conny's gaze shifted immediately to Johann. Oh, yes, he wanted to go very much. But did Johann? This was exactly the sort of thing they teased about in bed. Would Johann want to play those moments out in real life?

The look his lover returned to him made Conny's belly warm with want. Johann made his clockwork eye wink at Conny as the corner of his lip turned up in a smile. "Oh yes," Johann said, turning to Crawley. "It sounds perfect."

Conny sank into the velvet seats with a smile, biting his lip to try to keep it from becoming a ridiculous grin.

* * * * *

Johann had never been to a party.

There had been festivals in the city square every now and again, but even in simply driving up to the house where Crawley's merchant's party was to take place, Johann understood this event would be nothing like those village celebrations. It was not like the bawdy pub Conny and Val loved to frequent in Calais. Neither was it an *elegant* party the Bürgermeister told of attending in Salzburg in honor of the Archduke of Vienna's visit. This also was evident from the street, because the type of people entering and waving from upper-story balconies didn't seem like guests who would be allowed within fifty feet of a baron, let alone an archduke.

The host was Portuguese and younger than Johann would have guessed. He looked to be only a little older than Crawley, whom Johann knew to be in his middle thirties. All the successful merchants were fifty or older, their holdings passed down from a father or other relative. But this man had made his own fortune, which was apparently common in Portugal. It paid well, Crawley said, to trade in a nation completely uninvolved in the French-Austrian war.

The merchant's name was César Mateus, and he stood at the door greeting every guest as they entered. He was tall, though shorter than Johann, and closer to Conny's body type. He was handsome, but he had a look about him that hinted he was always up to a little bit of trouble. He wore a smartly trimmed beard, but his hair was unfashionably long and hung about his shoulders. Also draped on their host were two men, and both stroked Mateus like a lover. Casually, as if it were nothing at all to run hands over a gentleman as he stood in the foyer of his home. Occasionally Mateus paused to kiss one of them, which generally inspired the other to renew efforts to win a gesture of affection of his own.

Crawley introduced each of them to Señor Mateus. He took pains to talk up both Heng and Olivia as his senior officers, but he lavished praise on Cornelius, naming him as the best tinker in all of Europe. This seemed to interest Mateus, who kissed Conny's hand and spoke in fairly decent French.

"I look forward to getting to know you better this evening."

The statement dripped with innuendo, and the merchant's lips managed to caress Conny's skin in such a manner that the erotic nature of the gesture overcame Johann's jealousy and made him ache to watch Mateus kiss other parts of Conny's body. As they left the foyer and followed the others into the large drawing room where most of the guests gathered, Cornelius leaned in close to whisper in Johann's ear.

"Don't worry, darling. I won't do anything with Mateus or anyone tonight, unless you tell me to." He slid against Johann's side like a cat, pausing to kiss his shoulder. "I'll do whatever you ask of me. That shall be my pleasure. You can tease me, taunt me, display me, share me—or you can simply whisper all the dirty things you want to do to me in whatever language you like, driving me crazy until you can get me alone to have your way with my body. Any way you arrange it, love, it will be a perfect evening."

Johann wasn't certain what it was he wanted to have Conny do. He felt very out of place in the grand room of the suave young merchant. There were others with clockwork, but almost all of it was decorative, additions to otherwise perfectly intact body parts. A few pirates had clockwork legs or arms or eyes, but no one else had as much as Johann. This made him stand out, as did his height and his size, as did the fact that a pretty, flirty man held on to his arm at all times.

Conny seemed to sense Johann's unease and helped him through it. "Darling, let's find you something to drink or smoke." He undid the top button of Johann's shirt and kissed the center of his chest. "You need something to help you relax."

He well and truly did. Because even this subtle gesture of affection from Conny in front of all these people made him feel exposed—which was ridiculous, as three feet away from them a woman sat on a piano with her ample charms freed casually from her bodice. Olivia and Molly stood on either side of her, not touching the naked breasts but smiling and gesturing at them as they spoke to the woman. Nearby on a sofa a man sat with his head thrown back, mouth open and chest heaving as another man fondled him beneath the waistband of his trousers. Across the room on a small stage, a man in women's clothing lifted his skirt to reveal his nakedness beneath, and a woman in a man's suit beside him had her shirt undone and her cunt exposed. She palmed her quim openly, tongue sticking out of the side of her mouth as she leered at a crowd of squealing women and a few tongue-lolling men at her feet.

To feel uncomfortable merely being unbuttoned by Conny was ridiculous in this situation, and yet Johann could not stop feeling shy and embarrassed. He wanted it to end. He wanted to be free and relaxed like these other people. But he was nervous.

"I'm afraid I will make a fool of myself if I drink," he confessed to Conny.

Conny smiled and kissed the exposed hair above the undone button as he laid waste to another below it. "You won't be a fool. Even if you are, you'll be *my* fool." He stroked Johann's clockwork arm. "You work so hard. Let tonight be the night you relax and let go. Indulge and have fun."

Johann wanted to. He wanted this almost as much as he wanted Conny. "Is it safe to do so here, in front of so many strangers? How shall I protect you, if I let down my guard this way?"

For some reason this made Conny go soft and make French coos as he nuzzled Johann's chest. Then, with a saucy wink, he undid his necktie and tied it tightly around first his left wrist, then Johann's right. "There. Now we are joined. It will be easy to protect me, as I cannot leave your side. Also, now whatever pleasure we have, we take together. Let us start with a drink. Have you ever had absinthe, darling?"

Johann had not. "Isn't it strong? I heard soldiers say it can make you so undone you do not know yourself."

Conny's grin took up his entire face. "Yes. That's exactly what it does. It's wonderful. Best of all when it's laced, which I'm pleased to announce the Italians do even more so than the French."

He led Johann to a line of people waiting before a side table, and as they approached, he saw it housed a large glass decanter filled with water and an amazing quantity of ice. The decanter had five spouts from its base and stood on an elegant silver stand. All around the decanter were glasses, bowls of sugar cubes and several flat silver spoons riddled with holes. At the back of the table on a small shelf stood a dazzling array of bottles of various sizes and shapes, all written in French and all containing eerily green liquid.

When it was their turn at the table, Conny worked deftly with his free hand. After placing two glasses before him, he studied the line of bottles carefully before finally selecting two. "We'll start you with something a bit gentler, my love. The green fairy can be a bit cruel if you aren't mindful on your first approach." He poured a small amount of the liquid from the two bottles into each glass, then carefully placed two of the strange spoons over the rim before arranging a sugar square on the top. Humming softly under his breath, he set the glasses under two different spouts and lifted the handle on the spigot. As water drizzled over the cube, Conny settled against Johann and linked the fingers of their joined hands together.

"It takes a moment to prepare." He gazed fondly at the absinthe as the water slid over the edges of the spoons. "You must sip slowly. It might seem like any drink at first, but it will have you flying soon enough. It's not uncommon to feel as if you're in a dream. The world is soft, even magical." He raised their joined hands to his lips and kissed Johann's fingers. "But we shall fly tonight together, *mon petit loup.*"

The drink was quite pleasant. It was sweet, though not as sweet as he'd thought it would be, and it tasted of licorice. It did not seem entirely strong, but Johann made himself sip slowly as Conny suggested. This had the effect of forcing him to savor the experience, which wasn't at all a bad thing.

After several minutes, he felt the absinthe and cocaine begin to affect him. He laughed easier, and in addition to no longer objecting to Conny's undoing of his clothing, he began to undress his lover as well. When a woman seated nearby pushed up her tits until they spilled out of her dress, he didn't blush, he laughed and cheered with the rest of the crowd. When a man bent over and pressed a hand over his mouth, wiggling his backside at a group of men, Johann enjoyed watching the man get spanked like a child by his friends.

When someone pushed the man to the floor and pulled out a cock for him to suck, Johann forgot Conny's warning and drank deeply of the delicious absinthe as he boldly enjoyed the scene unfolding before him.

His glass wasn't half empty before the room began to float and spin. It wasn't as alarming an experience as he'd have thought it would be, though at times he could have sworn he saw objects from nearby tables floating away and dance about the room. He tried to set his glass free to join them, but it only clattered to the floor, spilling the remainder of his drink on the carpet.

This made him laugh, and everyone around them joined in, especially Conny.

"I believe my darling clockwork soldier has met the green fairy." Conny climbed aboard Johann, straddling his legs as he wrapped his free hand around Johann's neck. "Tell me, love. What do you think of my favorite drink?"

Johann thought absinthe was lovely. It made him feel so free and happy. He had no worries, no cares. Well, outside of one. He touched the open vee of Cornelius's shirtfront, caressing the smooth planes of his chest. "You have on too many clothes."

This made the people around them laugh, but though Conny smiled, it was a dark curling of lips, and it was accompanied by Conny drawing both his hands to his chest to undo his buttons. Johann's tied hand came along for the ride, which meant his fingers brushed every inch of Conny's skin as it became exposed.

When the last button came undone, Johann couldn't help himself. He leaned forward and pressed his mouth to Conny's skin.

He thrilled to hear the crowd cheering them on, and his cock swelled as Conny's sultry laughs became aching moans. Johann loved knowing everyone watched him kissing his lover's chest. He wanted them to watch more. So much more.

He began by teasing Conny's nipples—first with his tongue, then his teeth, and finally his clockwork fingers. Johann already knew Conny loved this best, that his tinker-surgeon took particular thrill in being seduced by the clockwork parts he'd helped create. The crowd seemed to enjoy this too, and so Johann gave everyone what they wanted. He pinched Conny's nipples with the delicate tips of his clockwork fingers. He ran them all over Conny's skin, using them to shove his lover's shirt over his shoulders. Through it all, Conny went softer and more pliant, and when Johann nudged him to stand so he could take Conny's pants off too, Cornelius obeyed without hesitation.

"Yes, darling." He arched his hips, pressing his erect cock forward as Johann freed it. "Do what you like with me. I'm yours to command. To undress. To touch. To fuck. What would you wish of me next?"

Johann saw the man who'd been playfully spanked now bent over the arm of a couch, sucking one man while others lined up to slap his now-bright-red bottom in earnest. He wondered what it would feel like to spank Conny. And to do it in front of all these people.

Conny followed his gaze and bit his lip against a grin. "Ooh, Johann. You naughty boy."

Then he climbed off Johann's lap and draped himself over Johann's legs, his naked bottom stuck pertly in the air.

Their bound hands had become twisted, and Johann tried to settle them into a more comfortable position, but it was difficult when he was so distracted by Conny's upturned ass. He ran his clockwork hand over the soft flesh, the metal sensors reading the sensation differently than his flesh hand would. Their audience seemed to like this—they were all clockwork fetishists in Naples, and this was a treat. A clockwork man caressing the naked bottom of his creator.

Well, Johann would give them more to savor.

He didn't slap Conny's bottom, more of a playful, experimental tap, but Conny gasped and arched into his hand, and the growing crowd around them murmured a susurrus of approval. Johann swatted again, harder this time, enough to make Conny's mounds of flesh shimmer like a pudding. He went in again, spanking the other cheek. Back and forth, harder, then a little harder, fed by Conny's mewls and wriggles and the audience's encouragement. He paused to knead at the pinking flesh, pulling at Conny's cheeks to spy the dark hole tucked inside, until he gave up and spread Conny's legs open to make the job easier. He ran his metal finger down the cleft, wishing he had their jar of lubricant, because wouldn't Conny love being fingered by Johann's clockwork hand in front of all these people.

As if they had heard his wish inside his head, someone appeared with a jar, open and ready for his use.

The crowd applauded as Johann pushed a slicked metal digit into Conny's body, and Conny spread his legs wider, inviting Johann to give him more. This had become one of their favorite bedtime games, Johann spearing Conny like this. Cornelius had added, in fact, some clever articulations which, with a few easy adjustments, let them bend in a manner that allowed Johann to push them all, even the knuckles, inside.

He wanted to do this now, in front of everyone. The very thought made his cock weep, made him finger faster and deeper inside of Conny.

With the absinthe, there was little hesitation between having this thought and withdrawing his hand and presenting it to Conny to make the adjustments. He didn't feel self-conscious while he waited, only eager to hear everyone gasp as he pushed, essentially, his entire hand into his lover—and that was what they did. Gasped and *oohed* as Conny cried out, arching into Johann's thrusts.

That was, he cried out until a man from the crowd came forward, freed his cock and plunged it into Conny's mouth.

Johann knew a flash of jealousy, an urge to pull his beloved back, but the beautiful drink smothered this, let him simply laugh and fuck harder into Cornelius's body as the strange man fucked his other end. It felt wicked and thrilling and perfectly right. He'd never watched anyone else fuck Conny's mouth, and it was erotic to see his lover speared in both his holes. When the man fucking Conny's mouth came, Conny choked as he tried to swallow.

That was pretty, Johann thought, and pushed deeper into Conny.

They were surrounded now, by men and women, though mostly men. Nearly all the men had their cocks out, pushing each other aside to get to Conny's mouth, the women fondling themselves or leaning back as other men and women touched them intimately. The scene was chaotic, rousing Johann's protective instincts even through the absinthe. He withdrew from Conny and settled his lover onto his lap, trying to decide what he wanted them to do next. Whether or not they should leave and find a quiet room.

Mateus appeared.

The crowd parted for him, every man yielding at the approach of their host. Mateus's gaze was fixed on Johann and Conny, his eyes dark with lust and want. The look made Johann ache. The man was so handsome, so powerful. Pretty like Conny, but different. The absinthe pushed aside his worries that he shouldn't think that about a man other than Conny, made him yearn to try this new flavor of man.

Then the man himself smiled at the two of them and held out his hand.

"*Venez avec moi.*"

Johann rose, bringing Conny with him as he followed their host through the crush. He remembered, belatedly, that Conny had left his clothes on the couch, but when he glanced over his shoulder, he saw a servant bearing all their discarded clothing.

How thoughtful.

Mateus led them into a smaller parlor, though it was not empty. A collection of men and women decorated the sofas and chairs, and in a few instances, tables. On one of them a woman lay sprawled, her breasts free and naked, skirt about her waist and her legs spread as two other ladies attended her. It was Olivia and Molly, Johann realized. Molly stroked the girl's face and nipples while Olivia's head bobbed against the woman's cunt. It looked wicked and delicious, and for a moment, Johann wanted to be between the woman's legs too.

A long couch with no sides, only a small roll at one end, stood empty in the center of the room, and it was to here Mateus led them. He smiled as he petted first Conny's face, then Johann's.

"You are precious," he said in his rough French. His hand lingered on Johann's neck, his thumb massaging Johann's collarbone. Then he pushed Johann's shoulder gently, then more firmly, until Johann had to yield and fall to his knees. He watched as Mateus freed his cock, which was longer and thinner than Conny's. He breathed in the musky, sweaty scent of the strange man, marveling at how similar and yet different this organ was.

He shivered as Mateus traced the outline of Johann's lips with the tip of his cock, and then, shutting his eyes, Johann opened his mouth and took the merchant inside.

Conny had fucked into Johann's mouth, but with Mateus it was rougher, a fact Johann found thrilling. Mateus used him, and Johann let him, losing himself in the sensation of having his throat fucked. He opened his eyes when he heard Conny whimper, felt him stiffen in their bond—Mateus had lifted Conny's right foot onto the couch and was thrusting into his hole with his fingers as above Mateus thrust his tongue just as roughly into Conny's mouth.

This Johann wasn't certain he liked, but he could hardly object with his mouth full of cock. When Mateus freed him, tugging Johann to his feet, he tried to say something—but then he was the one being kissed.

He had so many feelings at once. He knew he didn't truly want this, that the merchant wasn't the one he wanted to kiss, and yet the sensation was so decadent and perfect with the rest of the evening. When Mateus drew Conny into the kiss too, Johann stopped feeling conflicted and gave in to the sensation. Familiar, submissive Conny, different, confident Mateus. Two tongues in his mouth at once, then one, then none as Mateus kissed Conny alone. Then he came back to Johann, running his tongue along Johann's cheek as he made his way to whisper in Johann's ear in perfect German.

"Lie on the couch. I will show you how we can both fuck him at once."

Johann wanted to tell Mateus he already knew how to do this, that he'd done it with a stranger in the other room, though with his fingers, not his cock. He realized his clockwork fingers were still bent together, and he wondered if he should ask Conny to put them back to rights.

Then Mateus undid his trousers, encouraged them off his legs and eased Johann onto the sofa.

It was thrilling to watch Mateus arrange Conny on top of him. Their hands were still bound, and Johann brought their other hands together as well. He smiled as Conny absently fixed his fingers, as if he couldn't help tinkering, even in this moment.

Then Mateus took hold of Johann's cock and pushed Conny down so the organ went roughly into his hole.

For a few minutes this was all that happened: Mateus directed their fucking, urging Conny up and down, stroking Johann's chest and tracing his open, gasping lips. When he turned Johann's head and aimed his cock, Johann opened for him, moaning as he became overloaded with the duel sensations of having Conny ride him while Mateus fucked him. Mateus tugged on his hair, held him still while he fucked deeper, choking Johann, but still Johann yielded, loving this feeling of surrender.

He ached when Mateus withdrew, but he watched with interest as the merchant moved around the couch, climbing behind Conny. All around them in the room were the sounds and smells of sex, slapping of flesh and moans and the sharp, rich scent of musk and arousal. Part of Johann wanted to look around and see the decadence, but he couldn't bear to turn away from his lover and the wicked man behind him.

He saw Mateus's hand disappear, felt the brush of those fingers at his balls, against the base of his cock as Conny rode it.

Then he felt first one finger, then two work their way inside Conny beside Johann's cock.

Conny's eyes shut, rolling back in his head as he collapsed backward against Mateus. Johann groaned, transfixed by the sensation of Conny's heat and Mateus's cool, insistent fingers alongside his cock in that dark sheath. Conny made sounds Johann had never heard—desperate, terrified, eager sounds. When Mateus forced him into a kiss, he sobbed into it, his whole body shaking—until Mateus spread his fingers. Conny stiffened, almost screamed, but Mateus swallowed the sound. And pinched Conny's nipple with his other hand.

Johann took it all in, mesmerized. Nothing floated as it had in the drawing room, but he watched Mateus and Conny as if in a dream. Mateus spoke in

Portuguese, a language neither of them knew, and it sounded delicious. Conny wept, tears streaming down his face, but he couldn't stop touching Mateus. Until the merchant pushed Conny forward, arranging him on top of Johann. The two of them stared, drugged and delirious at one another as behind them, Mateus held Conny open enough to push his cock inside along Johann's.

Conny's cry rose in pitch until it almost became a song, and then he shut his eyes and babbled in rapid-fire French as Mateus directed the two cocks in and out of his body. Johann caught some of the words and realized Conny was begging—for more, for them never to stop.

Johann didn't want it to stop either. He felt so good, so wicked, so safe. Conny came undone above him, his body quivering. The hole Johann fucked with Mateus expanded to accommodate the two of them.

"*Je t'aime.*" Conny collapsed onto Johann, his body thrust forward by Mateus's thrusts as he fumbled for Johann's mouth. "I love you, my beloved Johann. You are my everything. You give so much to me. You understand me." He groaned, pushing back into the fucking even as he stroked Johann's face. "You are perfect. I want to be with you always. Your lover, forever."

Johann kissed him clumsily. "I love you too. I love you like this, Conny. Undone and open. Do you like this? Two of us inside you?"

Eyes still unfocused, Conny kept pushing forward. "It's only you inside me, darling. You told this man he could fuck me. It's you doing this to me. It will only be you forever, my love. You could give me to twenty men, twenty thousand, and I would know it was your cock inside me. Your command." He shut his eyes, lost for a moment as Mateus urged his legs wider and tipped him to fuck deeper. Glazed, nearly drooling, he spoke again, slurring as he stared down at Johann. "I could never rule you with a clockwork heart, darling. I could never rule you with anything. I am yours, utterly, for as long as you'll have me."

Johann's chest filled with love, with pride, with quiet happiness. He had no words to express this, so he kissed Conny instead.

They kept kissing as Mateus withdrew from Conny's body and removed Johann's cock as well. They kissed as Mateus lay them side by side, drawing the three of their cocks together and rubbing them against one another until they had to quit kissing and throw back their heads as they came.

Mateus smiled over them when it was finished, nuzzling their still-bound wrists with his nose. "You are delightful. You will play with me again someday. In my villa in Portugal. I will fuck you both as we gaze out at the beautiful sea."

Conny made no reply, his eyes shut, face pressed to Johann's neck as he caught his breath. He smiled too, looking content and almost serene.

Johann felt that way too. *He loves me. And I love him more than anything in this world. Enough that even after all of this, we are only closer, not further apart.*

"Yes," Johann replied at last, stroking Conny's disheveled hair with his clockwork hand. "I believe we will do this, someday."

* * * * *

Johann didn't remember finding a bed, yet he was in one with Conny when the shouting began.

He sat up, blinking and confused, surprised to see he was alone with Conny in a small but elegant bedroom full of fine antique furnishings and thick draperies on the windows. Hearing raised voices in the hallway, his soldier instincts kicked in, and he rose, seeking their clothing.

"Conny, wake." He tossed his lover's trousers onto the bed as he stepped into his own. "Something is wrong. You must get dressed."

Cornelius stirred to life, groaning and clutching his head. Johann's skull ached too, his brains feeling loose and sloshy. But he pushed past this, convinced something was wrong and that they must leave at once.

"You must get dressed." He helped Conny, urging first one leg and then the other into place. When the shouting drew closer, accompanied by several pairs of heavy boots, Johann's skin prickled as adrenaline pushed all his drunkenness aside. "Come. We must leave this place in haste."

"Who is here?" Cornelius yawned, frowning as he fastened his clothing. A loud crash and more voices from the floor below made him quickly alert, and now he looked to Johann with his eyes full of fear. "Do you think they're looking for the two of us?" He gasped and covered his mouth. "Oh, Johann, what if they know you have the heart?"

"We can escape through the window." Johann pulled back the curtain carefully and peered out with his body shielded by the wall. "There is a roof below us to another part of the house, and we can make our way to the ground and out through the garden."

He had the two of them on the small balcony, ready to leap over the edge, when the door burst open. Men in dark clothes bearing guns and short swords filled the bedroom, all of them descending on Johann and Conny.

"Hurry!" Johann tried to send Conny over the edge, but he was too late.

Johann attempted to reclaim Cornelius, but the intruders beat him back, then broke his hand—his flesh hand. Stomped on it with their boots. The bones crunched as Johann screamed, pain flooding him. Cornelius cried out too, and Johann reached this time with his clockwork arm. The soldiers stepped on this too, mangling the metal and sending confused, alarmed signals from the sensors to his brain.

They have come for me. They have come to kill me and take the heart.

Johann would not go quietly. He let them break what they would, because he had nothing to lose but his life. He swore in German, swiping at them with his ruined arms, tasting blood in his mouth as they punched him. Even when he lay on the floor in a wrecked heap, he fought, struggling to get away even though his body was too broken to move.

I will resist them. He heard Conny crying out to him, and he told himself he would not let his lover down. *I won't let them have the heart. I will find a way to escape them. I will come back to you, Cornelius Stevens. I swear on my love for you.*

The men converged, and Johann waited to be lifted, carted off to the belly of an airship, his final destination some terrible French dungeon or surgeon's table. But no one touched him now. They spoke in French too rapid-fire for him to follow. Conny told them *no* over and over again.

The men hadn't come for the heart. They'd come for Cornelius.

Cursing them in German, Johann pushed past the pain and dragged his bent and broken body forward. "I will not leave you, Conny!"

He had a brief, grisly view of Conny's pale, terrified face as he struggled with the men bearing him away. Then a boot came down on the side of Johann's head, and he saw nothing but darkness.

Chapter Fifteen

One moment Cornelius was screaming in an Italian bedroom as he watched his father's secret police brutalize his lover. The next thing he knew, he lay on a lumpy, dirty cot in a desolate castle tower whose ancient arrow-slit windows revealed he was somewhere in the Alps. One of the archduke's interrogation keeps, no doubt.

Was Johann here somewhere too?

Was there any hope he was still alive?

Conny's head throbbed as he stumbled, dizzy with aether hangover, to the door. It was locked, and a quick exploration suggested it was also bolted in a very tinker-unfriendly manner from the outside. He noticed the room was singularly devoid of potential tools, though with a bit of effort he thought he could do quite a lot with the cot. There was a bottle of sour wine and a hunk of moldy bread, which he ignored for now. The mold was encouraging, though. The few spy lessons he'd absorbed from his mother was *never trust the food*, though usually the poorer the fare, the less likely it was laced with poison or a hallucinogenic designed to encourage confession.

He kept himself busy mentally designing a handheld weapon and launchable deterrents from his bed and bedding, though he refrained from executing any of those plans until he knew what it was he was up against. This knowledge came at dusk, when soldiers escorted him down the long, winding stairs to the main floor of the keep, to a warm, finely appointed dining room where more guards and a burgeoning feast awaited him.

As did his father and Dr. Savoy.

The Grand Archduke, commander of the French-Germanic Army, Francis Cornielle Guillory sat at the head of the twelve-person table, already well into his meal. He drank deeply from a goblet of brandy and saluted Conny rakishly with a loaf of half-eaten bread.

"Ah, here he is at last. My son. Come, child, and share a meal with me and my friend, whom I understand you have already had the pleasure of meeting."

No apologies for having him abducted, drugged and tossed in the tower, as if that had been a misunderstanding, not crude calculation. "I don't wish to share a meal with you, Father. Not until you explain why you brought me here and why you did it in such a rude manner."

Francis wiped his mouth with a napkin and tossed it aside before motioning impatiently for the footman to refill his glass. "I brought you here in the manner most suitable to me and that will look the most pleasing to the damned newspapermen. This will allow me to be outraged and furious publicly over the abduction of my son and allow me to demand recompense when it's revealed you are likely dead." He winked at Conny. "I won't forget the favor you did me, making me hunt you down in Italy. I was being lazy, trying to take you in Calais, but this is so much better. Now I can insinuate the Italians helped. It's likely not enough to get them involved in the war, but it should at least help keep them quieter whenever I stray a bit over their border."

Conny sat down with a heavy thump on his chair. "That was you? You sent those thugs to kidnap me at The Alison?"

"Naturally. As I sent them to Italy for you. Took far too long to apprehend you, but Savoy's suggestion we always haunt the house parties, especially the risqué ones, was genius." Francis smiled and nudged a tureen toward Cornelius. "Do have the soup. It's quite good."

It took everything in Conny not to dump the tureen over his father's head. "Why have you brought me here? What could you possibly want of me, and why would you attempt to get it from me in this manner?"

"I did it in this manner because none of my ministers or the public must know my true plans, not until they see the wisdom of them. And I brought you here because *you*, dear child, will help me end this war. Just as you've always wanted." He speared a piece of beef and shook it at Conny with a cheeky wink. "You're going to build me a clockwork army, Cornelius. And power it with copies of that traitor Félix's clockwork heart."

Though Conny's heart sank and his soul filled with despair, he refused to let his father see him cry. He would mourn Johann in private. For the rest of his life. "So…you found it, then?"

Francis rolled his eyes. "*Found*. You make it sound as if I discovered it under my bed when chasing a button. No, I damned well scoured the country for it. I was certain he had it with him for a time, but of course I was too slow." He grinned. "But so was he, alas. We captured it from the gypsy he hired to transport it to one of his fellow conspirators. Lily-livered fool ran off at the first sound of steel."

The despair roiling inside Conny hesitated, uncertain. "You…found the heart…with a gypsy?"

"I did indeed. Just outside Marseille. Can you imagine if we were any later? It would have been bound for Africa or the damnable Americas. But now it's mine. You're going to study it, copy it and install it in my automatons. You can stand beside me as we watch them march across the fields and mountains and bring endless peace to all of Europe. United under one flag at last."

Savoy's smile was oily. "We will work together, dear boy. *Closely* together. I believe you'll enjoy seeing what I can do with some rudimentary electricity on a body. I've been able to animate a corpse for almost half an hour. Think what we can do when you make copies of the heart. What I can do when you show me how to build one myself."

Though Savoy's suggestions revolted him, Conny was overcome with joy at what their boasts told him. They didn't have Johann's heart. This must have be a decoy, what they'd captured. He didn't yet know if Johann had been captured, but he had a chance. Perhaps he was still alive and safe in Italy.

At least until Savoy's terrible clockwork soldiers stormed through Naples to take it for France.

Conny folded his hands in his lap and regarded his father calmly. "I will not stand beside you and watch you terrorize Europe, because I will not help you build your metal army. I will not copy the heart. No matter what you threaten or do to me. You can torture me all you like. I will not yield in this."

"Yes, well, Savoy in fact is quite good at getting you to surrender. But it would be needlessly complicated to achieve this and still keep you hale enough to outfit my metal men to suit my schedule. Which is why I brought along some incentive."

The sludge of sick terror rolled in Conny's belly, making him glad he'd declined to eat. Who did they have? Val? Félix? Oh dear God, did they have Johann after all?

Francis leaned back in his chair, patted his belly and grinned. "Goodness, but it has to have been *ages* since you last saw your mother. I'll have them pull her out of the stocks, clean up the blood from her lashes and let you wave to her from the observation area of the dungeon."

* * * * *

When Johann opened his eyes after the attack, it was the aftermath of the Siege of Calais all over again. Except this time, it was Master Félix who hovered over him. Because Conny was gone.

He wanted to rage, to fight off the tubes and pipes and insist they go after Conny's abductors, to find the traitors who'd given them away, but he could barely stay awake for all the aether, and all his speech was slurred and slightly crazed. Each time he closed his eyes, he dreamed of the raid, trying this time to stop Cornelius from being taken, but each time he failed and woke on the table with Félix peering worryingly at him through his tinker's goggles.

As he healed and they began to dose him with less aether, Johann realized his clockwork had changed. His left arm had been replaced, and he had a metal, articulated brace over his right flesh wrist. His legs were different also—subtly so, but he noticed. It made him ache, to lose not only Conny but his clockwork too.

Félix hushed him when he tried to ask after his lover. "Not now, child. The others are hunting him down, but right now your duty is to rest. You have a great deal of healing to do."

Johann wanted to ask more about this, to find out *who* was hunting Conny down and how, and were they coming back for him, but the aether claimed him again before he could organize the query. The next time he opened his eyes, however, Crawley, Olivia and Valentin hovered over him, looking relieved. Before they could begin speaking, though, Johann interrupted them. "Where is Conny?"

Crawley grimaced. "We're not sure yet, but we're starting to narrow it down. Félix put us in contact with Elizabeth's spy network, but we can only use the wireless to the French border, so the best information is delayed."

Olivia stroked his flesh arm above the cuff. "I've got someone on the wireless every hour of every day, looking for news. If anything comes through, we'll fly out in a heartbeat and bring him home."

That would be suicide, Johann wanted to tell them, but even thinking of explaining why made him weary. He contented himself to listening to them instead, glad they were there with him.

When the others left, Valentin lingered. He clutched the French-German dictionary in his arms as he approached the bed. "Hello. Are you feeling well?" he asked in butchered, horrible German.

Johann smiled through his weariness and answered in French. "I'm better. Thank you."

Val nodded and came hesitantly closer. He switched back to French to speak now, but spoke slowly in deference to Johann. "I'm doing my best to help find Conny. We all are. Thank you for trying to save him."

Johann averted his gaze. "There were too many soldiers. I couldn't be strong enough. Even with the heart."

"Félix says without the heart, you would be dead." Val sat on the edge of Johann's bed. "They brought you back in pieces. It was horrifying, but also revealing. I didn't understand how much you loved him until I saw it. The archduke's men wouldn't have wasted time torturing you if you weren't fighting them. But you fought them with everything you had in you, didn't you?"

Johann nodded woodenly. "It wasn't enough."

"Yes, it was. But now you don't have to fight them all yourself. We'll help you. *I* will help you." He flipped through the dictionary on his lap. "I wanted to ask you something. I've been studying this so I could speak with you more easily. But I don't understand all these marks. These lines above words or sometimes letters. Did you and Conny make these? Are they notes that can help me learn, if I know the code?"

Johann peered at the book, frowning. Yes, he remembered those marks from his own lessons. He'd assumed they were notes from whomever the book had initially belonged to. But this time when he looked at them, he assumed nothing. He remembered where the book had come from. What Cornelius's mother had done to the note she'd sent to warn him away.

"Have you shown this to Félix?" he asked at last.

Val shook his head. "No. Do you think I should? Why?"

"Because I think it might be a code."

Val's eyes widened, and he took the book back, clutching it hopefully. "A code that might help Conny?"

Johann hoped so.

Val left him then, and after another drift on aether, Molly appeared. She didn't weep, but her brown eyes shone, and she stroked Johann's face tenderly. Johann fumbled to take her hand, a gesture difficult with his new metal wrist.

"Molly." His voice was a rasp, rough with sleep and pain. "Molly, I'm afraid I won't get him back."

"We will, darling. I promise we will." She kissed his hand and held tight to the metal of his arm. "Félix and Olivia are poring over that book Val had. Heng and Crawley are bribing everyone they can find, trying to find a trail. Mateus is helping too—he feels sick the abduction happened in his house and wants to prove he had no part in it."

"I want to help too."

Molly smoothed his hair from his face. "Right now you do that by resting, love. Rest and get strong. Your tinker needs his soldier hale and hearty."

Yes, he did need to be strong. Stronger than he'd been. Stronger than the other soldiers. He'd tell Félix he wanted armor, enough to bash in doors and take down walls. He would find Conny again if he had to smash everything in France.

But first he had to rest just a little longer.

Just a little bit longer.

* * * * *

The first two weeks of Cornelius's imprisonment were a nightmare.

Nothing happened to *him*, outside of enduring Savoy's innuendo as they worked together. No, he was installed in what under other circumstances would have been the workshop of his dreams. He had every tool, every material he could dream of, workspace enough for an army of tinkers. Assistants who would lift and carry and work in whatever way he demanded. He had food and drink, even absinthe to his heart's content. His bed was as soft as an angel's wings, and his bedchamber adjoined his workstation. *He* was fine. But every night he did not produce the heart, he was escorted to the dungeons so he could watch his mother be tortured because he hadn't finished his work.

He pleaded with his workers, with his jailers, with anyone he thought might be able to bend the archduke's ear. On the third night when his mother's whipping sent him into hysterics, he held an improvised knife to his own throat until they brought his father to him.

"What is it, boy?" The archduke looked impatient, unimpressed with Conny's dramatics. "Why was I dragged out for this performance?"

Cornelius would not waste his audience. "I can't make it work. It's not the real heart. It's nothing more than a decoy. I've seen the real thing, worked on it, and this isn't it. Stop torturing her, because *I cannot make this heart what you want it to be."*

Francis clucked his tongue. "Dear boy. I've seen you build miracles out of bits of scrap simply because you were bored. You can make this heart work in a fortnight, no matter what it might be now. Because if you don't, I'll start taking your mother's fingers. And I'll make you pull the lever that lowers the knife."

With that he winked, saluted and sauntered back down the hallway.

That night was the worst. Conny sobbed into his pillow so hard he eventually had to stop and throw up. When even this didn't lessen his hysteria, he drank barely diluted absinthe and took cocaine directly through his nose until the world's edges didn't simply soften, they evaporated. He lay on his bed, staring at the ceiling as he watched it shift and transform. He drifted in and out of sleep, got up to piss.

When he stumbled back to his bed, he found Johann lying in it.

For a moment he was overjoyed, thinking he was rescued, but then he noticed Johann didn't have any clockwork, and if Conny blinked too hard, he vanished. So Conny stopped blinking. He sat carefully on the other end of the bed too, in case too much movement disturbed the mirage.

"I wish you were truly here," he whispered.

Johann smiled and leaned back on the pillows. "Don't think about that. Talk to me. Tell me your troubles."

Conny's laugh was strangled. "My troubles? I'm captive in some French fortress by my father, who is torturing my mother until I produce something I don't have the skills to create. My monitor tells me daily how he would like to fuck me, and I think he might be the one man in France I *wouldn't* let you order to have his way with me." He didn't wipe the tears leaking from his eyes. "Johann, I think I should kill myself. I don't want to, but it seems the only way out. I only wish I could save Mother first."

"Come now. There's always another way." Johann stretched, revealing large, muscular arms, both of which were hale and whole. "You're a tinker. This is what you do: you invent your way out of problems. Come. Stop panicking, and think about what it is you need."

It seemed like such a simple question, but when he tried to answer it, Conny's mind exploded with conflicting directions and goals. "I need to build a heart, but I can't. I need to get my mother out. I need to get *myself* out. If I could get us out without building the heart, I would, but I don't know if I can invent an escape before he starts taking her fingers. So I have to make the heart. But I can't."

"You know very well he won't spare her once he has the heart. He'll keep her constantly in peril until he breaks your mind. Turn you into one of his soldiers. Ironically, the kind of control I once feared from you."

Conny wagged a finger at him. "Stop that. You sound like me, not Johann."

Johann rolled his eyes and made a very French gesture with his hands, suggesting Conny was hopeless, but what could a man do? "Darling, of course I'm you. Once you've solved this snarl you've gotten yourself into, you can imagine me properly. But for now, isn't it better if I help you think?"

Why could Conny not stop crying? "I can't see the way out of this. I don't know how to invent around this trouble."

"That's because you aren't breaking it down. You need to get the two of you out, but you don't have the means, and you need more time. What means do you require? What is the tool you're missing to escape?"

Conny considered. "I could get us out of the castle, I think, but I'm not sure where we are or what we face outside the keep's walls. Even if there were no soldiers—which, of course there are soldiers—I don't know what direction to aim us." He lay on the bed, close to imaginary Johann's foot but not touching it, so he didn't have to watch it disappear. "I could build a small dirigible, I suppose. We could go out in the cover of night. But I'd still need time to do that, and some way to disguise it while I worked." He ran his tongue over his teeth, which he absently noticed were fuzzy. "I could possibly steal an airship, but my father isn't stupid. He'll have those well-guarded. If I knew the lay of the keep, I could possibly work around that, but I don't, and they'll make sure I never learn my way."

"What if you didn't have to build it or steal a ship? What if one came to you?"

Conny frowned at Johann. "How in the world would that happen?"

Johann shrugged. "You could call one. You could call *The Brass Farthing.*"

"Call? Like a bird?" He stilled. "Oh. On the wireless. Like Rodrigo's in Italy. Except even if there were a station here, it wouldn't be connected to Naples."

"You can connect it. Build your own wireless transmitter."

"*How?* If by some miracle I could manage it, they'd see it—*and* it would have to somehow get over the mountains. Never mind even if I could get this done in less than two weeks, you and the others would have to still arrive here. This assumes they're still in Italy. That you aren't dead. Meanwhile, my mother will suffer because I can't produce a heart."

Johann tucked his hands behind his head and smiled. "Then I guess you'll have to do both. Build a wireless transmitter and a clockwork heart."

Conny stared at him, certain his drunken projected self had tipped into the ridiculous. Johann stared back, still smiling.

Then the idea began to gel inside Conny's head.

It wasn't terribly intelligent to work with delicate tools when drunk and hallucinating, but Conny did it anyway, laying out schematics and building prototypes. His assistants were all asleep, and he didn't want to know what Savoy was doing, but he decided he preferred working alone, because it meant he could keep talking to his hallucinated version of Johann, which he found more helpful than thirty pairs of hands.

"I hope you stay once I'm sober." Conny glanced at Johann through his goggles. "I suppose I could stay drunk, but I worry I'd make too many mistakes."

Johann, perched on a stool near a window, smiled. "When you work hard enough and long enough, your mind will relax and I'll reappear. In the meantime, feel free to keep talking to me. Even if you can't see me."

Conny's throat tightened. "I miss you. The real you."

"Then keep working, so you can see me again."

Conny did. He worked that whole night, until it was morning and the servants tried to bring him his breakfast and his assistants tried to come in to help. Conny tossed them all out, not wanting to break his concentration. His first task was too critical, nearly impossible, and he couldn't afford any distractions.

The heart Félix had planted as a decoy was more than worthless—it was practically designed to confuse and entrap anyone attempting to use it or copy it. What it was good for, however, was reminding Conny what it *wasn't*. He had worked extensively now on Johann's true clockwork heart. He knew what it did and what it didn't do. He couldn't remember how all the internals functioned, and some parts of it of course he'd never seen. But the more he worked with the decoy, the more he remembered, and the more he understood.

By the end of the third day, he had the schematic, or enough of one to carry him through. But this was only step one of his plan.

His father watched him carefully. When he realized Conny wasn't flailing any longer, only working, he stopped the dungeon visits, but he never missed an opportunity to remind Conny what fate awaited his mother. He gave Conny everything he needed, but he began to install more monitors to report back on what Conny was doing. Sometimes the archduke watched him work too.

"It certainly looks like a heart," he remarked dryly, "but I'd hate for you to develop designs of heroism."

Conny ignored him and continued working.

The monitors never left him, trading shifts throughout the day and night, and Savoy demanded constantly for him to explain himself. None of it mattered, because Conny knew not even Savoy understood what he was building. He barely understood it himself, sometimes.

"What is this small box for?" Savoy asked, holding up the transmitter.

"It's a mechanism for adjusting small mechanics inside the heart," Conny lied. He held it up and shook it gently. "Would you like me to explain them to you?"

Savoy only glowered and turned away. This was because, as Conny had learned, Savoy was actually quite a miserable tinker. He was a passable physician, and he made an adequate tinker-surgeon, but for all his boasting of electronics, he was very poorly skilled. Conny suspected his "successes" came from his assistants in a lab Conny had yet to see.

And so Conny continued his plan without interruption, without Savoy or his father or anyone in the castle knowing what he truly did.

He finished his first heart on the evening of the fourteenth day of his incarceration. His father came to the workshop flanked by eight official-looking men. They peered curiously and a little suspiciously at the heart for a few moments, and then a patient was brought in.

At first they brought in a corpse, which Conny immediately sent out. "That will never work. Automation of that level requires brain surgery as well, and I don't even begin to know the ins and outs of that, let alone enough to restart one once it's been dead."

"I can do it," Savoy said with a leer, and snatched the heart away.

Of course, Savoy could not, largely because Conny had designed the heart not to.

"It doesn't work." The archduke glared at Conny, then waved at one of the guards. "Fetch Elizabeth."

Conny swallowed his revulsion. "It works. But not on a corpse. I can replace a failed heart in a living person, but I cannot reinstall life or animate a corpse."

One of the generals, a larger, older man, stared carefully at Cornelius for several seconds. "Can you prove the heart works, without a patient?"

"Yes. I can demonstrate it here on the table if you like. It's a terribly simple machine once it's working. It pumps blood. It must be cleaned and cared for, but yes, this heart is functional. Better than one of flesh, in fact."

The general nodded curtly and stepped forward. "Then you may install it in me." The others gasped, and the archduke paled, but the general held up a hand. "The doctors have told me I'll have another attack any day. Even if this fails, it will be worth the risk, and at least then I'll have died for my country."

And so Conny ended up installing the first heart not in a soldier, but a general. He tried not to reveal how much this excited him, but in truth it was more perfect than any scenario he could imagine.

He hadn't lied. It was a perfectly working clockwork heart, one that functioned better than Johann's, if he could be so bold. It was just that it wasn't *only* a heart. And as the general recovered from his surgery and made plans to travel to Marseille to check on the troops stationed there, Conny wished the general Godspeed.

Because he'd sent, in the French general's heart, a small transmitter emitting a coded frequency all but the most refined, modern tinkers would think useless noise.

This is Cornelius Stevens, and I'm being held prisoner in a French castle somewhere in the Southern Alps. The man broadcasting this message is bearing a clockwork heart that I was forced to produce. I am making more, and my father wants to use them for terrible things. Please follow the frequency link from this heart back to my main transmitter and give the location to Captain Crawley of The Brass Farthing *at Rodrigo Milani's villa in Naples, or to Félix Dubois, also in Naples. I wish to stop this war, and I believe I have the means to do so.*

It could all backfire, of course, but he counted on the fact that so very few people understood the new wireless code. Plenty of people in Italy used it, but few understood how it worked enough to look for this kind of signal. If anyone else were able to receive his message, they were likely liberal-minded and focused on economic future, not war. Hopefully they would pass the message on.

For weeks he agonized, waiting by the little box of wires and knobs and vacuum tubes, hoping for the transmitter to let him know he had been heard. He waited. And waited. He kept the box with him as he manufactured more and more hearts for his father, these with transmitters as well. He wasn't allowed to see his mother at all, except as display for motivation to continue working. It upset him, but he did not despair, pouring all his hopes into his transmitters.

Then one day, in the middle of a preparation for a second surgery, the bulb on the top of the box began to flash.

The assistant with him frowned at it. "What is that?"

Conny did his best to contain his excitement. "It's nothing of importance. A small calculation device set to help me work out fine motor improvements in the heart. The light simply means the most recent calculation is done." He dried his hands on a towel and moved as casually to the transmitter as he could. "I'll take note of the report, reset the calibrations and be with you in surgery shortly."

The assistant watched him as he scribbled nonsense on a notepad, eventually wandering back to his task. This allowed Conny to stop his charade and focus on translating the coded readout, hoping he was not reading the notice of his death warrant.

He could not help a brief, elated smile as he realized that no, he was receiving quite the opposite.

Chapter Sixteen

Johann had nearly despaired of being able to locate Cornelius when Valentin found the list.

He hadn't let up on the idea there might be something useful inside the odd code he'd discovered in the French-German dictionary from the magistrate's house, and he dogged Félix constantly to help him break the cipher. Félix didn't want to give him too much of his time, as he was busy outfitting the *Farthing* to more quickly and efficiently fly over the Alps while his network tried, in vain, to hunt down Cornelius's whereabouts. Eventually Heng took pity on him and sat with him one night with a bottle of port. That was when they discovered the key to the cipher, and that the entire dictionary was a list of names, cities and codes for a secret wireless network.

Félix did pay attention then, though largely he was stupefied. "What *is* this? I recognize several of these names—though why in the world…?" He thumbed through the deciphered list, amazed. "I don't understand. There are French and Austrian names, yes, which would make me think one set is full of traitors. But there are Italian names on here as well. And Spanish, and Portuguese. Egyptian, Moroccan, Turkish. Even American! This isn't a list of spies. This is the antiwar coalition I'd heard rumored about. This is their directory." He gasped and pointed to another name. "Elizabeth is on this list—Cornelius's mother!"

Heng pointed to a name and glanced at Johann. "That one's from a town near yours, correct? Do you know anything about him?"

It was a town near Johann's village, and the merchant was well-known in the region. "He's a good man, from what I've heard. Frustrated by the lack of economic development."

Heng grinned. "See? It fits. This is a list of people who want the war to end, I'd bet my life on it. And look at this one: a duchess in Vienna."

Crawley peered at the name and winced. "Heng, that's no good. That's the von Hohenburg by morganatic marriage. She has no power, low rank, and her children can't inherit."

"Yes, I thought that was probably the only way she could possibly be on this list. That doesn't mean she's without influence. What if we use this network to get an audience with her? Maybe she can help us figure out who might have Conny, since Félix's network is exhausted."

Crawley snorted. "You think *we* will get an audience with a duchess?"

Heng shrugged. "Stranger things have happened. Anyway, we have to try." He nodded at Val. "I figure Frenchie knows his way around a tea party. Félix too. And Molly looks good in a dress."

Johann liked this idea, not so much because it meant going back to Austria, but because it meant no longer sitting in Italy watching nothing happen. "They like tinkers in Vienna. Félix can present me as an example of his work. That should get their attention."

Félix, however, held up a hand. "I'm not ready to fly into Austria based on this list. I need to do some checking first. Caution is necessary in such an extraordinary matter. We can't risk antagonizing the war."

"I'm tired of caution, and I don't care anything about the damn war." Johann slammed his clockwork hand on the table. "Cornelius is God-knows-where, and we sit here milling about on street corners, hoping for gossip. He could be hurt."

He could be dead.

Félix would not be deterred, however, and so Johann paced the deck of the *Farthing* almost five more days after the discovery of the list before Félix agreed that yes, they could sail for Vienna.

"I have my network reaching out to the Duchess of Hohenburg, but I can't promise they'll be able to get us an audience." Félix tapped Valentin in the center of his chest. "Polish your charm and keep practicing your German, because we might well need both."

They flew out the next day. Rodrigo and his wife bid them goodbye, and then the crew, plus Félix, lifted into the clouds. *The Brass Farthing* had undergone over two months of repairs and refitting, inside and out, and as a result, she shone like a glittering jewel as she sailed swiftly over the Alps. The trip took little more than a solid day instead of the usual two, and they didn't need to stop for fuel at all along the way.

They could not, however, land inside the city limits of Vienna. There was an airship port in town, but it was strictly regulated and generally reserved for the army generals, merchants deemed essential by the state, and the noble families. *The Brass Farthing*, being foreign and unregistered with any country, had to sit for a lengthy inspection that involved also keeping the entirety of the crew on board. Johann paced the deck, nervous at being so close to the seat of the army he'd deserted—twice—and being yet still unable to do even the remotest thing to help Conny. It was clear the inspection would take days, possibly another week, and it was highly likely they'd never be admitted to the city at all. Neither Val nor Félix could charm anyone, because the inspectors were not the sort of men who went in for such a thing.

And then the princess came.

She arrived in a dirigible of her own, a small, short-range vessel of which there had been many in Naples and which there were precious few of in Vienna. This one outshone all the ships Johann had seen anywhere, even in pictures. It had filigree that was clearly gold, not polished brass, and it managed to bleed ornamentation without being grotesque, only seeming stunning and ostentatious. Once it landed, a pair of footmen lowered a set of velvet-lined stairs, with railing, and they stood on hand to assist as a young, well-dressed and impeccably poised gentlewoman exited the vessel.

Wearing clockwork was rare anywhere in Austria, but this lady would have stood out in gear-obsessed Naples. She stood tall on high-laced boots ornamented with gear and tinker filigree, and her height was exaggerated by a high metal collar etched with intricate design and bearing the Hohenburg crest in the center. Her left arm had a delicate clockwork casing, as did her waist, a sort of copper girdle with wires and valves and knobs clustered near her navel. All this was worn over an elegant gown, black taffeta skirt and bodice over loose white silk shirtsleeves. A maid behind her carried a black lace umbrella decorated with gears and laced at the ends with wires.

She marched up to the head inspector, who had ceased his lecture to Crawley as her vehicle approached and now bowed low before her. "Your Serene Highness. To what honor do we owe the pleasure of your visit? I thought your father and mother were at Court today."

"They are." She opened a reticule and produced a small envelope bearing an embossed, official seal. "I'm delivering this on behalf of the Archduke of Hohenburg. We commandeer this vessel in our name, thereby rendering your inspection unnecessary."

"The devil you are!" Crawley pushed around the inspector, who sputtered as Crawley tried to insert himself between the inspector and the princess. Johann too hurried to intervene, wondering how he could telegraph to the captain that he did *not* want to stir the hornets' nest he was about to step in.

Before either of them reached Crawley, however, the princess snagged her parasol from the maid with her left hand, turned a dial on her girdle and rammed the very pointed copper end into Crawley's side. There was a spark, a loud *pop* and an odd, sulfuric smell as Crawley yelped and fell backward into the inspector, clutching his side as he stared in stunned disbelief at the woman who had just felled him without so much as drawing a deep breath.

The princess calmly returned the parasol to her trembling maid, then turned back to the inspector. "As I was saying, you are no longer needed here. Thank you for your service. Please continue with your work on other vessels."

The inspector fumbled with the envelope in his hands as he glanced uncertainly around the dock. "Princess Gisa, I don't think it would be proper for me to leave you alone with these unsavory characters."

"It would be most improper for you to remain when you are dismissed. As for your concern for my person, I hope I have demonstrated I may take care of myself. However, if you remain unconvinced, I am happy to demonstrate my electric parasol to you as well."

The inspector hurried off quickly enough after that, offering to arrest the vessel's former occupants, which the princess declined. Once the man was away from their pier and well out of earshot, the lady turned to the *Farthing*'s crew. Though she had spoken in High German to the inspector, she spoke in flawless English now.

"Good afternoon. I am Princess Giselle Elisabeth Esterhàzy von Hohenburg. You may address me as Your Serene Highness initially and Princess or Princess Gisa after that. Who among you is Master Félix Dubois? And who is Mr. Johann Berger?"

Félix stepped forward with a bow. "I am Félix Dubois, Your Serene Highness." He gestured to Johann, who also bowed. "This is Johann Berger."

Princess Gisa curtseyed to them both. "It is a pleasure to meet you both. I have news I wish to deliver, but in private, please." She turned to Crawley, who had risen from the ground and stood wincing and holding his side where she had stabbed him. "Please direct us to the officer's meeting room of your vessel, Captain Crawley."

Johann had expected another outburst from Crawley, but the captain only nodded grudgingly and ordered Molly to lower the stairs. Princess Gisa sailed up them gracefully, her maid and wicked parasol in tow, then waited patiently on deck for the others to board. She glanced around with a critical eye.

"It is a fine ship. Solid in structure and pretty of ornament. Tell me, Master Heng." She turned to him, polite smiles and interest. "What sort of electricity do you have installed?"

Heng regarded her warily. "I don't know, Your Serene Highness. The regular sort?"

She waved this away. "That's fine. I'll take a peek myself."

Molly and Olivia had remained on deck during the inspection, and as they took in their first glimpse of Princess Gisa, they seemed not to know what to do with themselves. Molly in particular looked taken aback and was oddly shy as she was introduced. Except the princess seemed to know not only Crawley and Heng's names and titles, but everyone's. She clasped Molly's hand and smiled brightly. "When our business here is concluded, I should love to have a tour of the engines, Miss Taubner."

Crawley kept quiet as they filed into Cornelius's workshop, but once the door was closed, he turned to their guest with great suspicion. "Who are you, *Your Serene Highness*, and how is it you know so much about us and my ship? And what do you mean, you've commandeered it?"

She waved a black-gloved hand. "I had my father claim the vessel so you could fly freely into Vienna. That's of course not what *he* thinks, but never mind about that. Who I am, Captain Crawley, is an ambassador of the Austrian sector of the Society to Liberate Europe. I understand you came upon one of our less careful members, Mr. Tremblay of Calais, who wrote out the cipher key in a dictionary now in your possession."

The crew glanced at one another, uncertain how to react. Heng broke the silence cautiously. "We didn't see your name on the list."

"Of course not. It would be most unseemly for me as a member of the nobility to participate in such an organization. It would draw far too much attention. My cousin's wife, being somewhat outside society, is perfectly safe, and she serves as my shield." The princess folded her hands together over the table. "To get back to the cipher key. I will confess it alarmed us a great deal to find it had traveled outside the Society. However, before we could agree on how to deal with this breach, we received Mr. Stevens's transmission asking about you, and of course, that has changed everything."

Johann straightened, his chest growing tight and hot at her revelation. "Cornelius Stevens? You've spoken to him? He's alive?" He realized he'd practically barked at one of the most powerful women in Austria and quickly tacked on a low bow and a doffing of his hat. "Begging pardon for my rudeness, Your Serene Highness."

Gisa turned to him, smiling kindly. "No pardon needs to be begged. Yes.

Cornelius asked me to convey his warm feelings to you and to assure you he is well, enough as can be expected."

Johann wanted to weep in relief. "Thank you. Thank you so much, Princess."

"Not at all, Mr. Berger." She returned her focus to the rest of the table. "Mr. Stevens is in a remote keep near the Swiss border. His father has him held captive, producing clockwork hearts en masse. If he does not keep to the schedule the archduke requires, his mother, who is also captive, is tortured."

Johann ached, imagining what a horrible position his lover was in.

Félix frowned. "But how can he do this—replicate the heart? He does not have the original."

Gisa glanced again at Johann. "No, but he has worked on it extensively, and he had your decoy copy. It was enough. Mr. Stevens wishes me to assure you, however, he has made several modifications, which we shall soon find work to our advantage. One of these is that the hearts emit a frequency and a message as directed by Mr. Stevens in his prison. It was this which allowed us to connect, for me to give instructions as to how to improve his transmitter, and which have ultimately allowed me to pinpoint his location. All that remains is for your vessel, Captain, to deliver a rescue mission."

Crawley gaped at her. "You want us to attack a fortified French keep full of the archduke's finest soldiers, all bearing clockwork hearts? Are you mad?"

"I said nothing of the sort about attacking. I said rescue." She opened her reticule again, produced a roll of paper and spread it across the table. "These schematics give the finer details of the castle in which Mr. Stevens is kept. We will use them to plan our assault and escape. Of course, first we must consult with the Society and coordinate their efforts. While your mission is to retrieve Mr. Stevens, ours is to end this war. Though I daresay I have the tinker a hairsbreadth away from pledging to our cause, in which case our interests will be perfectly aligned."

Félix raised his eyebrows. "*We* will use the plans? Princess, surely you don't mean you will accompany—"

"I do indeed *mean*, Mr. Dubois. I will attend this rescue as the representative of the Society and as a competent woman interested in preserving a democratic Europe for future generations." She touched her hair lightly. "And as an electric-tinker. I understand from my conversations with Mr. Stevens neither of you are well-versed in electronics, and I am, to be blunt, Europe's expert in electricity and wireless transmitters. The only reason electronics haven't supplanted basic engineering tinkering is because men are too obsessed with designing things that can explode or go fast."

Crawley raised an eyebrow. "How in the world is it *seemly* for you, *Princess*, to engage in such a risky adventure on a boat full of pirates?"

Johann couldn't help admiring how breezily Princess Gisa dismissed all Crawley's attempts to bait her. "Perhaps you misunderstand, Captain. *I* do not find it unseemly to engage on behalf of the Society, or to belong to the Society, but others will. Therefore it is only in matters of public record where I cannot be named. Because of course the world believes the Society largely drinks tea and discusses politics. They would be aghast to see how involved we truly are."

She spied Valentin, then, who had come in last and lingered in the back of the room, unable to comprehend most of what was said. But when Gisa saw him, she rose, took his hands and kissed his cheeks in a warm way as she spoke in rapid-fire French, apologizing for not seeing him sooner, assuring Val that Conny was well and that they would soon be rescuing him. She explained how she should be addressed in his own language, and also gave him Conny's regards and his love.

Val nodded through all of this, looking enchanted and more than a bit besotted. He thanked her when she finished, then glanced about, as if trying to find an entry into polite conversation. "Your Serene Highness, your gown is beautiful, but it is all in black. Are you in mourning? May I give you my condolences?"

She seemed pleased by this, but when she spoke, she lifted her chin in a manner as only a princess could. "You may offer, Valentin, and how kind of you to notice. I *am* in mourning, for the state of women in our current society. I shall wear black until we achieve full equality in the eyes of the world."

Val blinked, then bowed and kissed her hand, appearing even more impressed than he had been before. Molly, on the other side of the room, looked ready to swoon.

Indeed, it was difficult *not* to be swept off one's feet by Princess Giselle Elisabeth Esterhàzy von Hohenburg.

* * * * *

Cornelius continued to produce hearts at his father's demand, but his work was much lighter now that he could speak to Princess Gisa on the transmitter. Their conversations were painstaking, as he had to translate the series of codes to form her words. She tried to have him build one of the Society's electronic wireless devices, a clever clockwork that could transform the codes into audible sound using electricity and secondary waves on primitive army radio transmitters in the Alps. It was, essentially, a more grand and flexible example of the telephone system commonplace in the Americas and rare in Europe because of the endless wars. Conny was tempted to construct the device to make their communication easier, but he feared discovery. It was one thing to convince his monitors the complicated transmitter was related to the construction of his surgical clockwork. It was another matter entirely to leave a revolutionary telephone lying about, or worse, be overheard speaking on one.

The princess was pragmatic, forthright and wildly intelligent, and she did much to bolster Cornelius's courage as he waited for her to arrange aid. She soothed him too, regarding his mother, who he still hadn't spoken with and now barely saw—a new tactic by his father to terrorize him, because of course Conny feared his mother suffered greatly, or worse, was dead.

This is an intimidation tactic, and you must not fall for it, Gisa wrote to him when he confessed his fear. *Your mother is a celebrated and valiant spy. She is likely more troubled by your mental suffering than her physical. Aid her by refusing to yield to your father's manipulations.*

Conny did his best to follow her advice and thanked her for being his emotional lifeline during this difficult trial. His gratitude overflowed, however, when she reported she'd had contact with *The Brass Farthing* crew. When she returned again to tell him she'd taken his friends under her protection and was preparing with them and the Society to launch a rescue, he nearly broke down and upgraded his transmitter, because he longed to hear Johann's voice more than anything in the world.

Is he well? How is his clockwork? Did the attack in Naples leave him with additional damage? Does he seem healthy? Happy?

He tried to keep his queries appearing to be those of a man inquiring after a close friend, but somehow Gisa saw through his ruse. *Your lover is well, but he is greatly concerned for you. He would like to immediately storm the castle keep with an uprooted tree, I think, but I've endeavored to convince him this plan would not result in success.*

Conny's heart swelled with affection, even as he worried what it meant that Gisa knew their secret. He decided to match her bluntness with his own. *You are not offended my lover is another man?*

That would be ridiculous, sir, as who you take to your bed is unrelated to my person and therefore irrational for me to take offense over. Though as a point of interest, it's especially unseemly for me to behave in that manner, as I too foresee myself partnered with a member of my own sex rather than one of the opposite.

This remark warmed Conny and made him wonder how Olivia and Molly were getting along with the newest member of their motley crew. He did not ask this, however, only requested she pass along his less veiled declarations of affection and his hope to be reunited with Johann soon.

They spoke intensely about a scheme to get Conny and his mother out, and of ways to use Conny's transmitter-enabled hearts to the Society's advantage. The archduke constantly urged Conny to make more hearts and at an increasingly rapid pace. He had tried to force Conny to teach other tinkers how to replicate his work, but Conny did his best to be a poor teacher, and of course neither Savoy nor any other tinker was able to learn on their own. Conny apologized, explaining each heart was a work of art and skill, not meant for mass production, and it would take him far more time to teach others how to make new hearts than it would to do the job himself.

This was partially but not entirely true. The hearts were complicated, yes, but he had already translated the schematics and instructions into Princess Gisa's electronic code and sent them to her via the transmitter. She then studied them with Félix and offered her critique of his work, not on the function of the heart as a pump but of the embedded transmitter.

You do understand you could do so much more than broadcast the location of the heart and by extension the person carrying it. You could control the heart remotely by electricity and wireless transmission. This would of course not allow you to repair physical damage—though I believe it's possible to construct miniature, even microscopic clockwork designed to travel places human hands cannot go and do the work of flesh and mind via electronic command. It is, unfortunately, only a theoretical, not practical vision at this time. What is entirely possible however is affecting the function of your transmitter-enabled hearts. You could give an electrical charge via wireless to restart them. You could also send a message for the heart to slow, behave erratically or even stop.

Cornelius had become fluent in the wireless code almost as a language, no longer seeing it so much as French but as its own type of speech he could read and respond to with reasonable ease. This message from Gisa, however, he read several times, then wrote out on paper so he could stare at it for several minutes before burning it in his brazier, his gut churning in horror both at her suggestion and his own temptation to give in to it.

What she suggested building into the hearts was the possibility of murdering every soldier given the clockwork. Not only the generals but the men who hadn't joined the army to have their life put in the hands of an Austrian princess and her liberal collective. Men who had not even joined the army at all but had been drafted to serve Cornelius's father's vision of a Europe dominated by France. Men like Johann.

To do what Gisa suggested would do to his own countrymen what he had sworn to Johann his own clockwork heart would never do: control them and their destiny. It was the sort of invention his father would thrill to have and would exploit in ways cruel and terrible, all to justify his vision. To add this capability to the heart would go against everything Conny believed in, every vow he'd taken as a tinker-surgeon and every belief he held as a free-thinking man. It would undo his defiance of his father's way of viewing the world in a simple collection of wires and circuits designed to receive transmitted code.

Yet if Cornelius installed this modified heart in enough French soldiers and generals, that collection of wires and circuits would not only ensure his freedom but that of Europe from the archduke's war machine.

Conny did not reply to Gisa's transmission, but her words haunted him all that day. His father had been gone to the eastern front, but he returned that evening, and as had become ritual when the archduke was in residence, Conny was brought first to dinner with him and Savoy and then taken to view simple but significant torture of his mother. Normally during these evenings Conny spent the meal attempting to keep his rage and helplessness from showing, as he knew this was what his father hoped to see. The day of Gisa's terrible suggestion, however, Conny's struggle was to keep from sinking into his own reach for power. When he thought objectively of the idea he install a remote control mechanism in the hearts, he knew he would never agree to such a move. When he sat in front of his father, playing the sick game of dining formally before they viewed his mother's latest lashing or beating or branding with hot iron, Conny's objectivism evaporated and he wanted to install not only a potential means of control but a literal time bomb in his father's own chest cavity.

This thought, once germinated in Cornelius's mind, was potent enough on its own merit. After watching his mother weep and plead as the guards waved red-hot coals before her face and tugged at her ragged dress, slapping her cheeks and kicking her behind her knees so she nearly fell into their torture brazier— the idea of giving his father a weaponized clockwork heart was not simply a temptation, it was a cancer.

He rarely slept the evenings after those performances, but that night he paced the workshop, mind spinning crazily as he wrestled with himself. Though he worked with scores of assistants and stood under the gaze of countless monitors, he craved an advisor, or better yet a master to take this decision from his hands. He could not bring himself to allow this person to be Gisa—he would betray his father and the army, but he could not shed his patriotism so far as to defer wholeheartedly to an Austrian noble. He considered for the span of an hour a scheme to demand an audience with his mother, but even if he could arrange their ability to speak freely, he doubted she could be a voice of reason after her months of imprisonment and abuse. Out of loyalty he considered speaking to Valentin, then acknowledged the person he should seek counsel from was his mentor.

Except as he began to tap out a message to Gisa, he found himself instead begging her to explain her suggestion in full to Johann, ask his advice and relay his response, whatever it might be.

He prepared himself for hours of delay, as it was well past midnight and everyone would surely be in bed. To his surprise, however, her reply came in less than fifteen minutes.

I will brief Mr. Berger now and bring him to the transmitter as soon as he is ready to respond. In the meantime, I am sending the instructions for building an audio transmitter as well as a device for isolating the auditory transmission and delivery. At this point I imagine even you can see the benefits outweigh the risks.

It was difficult to keep his hands steady as he constructed the wireless telephone. The knowledge that he was about to not simply speak with Johann but *hear* him overwhelmed Cornelius so much he could scarcely follow Gisa's instructions. He did his best to pack his emotions away as he had become so accustomed to doing during his imprisonment, but when a blinking bulb that indicated he was receiving an auditory signal began to flash and he put the transmission device to his ear and heard Johann's hesitant query—"Conny?"—Cornelius burst into tears.

"Darling—oh, Johann, *darling*—it's you. Your voice." He pressed his hand to his mouth, stifling his sobs lest he draw attention from the night watchman in the hall.

Johann's reply, after the transmission delay, crackled with an odd static, fading and breaking in places, yet it remained unmistakably him. "Are you well? Have they hurt you? How is your mother?"

How like Johann to caretake even from a mountain range away. "They don't let me see her much, only as a torture. I keep hoping her despair is part of an act—knowing her, she's playing the part of frail woman to keep them from trying to break her in truth, but it's still difficult to see." He shut his eyes, the first tide of emotion at their reunion receding and allowing him to return to the reason he had taken the risk of building the electronic wireless. "Johann, did the princess tell you of her suggestion, of what she thinks I should do to the clockwork heart?"

It was hard to remember the pause was not Johann's hesitation but the transmission lag. When his reply finally arrived, it was quiet and full of weight and careful consideration. "She has, and that you want to know what I think about it." Another pause. "I should tell you we all discussed it here, even before she suggested it to you. At great length, in fact. She suggested it only after both her Society and the *Farthing* crew and Master Félix agreed it was the best solution."

The pause at the end of his speech went on long enough Conny felt he should fill the silence. "But do *you* think I should do it?"

He breathed slowly and carefully as he waited for Johann's reply. In and out. A conscious act, willfully controlling his breath, yet at its core an involuntary mechanism of the human body. As was the pumping of a heart.

The credo he'd vowed to serve when he took his apprenticeship to study clockwork surgery was to always build clockwork that would serve the body, not supersede it. Was it worth breaking that vow to end the war? To stop his father? To free himself and his mother?

Would Johann still love the man he'd become?

Would he be able to live with himself?

Johann's first response was a weary sigh that crackled and broke apart in the signal, yet still managed to wrap around Cornelius as warmly as a pair of arms. "I don't know that I can answer that fairly. I know you want my advice, but I'm not certain it would help you."

Conny's flesh heart slowed, constricted and ached in his chest. "Because you don't want me to. Because you would hate me if I did it, but you know it's the only way to stop my father."

The delay was almost nonexistent, meaning Johann must have begun speaking before Conny finished, and his voice crackled not with transmission static but the force of his passion and anger. "*No.* I would never hate you, and I *do* want you to do it. That's the problem. I can't advise you because I don't just want you to install those terrible hearts. I want you to make them all explode. I want to burn down that castle, then find your father's burned corpse and grind his bones into meal so I can eat them and consume him completely in his defeat like some barbarian warrior. I don't care if the whole of France falls, so long as you escape whole and safe into my arms. I want anyone in the world who might exploit you like this destroyed so they can't ever hurt you again."

Conny cried. He wept as softly as he could, but this ocean wave of feelings rolled in from the depths of him, rousing emotional responses he couldn't hope to control. Any effort to cling to rational discussion of a grave ethical matter crumbled into the surf of decades' worth of longing for something he had never allowed himself to acknowledge he so desperately wanted.

That passion and anger was for Conny. Almost a possession, as if he were Johann's most precious belonging stolen away, and he would lay waste to the world to see his return. No judgment about Conny violating his surgeon's oath. No condemnation or accusation that here was what Johann had always known Conny would do to him, an act about to be made so much worse than Johann had ever feared. None of this mattered, because all he wanted was Cornelius's safe return. By any means. At any cost. This ferocity, this consuming demand, this overwhelming instinct to protect—this love.

This was what Conny wanted more than air. This was what Johann gave him, even from fifteen hundred kilometers away.

"I'm sorry to be so ruthless." Johann's voice was still gruff, though tempered now with apology. "It's why I cannot help you. I have no objectivity. I only want you safe. I love you, Conny."

"I love you too." Conny wiped his tears away with his fingers and tried to compose himself. "I don't want to kill innocent men to be with you. I don't judge you for having killed as a soldier. I wouldn't care if you carried out your threat and destroyed the castle, or if you or Master Félix installed those self-destructive hearts. But I don't know that *I* can do it." He drew a deep breath and sank into the tide of safety and calm Johann's passion had aroused. "Yet I will, if you ask it of me. Please, Johann. Tell me what I should do. Please don't make me be the one to decide. I don't care if your reasoning is sound or not. I only want you to still love me when this is over."

"Then I want you to do it. If you can find a way to make sure as few innocents as possible suffer, then do so. But alter the hearts with clean conscience. At least as far as judgment from me. And from all of us."

It was astonishing how much freedom this permission gave Conny, not only to calm but to *think* more clearly, as if Johann had removed obstructions to a thousand alternate paths. "I could have the transmitter only *slow* soldiers' hearts. For the generals, it could be a more compelling arrest." He breathed a sigh. "I've installed so many clockwork hearts, darling. They make the pieces at my direction, and I assemble them until my fingers bleed."

"So there are many out there with a transmitter, but no remote control. Yet they won't know that. You could feint and tell them the ones affected are only a demonstration." A pause. "You've installed them in officers? How many?"

"Only a few, but there are more and more interested, as they see how my patients improve with the clockwork. My father wants one as well. I think he is working up the courage to go under my knife but doesn't want to admit it."

"Then there's your answer. Install the weaponized heart in as many officers as you can, and do whatever you must to get one inside your father. Call back those men you've already worked on and offer an upgrade. Can you do something to enhance them further? Make them want new hearts even if they don't need them?"

Yes, he could, but oh, that felt terrible. But if Johann wanted him to, he'd do it. "I can. I will, for you."

"Don't bleed for the officers, Conny. If you know one is a good man, then lie and tell him he's not a suitable candidate. Encourage your father to only give this upgrade to his closest and most trustworthy officers—that will ensure only those who think torturing your mother is an acceptable plan will end up in our crosshairs."

That was quite clever, actually, and very helpful. "You're a fine soldier, Johann. An admirable leader."

"I'm a crafty pirate who wants his lover back. As soon as possible."

They spoke a bit longer after that, more tender reconnections and wistful plans for their reunion. They couldn't linger as long as they'd have liked, because Conny needed to maximize time to conference with Princess Gisa about the specifics for these new hearts. All too soon, Johann surrendered the wireless to her. She had the clipped gruffness of an Austrian, but her French was impeccable, more eloquent and polished than his own.

"Mr. Stevens. How good it is to hear your voice at last. I gather Mr. Berger has effectively eased your conscience regarding our proposed strategy?"

"I believe so. I assume you will send me appropriate instructions for the new transmitters?"

"Mr. Dubois is preparing the code as we speak. You should begin receiving it shortly. I urge you to keep the wireless telephone disconnected but assembled so we may further converse easily should you run into trouble. If someone questions what it is, invent a fiction about something to do with the construction of the hearts."

"I will do so. Thank you, Princess."

"We have plans in hand to covertly enter the castle, but we shall await your confirmation that the hearts have been installed in as much of the Army leadership as possible. Do not hurry yourself. Once you convince them they can have the prize you offer, they will delay and possibly alter any other plans in order to slake their greed." Her voice tempered, less imperial though still bearing velvet strength. "Do not worry for your mother. I am personally acquainted with Miss Clarke. Not as well as you are, I acknowledge, but I recognize a woman of strength when I meet one. I also know how much she loves you, despite her frequent absence in your life. She would gladly bear any pain to keep you safe. And if they harm her body, you will make her beautiful clockwork when this is over. She will be the envy of Europe for her distinctive elegance and proof of the strength of her spirit."

Conny could not help but smile. "Princess Gisa, I didn't know I could have so much affection for Austrian spirit until I met you and Johann."

"And I have learned to appreciate the aesthetic and grace of the French. The world is a better place when we carry empathy. And an electric parasol."

Conny blinked. "An electric parasol?"

"I will send you this schematic as well. I'm certain you will find it stimulating."

When Conny finally went to bed that night, after speaking briefly with a tearful Val and an encouraging Félix, he slept deeply and peacefully, his dreams full of clockwork women flying about the clouds with electrified umbrellas. When he rose, he fell to his work, absorbing Gisa's schematics for the new transmitter, and set his assistants working double-time to create them. He read her notes on the electric parasol too, with a thoughtful expression and his eyebrows raised.

He incorporated *them* into the design he'd begun for his father's heart, letting his hands dissolve into the flow of work while he contemplated the best way to convince his father to go under his knife.

Chapter Seventeen

Johann understood Conny needed time to install transmitter-enabled hearts in as much of the French Army command as possible, and that the Society needed to fully coordinate its behind-the-scenes work to establish peace after what they hoped would be Archduke Guillory's surrender. Princess Gisa had been adamant that simply defeating him would create a power vacuum too easily filled by other war-minded leaders. The Society was far-reaching and diverse in its membership, including a number of men and women of influence, and there was still much discussion to be had over their secret network. Yet Johann couldn't help thinking every day gave the French more opportunity to learn about their plans and put Cornelius in greater danger.

It helped that he could dispel his fears with daily conversations with Conny. They spoke rarely on the wireless telephone, relying instead on the coded transmitter. It was cumbersome, but it was safer than risking someone hearing Conny engaged in conversation when by rights he should have been alone. This signal, Gisa assured him, was isolated now between the castle keep and the *Farthing*, and so Johann did not hold himself back when professing his love of Cornelius and his determination to reunite the two of them.

I will make love to you for seven days straight once I have you in my arms again. I won't take you out to let you indulge your exhibitionism either. I will keep you all to myself until you're so sated all you'll be able to do is lie in bed and breathe.

I look forward to my forthcoming exhaustion, my love.

Val was quite a comfort too. He spoke with derision as he always had, but it was all teasing now, designed to keep him distracted as they waited to act.

Sometimes they drank together, and during those times Val wept with him, alternating between fretting over Conny's safety and vowing ferociously they would get him back if they had to climb the mountains alone.

When the day finally arrived for *The Brass Farthing* to lead the Society to Liberate Europe into its best hope to end the war, Johann thought his pent-up yearning to damn their plans and go rescue his lover could possibly fill the balloon and carry them over the Alps with a single sigh from his clockwork-assisted lungs. They flew over Austrian and Italian airspace as much as they could, and once they entered French territory, Crawley ordered them into their oxygen masks and had them sail high into the atmosphere.

Félix and Gisa had designed the breathing apparatus and assured them it was perfectly safe at their altitude for the short flight to the castle, so long as they had an oxygen assist, but Johann couldn't help being nervous at being so incredibly high from the ground. He'd heard stories of men passing out and dying at high altitude, and one tale of a man who had practically imploded. Valentin seemed uneasy as well, though Johann couldn't be sure if this was because he feared the dangers of high altitude, because he was too conscious of the perils awaiting them, or because of some unknown and inexplicable reason only Val could invent.

They had used Conny's transmitter to locate the castle, and when the keep Gisa insisted the signal came from appeared in Heng's spyglass, they landed the *Farthing* in the forest and prepared to cover the remainder of the distance on foot. As they made their way along the edge of the woods, the princess fell in beside Johann. She had shed her elegant clockwork dress in favor of a more serviceable pair of trousers and leather bodice reinforced with steel plates over her white blouse, but she still had her electronic cuffs, waistband and her parasol.

"It's time to arm your own electronic apparatus, Mr. Berger. Do you remember the settings?"

He nodded and demonstrated his knowledge of the knobs and dials she'd installed on him. Félix had made minor improvements to his clockwork when restoring it after the attack, but Princess Gisa had for all intents and purposes turned his left arm and right wrist plating into some mad kind of electronic pistol. The grounding wire and the shielding ensured he only electrocuted others, not himself. The ejection mechanism for the slim rods could extend from his wrists and send a significant burst of voltage into his victim, a trick similar to Gisa's deadly parasol. And of course there was the last, most stunning and powerful setting, which he could only use once: the electric fingers. With a push of a button, he could send high voltage up to fifteen feet away, shooting in five arcs from the housing. It would fell his enemy, but it would also burn out the apparatus and damage some of his permanent clockwork.

Gisa listened patiently through his recitation of how to use his weapons, nodding approval as he finished. "Well done. As much as you are able, refrain from using the electricity. If you run out of charge, you will not be able to refresh it until we return to the airship. I suspect Mr. Stevens will have ideas on how I can loop the electricity to be powered by your heart and not damage your circuits, but of course that must wait for another day."

It was Johann's fondest hope he'd never have cause to weaponize his body parts again. "How will we enter the castle?"

"Through the sewers. This is an old keep, and the drainage and water-carrying systems are large enough for us to walk through in most places and are accessible by crawling through the rest. They will no doubt have a few token guards on duty there, but if we subdue them before they sound an alarm, we shall have full access to the dungeon levels of the castle. Freeing Miss Clarke is our first priority, which makes that access point doubly convenient."

Johann didn't like that they were saving Conny to rescue *second*. "Won't freeing her alert them and put a lockdown on Cornelius?"

"Freeing her removes their leverage over Mr. Stevens, and he isn't without resources to fight back. My only concern is that he will need to deploy the heart transmitters before we can negotiate a surrender. It will be a much more prolonged siege if he must act out of turn."

She spoke so calmly about invading the command center of the French Empire and negotiating what would essentially be a major act of treason. Johann envied her self-assurance. "What will happen if we succeed? What will Vienna do?"

"The emperor and every male member of the Austrian ruling class will likely need one of Mr. Stevens's non-weaponized clockwork hearts after finding out what we've done. They'll be furious with me and tell me how I've betrayed my country. They'll do their best to take their fury out on you, I'm afraid. You'll want to ask your pirates to keep you well out of Austria's reach until matters have settled. But they'll also be reckoning with the Society, who are preparing even now to go public and work to maintain the peace our blow today should realize. I look forward to this, as I know neither France nor Austria has any concept of how many of their citizens, particularly the nobility and economic elite, have no stomach for these prolonged conflicts. Europe is ready for peace and prosperity, and the Society shall lead us to that destiny."

She spoke with so much passion and quiet conviction she managed to make even Johann's jaded heart lighten. "Austria would be well-served to have you among its leaders, Princess."

She waved this idea away with a gloved hand. "I considered leadership, but I find it too pedantic and shortsighted. Revolution is far more to my liking."

As they approached the back of the castle and the entrance to the drainage corridors, they went quiet. There were indeed two guards at the entrance, looking bored and half-asleep. Olivia and Heng aimed crossbows at the men and took them down with only the *snick* of the mechanisms' release and the muffled tumble of two bodies to the ground. The men were not dead—this had been decided by careful debate, which had been settled when Félix said he could easily tip the arrows with a swift-acting paralytic. This meant they spared several minutes binding and gagging the wide-eyed soldiers before they entered the castle, but it also meant they had not yet taken the lives of any men whose only crime was following orders.

Johann found, as he passed the men to crawl awkwardly through the opened grate, he appreciated the gesture more than he'd anticipated.

The drainage passages were damp, slippery and stank of refuse, but within fifteen feet they were indeed able to stand and sometimes able to walk along raised brick access paths. Félix and Johann had the most trouble navigating themselves, Félix because of, as he put it, his "damnable knees", Johann because his clockwork legs decidedly did not care for sloshing through sewage and because he was petrified of stumbling into it face-first and ruining his electronics. When they finally made it out of the passages and into the relative dry of the dungeon level, he exhaled in relief as Félix double-checked his limbs to assure they had indeed survived the wet. While he and Princess Gisa fine-tuned him, Crawley, Heng and Olivia scouted the level.

"Only a handful of guards. If we divide up and use more of Félix's paralytic, we should have no trouble." He touched his ear, to the small wireless transmitter the princess had built for him and each one of them. "Will we be able to communicate with these?"

Gisa shook her head. "The walls are too thick. We must rely on planning and visual signals until we rise to a higher level of the keep."

Johann's clockwork heart didn't alter its beats as he crept with Molly down a passage to the pair of guards they'd been assigned to stun, but his body filled with adrenaline all the same. It was easy enough to aim and shoot Félix's paralytic, but with all the guards so close to one another, once they began to fall, they noticed each other's struggles and shouted out. Fortunately the same thick walls that prohibited their transmitters also muffled the guards' calls for aid, and soon one of the dungeon cells was full of paralyzed, bound and gagged French soldiers. Now all they had to do was free Conny's mother, and they could make their way through the castle to Cornelius himself.

They found Elizabeth's cell easily enough—she was the only prisoner in the dungeon, and she was easily visible by the central location where Heng, Olivia and Gisa had felled four of the guards. As they approached her, she lay still and silent on her pile of dirty straw on the farthest side of the room. Johann's breath caught as he saw the bloodstains on her ragged gown, the cuts and burns along her exposed arms and feet. Her hair had been shorn as well, not shaved but hacked off in cruel, uneven patches. When she continued to remain huddled and shivering, Johann feared they had arrived too late, that the archduke had damaged her spirit beyond recovery.

As Heng struggled with the rusty lock, however, Princess Gisa stood straight at the bars and spoke clearly into the cell. "*Oderunt dum Metuant.*"

The huddled figure stilled, then straightened slightly. She replied in a quiet but steady voice, "*Per Ardua Ad Astra.*" Elizabeth sat up, hissing in her breath and grunting for the effort, but she turned to face the group of them calmly, with a resolve matching and perhaps surpassing the princess. She didn't smile, but there was an admiration in her gaze as she studied Gisa. "You must be Princess Gisa. But I can't imagine your compatriots are members of the Society."

"No, but they will directly be commended for their service. They are companions of your son, here to secure his freedom and aid our effort to end this war." She stepped to the side and gestured to Félix. "This gentleman, I believe, you know quite intimately."

Elizabeth's face transformed to happiness as she stumbled clumsily forward. Heng had the cell door open by this point, allowing her to tumble weeping with joy into Félix's arms. She spoke animatedly in French. "Darling Félix! But what in the world are you doing here? You're too old for this kind of adventuring."

"A fact of which I am well aware, my dear. I'm here entirely for you. We will slip out of the sewers together, and when we're at the ship, I'll fix you up properly."

"You will do no such thing. Since I began feigning a broken spirit, they stopped blindfolding me as they carried me around the castle. I know the layout better than anyone here, and if you have a spare pistol and a knife, I'll be happy to give back to those who've been so generous to me during my incarceration."

Crawley's lips flattened as he took in Elizabeth's battered form. "Yes, love, but can you walk up to them to drive the knife home?"

"I can if Félix builds a support for my leg. And yes, before you ask, we have time enough to linger. They won't be down here again for hours. I promise you, I'm worth the wait."

Princess Gisa glanced around the dungeon chamber. "We need something stiff, preferably metal. And twine, or wire."

Johann gestured to himself. "Can you use something from my clockwork? Perhaps one of the electric rods? She wouldn't be able to use it as a weapon without the charging unit, but it should do for a leg brace."

Elizabeth had largely overlooked him until that moment, but she smiled as she regarded him now. "That's my son's work, if I'm not mistaken. My, my, aren't you a dashing figure. If my son isn't half in love with you, child, I'll wonder what's become of him."

Johann blushed and inclined his head in a shy nod. "He is, and the condition is mutual. Though by much more than half."

Elizabeth beamed. "Oh, how wonderful. What was your name, darling?"

Princess Gisa waved Johann into silence before he could reply. "Despite Miss Clarke's insistence we can linger, we aren't the only intruders converging on the castle. Yes, Johann, I will remove the rod from your left arm. Your right is more stable for extension of the weapon, being still largely flesh and bone, and I can retain the electric fingers in your left even without the rod. I'll reduce them to a simple stun, however, so that they're more serviceable."

Johann did get to tell Elizabeth his name and a bit of how he and Conny had met as Gisa and Félix worked, but soon she was patched up enough they asked her to try out her reinforced leg, and shortly after that they were on their way.

They moved through the castle like ghosts. Once they were on the main floor, the princess announced the transmitters were live, and they broke into teams, speaking low into what Princess Gisa called a micro-phone, listening to each other navigate their way to the third level, which was where Elizabeth believed Cornelius was being held. None of the guards they passed were on high alert, and the ones they had to subdue to pass through an area fell almost too easily.

Princess Gisa didn't seem concerned. "They don't anticipate a threat, and they believe themselves invincible, especially with Mr. Stevens's hearts. Matters will be different as we reach the third level, however."

This proved to be true. Once the living quarters of a ducal family, it was now the swarming headquarters for the French Empire's war. On one end of the level, high-ranking generals and other officers milled about examining maps and mockups of cities they wished to conquer. At the other end was Cornelius's lab, which was surrounded by guards on high alert. Their attention was fixed on the laboratory, not invaders slipping through the halls, but there would be no easy disruption of their number with the officers less than fifty feet away.

"How will we get through?" This question came whispered over the wireless from Heng, though Johann wondered much the same as he huddled in a stairway with Molly.

A familiar, beloved voice sounded over the wireless. "You wait for my signal, then rush the lab."

Johann's eyes fell closed, his throat full of emotion. "Conny?"

Cornelius's voice softened, but only a little as he replied. "Yes, darling. Hold fast." There was a scuffle and a crackle. "Don't linger fighting in the hallway. Get yourselves to the lab. Once you're inside, I'll barricade us in."

Johann was about to ask how they'd know when to move, thinking he must have missed the instructions on what this signal would be—and then the castle shook with an explosion from the floor below. Drawing a breath, readying his weapons, Johann burst into the hall with the others, bent on reaching the door beyond which Conny stood.

The castle was in chaos, soldiers rushing for the stairs and officers shouting and demanding to know what was going on, peering out the windows to look for advancing armies. When the guards at the door saw the pirates coming, they shouted the alarm and formed rank to block the crew of the *Farthing*'s advance.

Then the stones beneath their feet exploded, and the lot of them fell headlong into the floor below.

The doors remained largely intact, swinging inside with the force of the blast. Cornelius was visible at a central table, fingers on an apparatus, his gaze on his rescuers. It lingered on Johann, and for a fraction of a moment, it was only the two of them in the world, reassuring one another they were both well and happy to see each other again. Johann saw there were no scratches or even bruises on his lover, and that somehow he had managed to grow more handsome in their time apart.

Then more guards swarmed them, Cornelius's assistants in his laboratory swarmed him, and the tender moment was over.

Once Johann and the others scaled the gaping section of the floor, it was easy enough work to subdue Conny's assistants and bar the door. Johann and Conny embraced and kissed, and the others gave a quick smile and pat on the back before they allowed mother and son a moment to reconnect.

Cornelius wept as he clutched her, all his bravery falling away. "Oh, *Maman*, I thought they'd broken you. They hurt you. I couldn't stand it. I had to do what they said."

"I know, darling. It's all working out for the best now, so don't fret." She kissed him on the cheek and ruffled his hair. In the hallway behind them, the soldiers were scuffling and shouting, and from the sounds of things readying a ram to batter down the door to the laboratory. "Now, what's the next step in the battle plan?"

Cornelius handed them all small weapons that looked like pistols, but Johann recognized several of the princess's electronic circuits. "These will stun anyone you wish to slow without causing more bloodshed. There's a risk someone with a weak heart will be killed, but it's the best I could do. Avoid the generals in my father's inner circle, however, and do not shoot my father. It won't do much to anyone with a clockwork heart except tickle. The calibration would have to be set much higher to do them any damage, and it would overheat the heart, killing them instantly. Which wouldn't be a terrible event, given they are all the worst offenders, but I didn't have expertise enough for a two-channel weapon, and we agreed we preferred stunning over death for the lower-ranking soldiers." He handed an electric pistol to Princess Gisa. "Is the plan still to wait for the Society's forces to move into position? How many units do they have?"

"Yes, that's the plan, though they have no units, only a delegation. They knew the explosions were the signal for them to move forward, but it will take a moment for them to advance. They have a signal cannon, and when it fires, you may consider yourself free to engage in the final stratagem. Your transmitters are the only soldiers we have until then."

Conny nodded, looking pale and grim. He softened, however, as he approached Johann and took his metal hand. "Will you fight beside me, my love?"

Johann squeezed Conny's hand back, the metal digits curling now as easily at his brain's command as his flesh ones did. "Of course."

The doors to the laboratory burst open, the French soldiers swarmed forward, and Johann shifted his stance to guarding position, ready to shield any blows that might come his lover's way.

The world exploded all around Cornelius, every facet of his life colliding in one terrible climax, and yet Conny could not stop himself from indexing his lover's new parts, hating that someone else had been the one to do the surgery, despising the world that kept him from falling into Johann's arms and memorizing every new scar, wire and rivet of his body.

He hated most of all the way Johann felt it acceptable to put himself in the line of fire. When Conny tried to push forward, however, Johann dug his heels in more firmly and shook his head.

"No. You have no armor, no shield."

"Neither do you, not enough to stop—"

An officer aimed a pistol at Johann, shooting before Conny could cry out. Instead of penetrating Johann's chest, as it should have done, it clattered uselessly to the floor. Conny's mouth fell open. "What in the world?"

"I don't understand it entirely. Something to do with electricity and magnets." Johann thrust out his right hand at one soldier advancing for them and gripped another with his left. There was a buzz, a blue-white crackle of lightning and a nauseating burning smell as both men went down. "The princess had a bit too much fun kitting me out, I think."

"I should say so." Conny clutched his transmitter with one hand as he gripped Johann's waistcoat with the other, which he now realized was made of rubber. He tucked his hand more firmly against the grounding material as Johann stunned another pair of advancing soldiers. The room was chaos now, glass breaking and clockwork parts falling from shelves as the pirates, the princess and Elizabeth fought against the elite members of the French Army. Even Val managed to fell a few with his electric gun.

Then a sharp whistle rang through the room. The French soldiers fell back, snipers aimed rifles at their heads, and Archduke Francis Cornielle Guillory entered the room.

"Enough of this." He sauntered forward, smirking at the crew as they closed ranks around Cornelius. "You are surrounded, and you are trapped." His gaze shifted to Conny, and his smile was without mercy. "Dear boy, I'm afraid you'll watch many people you love die today. Though what you were thinking bringing that ridiculous fop along to your rescue, I'll never understand. Valentin, your father will be most displeased with you."

"I don't give a damn what my father thinks." Val, who stood beside them, spat over a table and sneered at Francis. "You are a monster, and you are not the leader of France. You are a servant, and it is time you are taught to behave as such."

The archduke laughed. "I am France's savior. That fat fool calling himself emperor can barely direct the drawing of a bath. I doubt he'll notice he's been deposed until we relocate him to La Santé. He's not fit to lead the Empire, and everyone in France knows it."

Princess Gisa, who stood tall and proud beside Captain Crawley near an as-yet-undisturbed pile of switches and transmitters, lifted her chin a little higher. "You will take no throne and hold no office, French dog. On my honor as a Hohenburg, I shall see to it *you* are the one to rot in prison. Or better still, I shall see your head placed on a pike."

"Ah, this must be the always-charming Princess Giselle, who fancies herself a revolutionary. As for Austria, that backward country full of peasants and lordlings, you will be ground beneath my heel like the bothersome rodent you are." The archduke laughed. "Oh, but I'll make great use of *you*, Highness, don't worry. I'll make you lead the head of my human automatons. Though I'll torture you first, to make certain I've gleaned every bit of information from you."

Conny pushed around Johann and glared at his father. "I've told you over and over, you can't make human automatons. You can't control the brain so easily."

"I can if the right part of their brain is severed, which Dr. Savoy has just this morning learned how to do." He gestured to the physician smirking beside the archduke. "Dr. Savoy might not be able to replicate your hearts, but he has put them to good use with quite a few improvements. *His* soldiers operate by the new wireless transmitters, which I see your friends have put to some creative uses. We'll be gleaning that information from you as well. The princess's electric parasol will suit my soldiers nicely."

Conny felt sick, imagining the men and women who must have died in horrible ways for these experiments, and those who were not so fortunate. "I will *never* aid you in such a venture. No matter who you threaten to torture."

"Then I will torture *you*, my dear boy, or better let give you to Dr. Savoy, who will make use of you one way or another."

Conny's mother bared her teeth. "You are a burrowing pig, Francis, to threaten your only son in this way. Where is the affection you always carried for him? How can you so easily toss him away for your ambitions?"

"The affection I have for him has been and will ever be subservient to my country." He gestured to the room as if he were already the emperor, on his dais at Versailles. "You accuse us of reaching for power, because you are mongrel fools. We are the leaders of the new world, the Europe which *will be*. United and whole, at peace because there are no more borders to squabble over. With our glorious clockwork hearts, we are stronger and faster than any other men who stand against us. With Savoy's soldiers at our side, we will take Austria, then Italy, Portugal, and even Russia, if she stands in our way. We will make every man, woman and child who stands against us work for us by taking away their will. This includes all of you, if you do not surrender immediately."

Conny had hoped for his father to keep pontificating, buying them more time, because no cannon fire had come from the hills. A glance at Princess Gisa told him she was worried too, that the Society should have approached by now. When she met his gaze, he raised his eyebrows in silent question. *Should I proceed?*

After a moment's hesitation, she inclined her head.

Drawing a deep breath, Conny turned back to his father. "We will not surrender. But you will." Gut twisting in distaste, fighting the urge to shut his eyes, Conny pushed the first button on his transmitter.

Every man he'd put the clockwork heart inside, including the archduke, stumbled forward, clutching his chest. As they recovered, Conny held the controller in his hand higher.

"This is a wireless electronic transmitter. It operates differently than your radio waves, and it has been attuned to the micro transmitters fashioned into each one of your clockwork hearts. You will surrender, or I will push the other button. The one that will kill you all."

For a moment, the archduke looked stricken. He shot a furious glance at Savoy, who frowned as he studied the archduke's chest. Then Guillory narrowed his gaze at Cornelius, relaxed and laughed.

"No. You won't. You don't have the stomach for so much death. You might slow us, but not every soldier in the room has your heart, and they will take you down. As for our clockwork hearts, Savoy and his team will undo whatever damage you've done." He motioned to a captain. "Seize them."

"Now, Mr. Stevens!" Princess Gisa cried, extending her parasol.

The room exploded in chaos. Heng and Crawley went down with terrified cries, and Olivia and Molly kicked and screamed obscenities as they fought off their attackers. New soldiers had entered the room, the human automatons Savoy had created. Their eyes were fixed and without light, their bodies ambling forward without care or pause, unmoved by the electric guns or even regular bullets. Elizabeth and Félix held their own, sheltered as they were behind Princess Gisa, but they too would fall quickly.

It would all stop if Conny pushed the button. Except his father was right. He couldn't do it.

The others urged him on, shouting his name, telling him not to let his father get into his head, but they didn't understand. Conny *couldn't*. He turned to Johann, trying to explain, but Johann was busy fighting off the soldiers trying to take them down. It was nearly over, and everyone Conny loved was about to die or become one of his father's horrible creatures, all because he didn't have the strength to push a button. With a tear running down his cheek, he turned to Val, hoping his friend would have the presence of mind to talk him into doing what he had to do.

Except Val was already in front of him, reaching for the transmitter.

It all happened so quickly. Val's arm extending, hand closing over the mechanism. The archduke barking out an order for the soldier whose rifle was trained on Val. The shot ringing through the air, the electric arc of Johann's modified clockwork zinging across the room, taking down the shooter and the entire regiment of automaton soldiers. In the distance, the surreal multi-tonal sound of the signal cannon told them the Society had arrived at last. Nearly too late.

With the cannon's song still ringing in the distance, every man carrying a clockwork heart, save Johann, fell convulsing to the floor.

So did Val, clutching his chest as his shirt and waistcoat stained with blood.

Crying out, Conny caught him, applying pressure to the wound as he wept over his longest friend, who now stared up at him in shock. All around them chaos reigned, the soldiers hesitating as their officers sputtered and died, and the pirates took quick advantage of this. Princess Gisa barked out demands, explaining what she'd meant to say when the archduke was still alive, that the Society to Liberate Europe had arrived with their armed escorts and their intent to seize control of the keep and the command of the war itself. The French Army had lost. The Society was about to carry the day.

All the while, in Conny's arms, Valentin bled out.

"Oh, Val—" Conny choked on his sob as he pressed harder on the bleeding area, unable to deny how close it had come to the heart. Likely damaging a major aorta. He had almost no time. All because Conny could not bear to take a life. Because he had hesitated like a coward. Because he had failed them all.

Val raised a hand weakly, his fingers barely brushing Conny's face, though his glazed gaze lingered. "No. Don't...look like that. I never meant to let you push the trigger. You—" He broke off, coughing, blood coming out of the side of his mouth. "You wouldn't be Conny, if you killed so many men."

"But I don't want to lose you," Conny whispered.

Félix crouched beside him, assessing Val with a surgeon's eye. "If we can get him onto a Lazarus, we can keep him alive long enough to sort out his injuries."

Conny shook his head, biting his lip. "It's his heart, Félix. I'd have to build him a new one. They take *time*, as you well know, and my lab has been destroyed. We need far more time than we can afford to have him on the Lazarus."

Crawley appeared on Cornelius's other side. He looked pale and distraught, unable to take his gaze from dying Valentin. "Why can't you take one from the dead officers?"

"The hearts were ruined by the pulse I sent." He clamped a hand over his mouth. "My darling Val, I'm so sorry."

Johann put his clockwork hand on Conny's shoulder. "Can he use mine?"

Conny shook his head, ready to explain *no one* could live that long on a Lazarus alone, but Félix eyed Johann speculatively. "He has the original, not your copies. It has the best, rarest metals in its interior. It's been improved by the both of us, and tempered by Johann's use. It's strong. Strong enough to beat, at least for a short while, for two. They would both have to be under aether, and it would have to take turns pumping for each of them. Two Lazarus machines. Two patients. One heart. And an incredible amount of surgeon skill."

The idea of the men he loved most in the world having their lives hang in the balance made Conny want to vomit. But Val was fading before him, and Johann crouched beside him, looking Conny earnestly in the eye. Waiting to be given his orders.

Conny wiped away more tears. "None of this would have happened had I not hesitated."

"No," Crawley said. "We were cruel to leave it in your hand. Our intention was never to have to follow through, but we shouldn't have relied on the Society's arrival. We should have had a dummy transmitter in your hand and a real one in someone else's. Val was right, you never should have had this burden. And it would have been you dying, if you'd looked ready to make the move. They'd have shot whoever put their finger on that button. The only reason Val made it was because they didn't see him coming." Crawley nodded at Conny, the glib curtness of his tone belying the stricken look in his eyes. "Stop taking the weight of the whole war on your shoulders and do what you do best, tinker. Fix it. Fix our Frenchie."

Conny drew a steadying breath. He glanced around again, saw Gisa had the room in hand, that some of the Society members and their soldiers had begun to enter the lab. The castle was seized, the battle won.

Now all that was left was to heal.

He straightened, drew a steadying breath and nodded to a large cabinet across the room. "There's a Lazarus in there, and we'll likely find another in Savoy's lab." Keeping one hand on Val's wound, he grabbed Johann's face and kissed him hard on the mouth. "You will not die, do you hear me? *You will not die.*"

"Not unless you tell me to," Johann promised.

Chapter Eighteen

In the ruined remains of the room where he'd been held prisoner, with his father lying dead on the floor beneath a sheet, Cornelius Francis Stevens performed the most technical, terrifying and tender surgery of his life.

He'd had curtains set up to enclose them in their corner of the room, but there was no escaping the activity near the door, where Society officials and their underlings moved bodies, set up makeshift floorboards where they'd been blown away, and in general cleaned up after the mess. Princess Gisa did what she could to keep them quiet, but it was difficult.

Cornelius tried not to care, tried to focus on his work. It was easy enough when he was tending to Johann or Val, because while he checked their vitals or adjusted who between them used the heart and who used the Lazarus, he thought of the two of them and how humbled he was by their sacrifices, of how much he loved them both. When he returned to his worktable and helped Master Félix build Valentin's new heart, however, the gravity of it all overwhelmed him.

"Hush, lad. Focus on your work, and let the rest of it go. There will be time enough to dwell on things when the boys are sewn up again."

Conny understood his mentor was right, but he still couldn't bring his mind to heel. He was never like this in surgery. Even when he'd installed Johann's heart, committing seven kinds of treason, he hadn't faltered. But he hadn't been in love with Johann then. He hadn't been racing to save Valentin's life, who had arguably just put his life on the line for his country—for Europe—in a manner incomparable by any of her other citizens.

Now their lives were, literally, in Conny's trembling hands.

The hearts he'd made under duress were serviceable and everything he'd promised his father they would be—but Félix was right, there was nothing to compare to the original Johann carried. Conny would only consider something as good or better for Val, which meant he and Félix built slowly, consulting one another over their designs, combing the castle for suitable materials. Some of it had to be brought in from parts beyond. Princess Gisa sent the swiftest couriers, and Crawley flew them personally in the *Farthing*, but meanwhile Conny and Félix worked, trading shifts to sleep and eat and, occasionally for Conny, stand on a balcony and stare into the Alps to see if the majesty of the mountains could provide him with calm.

On one of these occasions, the princess came to stand with him. At first she said nothing, only gazed with him with an appreciative eye for the landscape. Eventually, however, she spoke.

"It is comforting, this view. The craggy peaks know nothing of the cruelty and horror your father planned for the world they oversee. They have lived through and forgotten ten thousand tyrants and madmen. They have harbored ten thousand saints. In the end, they remain mountains. They are constant where we all fade away."

Conny leaned into a pillar supporting the balcony's overhang. "Even the mountains will pass on someday. The mountains in the eastern Americas were once towering giants, but now they are little more than hills."

"Fair point and a more poetic thought." She glanced at him, her expression uncharacteristically gentle. "You seem to be having difficulty surrendering your cares to the mountains or gods of any mettle. What ails you, Mr. Stevens?"

He sighed. "I don't know. That's the trouble. I don't think it's anything in particular. I suppose it's that ever since I brought Johann into my life, everything has been chaos. Clearly it would have come to this in some way regardless—more grisly, to be honest, because without him I would not have found the *Farthing* crew and by extension you and the Society. I would have died my father's slave."

He indulged in a glance backward to the castle, toward the laboratory where Val and Johann lay waiting. "All I've ever wanted was to help people. To do good. To love and be loved. It upsets me that there are people in the world like my father. That *my father* was the worst of those kind of people." He threw up his hands. "Why are there men like him? Why must people be so cruel?"

"Because people are complex and wonderful and terrible. You may create the most intricate clockwork in the world, power it by my electricity, turn your clockwork heart into the most incredible machine a human has ever built. But nothing you or I or anyone alive will ever make can compare to humans themselves. To allow us to be as kind and pure-hearted as you are, we must allow ourselves also to be as cold and cruel as your father. There is no world in which one exists without the other—unless it is a world where we are all reduced to your father's terrible human automatons."

The princess's words, while ringing of truth, brought him little comfort. "I wish to be done with the likes of my father. Forever."

"Alas, I suspect your life will always put more than your fair share of those type of men and women in your way. Which is why I suggest focusing your energies on restoring two of the people who most help you alleviate the pain of dealing with the monsters." She put a hand on his shoulder, a simple but substantial presence. "You cannot erase the darkness. But you may bring as many candles with you into it as you like."

Those words, at last, penetrated his fog of fear and helplessness. She was right. His candles lay in his laboratory. They had stood beside him through every dark cavern, supporting him, advising him, carrying him. Now they had both offered their lives for him.

He would give them their lives back. Better and brighter than they had ever hoped to know. Then he would do everything he could to keep both of them by his side, lover and friend, forever.

It had been two days since they began working when Gisa spoke to him on the balcony, and there would be three more before the Lazarus was removed and both men could rise on their own power, but from that moment forward Cornelius worked with a focus and intensity he had never known before. He built Val's new heart not haunted by terror or fearing what other horrors the world might have in store, but determined to give his friend an engine the world would find it difficult to challenge. When he and Félix discovered an improvement over the original design, he gave the upgrades to Johann's heart as well. They would both, he insisted, rise from their surgeries with his skills and his love fused inside their hearts.

Rise they did. Slowly, groggily, a week of aether and clockwork surgery exacting its toll. But when they saw him, they smiled and reached for him.

Conny took each of their hands, kissed their knuckles and sat patiently, waiting for them. His two candles, Valentin and Johann, who he knew, once they were healed and rested, would go with him into any darkness. And he, Conny vowed, would always be there to make sure they were more healthy and able-bodied than anyone else on Earth.

Chapter Nineteen

November, 1910

Alcochete, Portugal

On a lazy afternoon while the rest of the crew of *The Brass Farthing* sat joking and teasing one another in a bistro across the street, Johann pressed Conny's head farther out the window of their third-story rented room as he fucked his lover enthusiastically from behind.

It had been some time now since they left the chaos and pain they both associated with their homelands, but Johann had learned his Cornelius fared better when he was well-fucked, which meant indulging his need for exposure. He intended to take Conny to a private party tonight, one Crawley and the others planned to attend as well, but in the meantime the window had presented itself so handily, and it was the sort of neighborhood that wouldn't be shocked by much of anything.

When they finished, they curled together on the bed, which had been terrible when they arrived but was quite comfortable now, between the fresh linens and featherbed Johann had brought in and the tinkering Cornelius had provided.

Conny traced circles in the whorls of hair over Johann's chest, lingering on the edge of the flesh door concealing the opening to his clockwork heart. "I received another transmission from Princess Gisa today. She says the Austrian Emperor has tripled the offer for me to be the official court tinker. He's made us both barons and issued official pardons for both your desertions of the army."

Johann kissed Conny's hair and smoothed his clockwork hand down his lover's back. "Are you interested in accepting?"

"Oh, heavens, no. With all the work we've put in to making our suite on the ship? Besides, it's exciting to never stay in the same place. I'd be bored in a week in Vienna." He sighed. "Though it would be lovely to work with the princess again."

"Any further word on the Society?"

"Nothing more than we read in the papers. France is in chaos. Germany, Poland and Spain have broken away, and Brittany is considering forming its own government as well. There was a small hint about Emperor Éloi stepping down, but I think the Society would rather let him fade away. Put the focus on the parliament. And of course the dismantling of the army."

Johann kissed Conny's neck, urging him onto his belly. He worked the tension out of that slender back with the meat of his flesh palm and the gentle kneading of his clockwork. "Would you like to visit Calais again? Crawley was hinting we might travel to England next. It would be easy to arrange a night away over the Channel."

"I don't know. Yes, because I miss the sight of it, the familiar feel of the cobblestones beneath my feet. No, because it won't be the same, and it might make me sad."

Johann trained his left hand over Conny's buttocks and teased the tender opening between them. "What if I promised to take you to The Alison, get you drunk on absinthe and fuck you over a table while friends and strangers fight one another to be the one who feeds you their cock?"

Conny shivered with pleasure and pushed his bottom into Johann's hand. "When did you say Crawley wanted to leave? Do you think he'd let us stop on the way?"

They made love again, a slower, more lingering encounter which remained entirely on the mattress. After a nap, they wandered to the dock where the *Farthing* waited, because Cornelius insisted he wanted to see his lady.

Though the manifest still listed Crawley as the owner, every pirate in Europe knew the soul of the airship now belonged to its tinker. She was leaner now, her gondola's bottom shaved and shaped, her casing made of reinforced aluminum, which allowed for more cargo *and* individual rooms for each member of the crew. All but Conny and Johann, who'd turned their space into a series of open chambers, complete with an elegant clawfoot bathtub fitting two. Especially when one of the men had removable legs.

But the true glory of the *Farthing* was her balloon. It was sleek and silver, the hide made of material Johann didn't understand except to know it was beautiful, shining even when the sun was behind the clouds. It had elegant brass casing, intricately molded filigree and curves making her the envy of air and sea.

She shone bright and proud as Johann and Conny approached, snug in her berth, moored and secured with electric locks no thieves could hope to crack. Conny leaned against Johann as they regarded the ship across the street.

"Crawley keeps offering to cancel our contracts if we want, but to be honest, Johann, I don't ever want to go to Calais or anywhere else to stay." He turned in Johann's arms to look at him, touching his face. "What about you, darling? Do you have any wish to go home?"

Johann kissed Cornelius's hand and smiled as the evening sun set his lover's hair alight with fire to match the glint of the *Farthing*'s gilded casing, his face full of joy and peace and years of promised adventure.

"I'm already there."

About the Author

Heidi Cullinan has always enjoyed a good love story, provided it has a happy ending. Proud to be from the first Midwestern state with full marriage equality, Heidi is a vocal advocate for LGBT rights. She writes positive-outcome romances for LGBT characters struggling against insurmountable odds because she believes there's no such thing as too much happy ever after. When Heidi isn't writing, she enjoys cooking, reading, playing with her cats, and watching television with her family. Find out more about Heidi at www.heidicullinan. com.

To seal their bond, they must break the ties that bind.

A Private Gentleman
© *2012 Heidi Cullinan*

Painfully introverted and rendered nearly mute by a heavy stammer, Lord George Albert Westin rarely ventures any farther than the club or his beloved gardens. When he hears rumors of an exotic new orchid sighted at a local hobbyist's house, though, he girds himself with opiates and determination to attend a house party, hoping to sneak a peek.

He finds the orchid, yes…but he finds something else even more rare and exquisite: Michael Vallant. Professional sodomite.

Michael climbed out of an adolescent hell as a courtesan's bastard to become successful and independent-minded, seeing men on his own terms, protected by a powerful friend. He is master of his own world—until Wes. Not only because, for once, the sex is for pleasure and not for profit. They are joined by tendrils of a shameful, unspoken history. The closer his shy, poppy-addicted lover lures him to the light of love, the harder his past works to drag him back into the dark.

There's only one way out of this tangle. Help Wes face the fears that cripple him—right after Michael finds the courage to reveal the devastating truth that binds them.

Warning: Contains wounded heroes, bibliophilic tendencies, orchid obsessions, a right bastard of a marquis, and gay men who get happily-ever-afters.

When your deepest, darkest fantasy shows up, get on board.

Special Delivery
© *2014 Heidi Cullinan*

Love doesn't come with a syllabus.

Love Lessons
© *2013 Heidi Cullinan*

Love Lessons, Book 1

Kelly Davidson has waited what seems like forever to graduate high school and get out of his small-minded, small town. But when he arrives at Hope University, he quickly realizes finding his Prince Charming isn't so easy. Everyone here is already out. In fact, Kelly could be the only virgin on campus.

Worst of all, he's landed the charming, handsome, gay campus Casanova as a roommate, whose bed might as well be equipped with a revolving door.

Walter Lucas doesn't believe in storybook love. Everyone is better off having as much fun as possible with as many people as possible...except his shy, sad little sack of a roommate is seriously screwing up his world view.

As Walter sets out to lure Kelly out of his shell, staying just friends is harder than he anticipated. He discovers love is a crash course in determination. To make the grade, he'll have to finally show up for class...and overcome his own private fear that love was never meant to last.

Warning: This story contains lingering glances, milder than usual sexual content for this author, and a steamy dance-floor kiss. Story has no dairy or egg content, but may contain almonds.

It's all about the story...

Romance

HORROR

www.samhainpublishing.com